Also by Ann Aguirre

Witch Please
Boss Witch

EXTRA Witchy

ANN AGUIRRE

sourcebooks
casablanca

Published by Sourcebooks Casablanca, an imprint of Sourcebooks
P.O. Box 4410, Naperville, Illinois 60567–4410
(630) 961-3900
sourcebooks.com

Library of Congress Cataloging-in-Publication Data

Names: Aguirre, Ann, author.
Title: Extra witchy / Ann Aguirre.
Description: Naperville, Illinois : Sourcebooks Casablanca, [2022] |
    Series: Fix-it witches; 3
Identifiers: LCCN 2022019559 (print) | LCCN 2022019560 (ebook) |
    (trade paperback) | (epub)
Subjects: LCGFT: Novels.
Classification: LCC PR9200.9.A39 E98 2022 (print) | LCC PR9200.9.A39
    (ebook) | DDC 823/.92--dc23/eng/20220420
LC record available at https://lccn.loc.gov/2022019559
LC ebook record available at https://lccn.loc.gov/2022019560

Printed and bound in Canada.
MBP 10 9 8 7 6 5 4 3 2 1

For Dixie:

Who tried her best to displace my laptop
and claim lap supremacy for all time.
You are the best dog ever.
It's too bad you can't read.

CHAPTER 1

LEANNE VANDERPOL GOT THE CALL she most didn't want in the middle of a meeting she would've preferred not to attend.

Once again, the deputy mayor had off-loaded his responsibilities to her with an unctuous smile. Strictly speaking, *she* wasn't obligated to attend, but someone from the mayor's office had to, and those assholes had slacking down to a fine art, usually executed under the guise of "important business." Since she'd be responsible for writing the press release anyway—to cover Mayor Anderson's behind when he refused to fund the center's current proposal—it seemed like the lesser of two evils to get firsthand impressions without relying on someone else.

When she took this job, she'd thought it was the best way to make the world a better place without braving an election, but the longer she worked in politics, the more she realized she needed to get her ass in gear. Unmarried women often had a hard time getting elected, and since she was twice divorced, it would be even tougher for Leanne. She could imagine the smear campaign now:

She can't even commit to one man. How can you trust her to do what's right for you?

If a potential husband dropped out of the sky, that would be awesome, preferably one who stuck around until she got a seat on the city council. If she had to attend these meetings, her voice should matter, right? She wished she could approve the funding for the community center herself, but in her current role, she lacked the power to make any lasting changes.

With a sigh, she stared at her vibrating phone and tiptoed out the back—not easy in a pair of designer heels. She didn't let the backs touch the floor until she pulled the door gently closed behind her. At least the lights had been dimmed in the middle of the presentation, providing cover for her exit. Her mother wasn't the type to give up, so she'd keep calling until Leanne answered. She took a few more steps away from the conference room then picked up.

"What's up?" she asked.

"What time will be you home?"

Based on precedent, the question sent cold chills down her spine. "Why?"

"Hurry back! I'm making margaritas!"

Those prescient shivers ripened into full-on foreboding, and she raised her eyes to the ceiling that bore an ominous water stain in the shape of a turkey leg. The mayor really did need to allot more funds for community use, not that doing the right thing ever pinged on his radar. This center had seen better days, and the lighting was shit. On the other end of the call, a blender whirred in the background.

Leanne counted to ten, wishing she had a normal witch for a mother. *Danica's mom enjoys gardening. I bet* she *never spent the summer following Phish in a van with a guy named Noodles.* The only good aspects of that? Leanne had been left to her own devices when she was old enough to manage, and her mom didn't marry Noodles.

"You're in my kitchen, aren't you?"

Sunshine and cheer sparkled across the line. If there was a project glitter spell, her mom would be casting it. "I landed three hours ago! Wanted to surprise you."

Surprise was one word that could apply to her mother's unexpected arrival, but not the one Leanne had in mind. "We've talked about this. Boundaries, remember? Popping in isn't—"

"They're mango margaritas!" her mom cut in.

For this interruption, Leanne was missing the main point of the meeting she shouldn't have agreed to attend. "It's two in the afternoon."

"It's booze o'clock somewhere."

Leanne sighed. There was no point in trying to reason with Juniper "Junie" Vanderpol. She'd never get Junie to understand that Leanne had an actual career, not just a place where she showed up to occasionally earn cash to pay the rent. Junie preferred living as the spirit moved her; Leanne's middle name had been "Moonbeam," though she'd legally dropped it down to a mysterious *M* when she reverted to her maiden name after her first marriage. People could do that free of charge during divorce proceedings, no separate name-change decree required.

"I'll be home around five," she said. "I'll have a drink with you, then *I'm* going out. If you'd called ahead, you would know my coven's having a party tonight."

"Sounds fun…" The wistful tone came across crystal clear.

Leanne knew her mother was angling for an invite, and

she'd be damned if she added that much chaos to an occasion
that already might blow sky-high. Between Danica and Clem, the
coven had as much tension as it could hold. They didn't need
Junie adding her special brand of spontaneity to the mix.

"I'm sure it will be," she said briskly.

She swallowed the rest of her words. *You're my mother. We're
not besties.* That wasn't how Junie had raised Leanne, however.
She had been twenty when she chose to get pregnant, twenty-one
when she had Leanne, and she'd raised her as if they were friends
who cohabitated. There were never any rules—Leanne ate cookies
for breakfast, cereal for dinner, or whatever she could find, and
there was always another handsome man promising Junie the sun
and stars. More often than not, she'd believed them, and she had
been married six times. Oddly, the one person Junie hadn't married was Leanne's father; Leanne had never met the man, as far as
she could recall, though there had been so many "uncles" that she
was sick of the word.

"See you later," Junie said, some of the brightness seeping out
of her voice.

Leanne cut the call, wishing she could siphon away the insidi-
ous guilt as easily. It was easy to tell that her mom was lonely, but
it wasn't Leanne's fault that she'd lived like a nomad, never putting
down roots. Unlike her mother, Leanne had *chosen* St. Claire after
doing significant research on the place and finding a coven that
fit her. She'd moved here intentionally after college, selected this
as her home, and never regretted that decision. If Mom wanted to
live in St. Claire, she could find a place here, but she couldn't burst
into Leanne's life and expect everything to work out long-term.

Quietly, she crept back into the meeting in time to hear the main point. Unfortunately, all eyes locked onto her as she returned to her chair. Lorraine Talbot, the director of the community center, seemed particularly perturbed that Leanne had ducked out. Lorraine frowned so hard that her eyebrows touched, her rust-lipsticked mouth compressed in a firm line. The color didn't suit her even slightly, rendering her freckled complexion sallow.

"We were under the impression the mayor's office takes our concerns seriously," she snapped, skewering Leanne with a gimlet stare.

Damn Deputy Mayor Dudley. I'm not even meant to be here. This day sucks.

"We do. I'm truly sorry for the interruption. You have my full attention."

She spent the next hour listening to valid agitation regarding budget cuts. As director of communications, Leanne shouldn't be dealing with any of this. Both Mayor Anderson and Deputy Mayor Dudley were prime examples of people failing upward, until they plateaued and became someone else's problem. If the people who'd voted for them had any inkling how much time they spent on the golf course while making staffers pull their weight—

Best not to dwell on it. I'll end up with resting witch face, and Lorraine will think it's about her.

At last, the meeting ended, and Leanne offered vague assurances about presenting their reasonable requests to the mayor. Who wouldn't listen, because he never did. The man had perfected a jovial expression, one that seemed attentive and sympathetic, while he pondered something else. If her job wasn't to keep his office smelling like roses, figuratively speaking, she'd have let him fall on his face years ago.

If only I'd known what a tool he is before I took this job…

Dan Rutherford, a city councilman, stopped her before she could make her escape. The man…loomed. There was no other word for it. He was tall and broad, dedicated to working out, and she had no doubt that he considered himself a vital and exciting man. Though he dressed well, she hated his affectation in wearing a bolo tie. *And don't get me started on the cowboy boots. It's not like he's from Texas or Arizona.* His skin was deeply weathered, and he kept his haircut high and tight, showing off a faint and involuntary tonsure at the back of his head.

"Looking beautiful today, Ms. Vanderpol." His gaze dropped to her boobs, lingering a while before it returned to her face.

She refused to say thanks for a compliment she didn't want; instead, she folded her arms across her chest. "Did you need something, sir?" Goddess, but it galled her to add that respectful word at the end. She'd rather kick his shins.

"Can you ask your boss to call me? He said something about setting up a tee time, but I can't get him on the horn."

"You could call the office," she suggested.

This is so sus. Send him a text. Or an email? Try his assistant, even. Why are you bothering me with this?

"But you're right here." His tone became cajoling. "I'll make it worth your while. Hell, if I had my way, you'd be on my arm, brightening up every room you enter. You wouldn't need to work another day in your life."

Wow. I just threw up a little in my mouth. Did this bastard seriously just ask me to be his trophy wife? Well, he hinted at it anyway.

She counted to ten because if she told this asshole off, he'd complain to Mayor Anderson, then the mayor would find creative ways to make her life worse. Nothing actionable, of course. He was too crafty for that, even if he wasn't brilliant in other ways.

The lesser of two evils was to comply with this request and end the conversation. "What days and times work for the golf meeting?" she asked briskly.

"That depends on you," he said with what he likely intended to be a flirtatious smile. "When are *you* available?"

Just as she'd suspected, this was an excuse to ask her out. "I don't play golf, but thanks anyway. If you need to check your schedule first, I suggest contacting the mayor via text. He tends to dodge actual phone calls."

Rutherford let out a booming laugh. "You're feisty. I love that. Never mind, then. I'll get in touch with him sooner or later. Man can't run forever—he owes me money."

Uh, what? That was way more than she wanted to know about their personal business.

"I have a meeting. If you'll excuse me..." Leanne strode off, taking that permission for granted, mostly because she didn't care about Dan Rutherford's response.

I can't believe that jerk represents my district.

Without looking back, she hurried to her car, feeling vaguely grimy from that interaction.

According to the time, she should return to the office for an hour, but if she did that, they'd suck her into some other crap that wasn't part of her job description. It didn't seem so bad, suddenly, to go have a margarita with Junie. Fudging the truth a little, she called the receptionist to say, "I'll be out of the office this afternoon. Let anyone who might be looking for me know that I'll be in at the usual time tomorrow."

The nice part about her job was that she did sometimes work off-site, so the mayor wouldn't follow up. Neither would the deputy mayor, as they were teeing off by now. Maybe Rutherford could join them. And nobody else had the *right* to check up on her, so she could get away with being a little irresponsible today. Leanne headed straight home from the community center, passing through the residents' gate with card access. Junie's skill with illusion meant she'd probably pretended to be Leanne to gain entrance earlier. That was the way she operated: convenience before honesty in most regards.

The guard stared so hard that Leanne paused as the gate lever rose. "You probably didn't even see me leave, did you?"

"I sure didn't."

Which meant she was right about Junie. "Watch less court TV, Ernest."

He shot her a rueful look as she pulled away, making room for the car behind her.

Leanne's condo was on the fourth floor. The building had an elevator, and she appreciated not having any neighbors above her. The view was nice too; she faced the back of the community, overlooking a man-made pond. Landscaped with carefully shaped topiary and a profusion of flowers, the little lake even had ducks that flocked to it. Leanne had no idea if they had been part of the plan or if they'd moved in on their own. She'd heard the grounds keeper bitching about cleaning up after them, though.

She input the code to let herself in and found her mom chilling at the breakfast bar with a margarita in hand. The kitchen was a mess, as Junie never did anything neatly. "I see you made yourself at home."

"It's where the heart is," Junie said cheerfully.

"And I'm your heart?" She didn't mean to sound so skeptical.

"Of course you are. You're my little LeLe Moonbeam."

Please, no.

For the first time ever, she asked her mother for advice, mostly because Junie was here. "What would you do if a man made you feel grubby as hell just by looking at you? He's such an awful, arrogant son of a bitch."

"Find some way to make him sorry," Junie said promptly. "You could hex him?"

"I don't want to be that witch. It's not like he wronged me in the Victorian sense, but he's such a gross chauvinist. Ugh."

"If it's a matter of disrespect, take something that belongs to him. I once hot-wired this asshole's Toyota, but I magicked myself to look like someone else during the theft, and I only drove it for half an hour because I didn't want to get arrested. I wouldn't do well in prison."

Apart from grand theft auto, that was...surprisingly on point—and in line with Leanne's own thinking. She needed more time to ponder, but the seeds of an idea were already germinating, and in the meantime, the cocktails were delicious. Leanne had one, then two, and giggled with her mom while figuring out what to wear to the party later.

If she couldn't escape Junie's influence, maybe she'd lean into it.

Trevor Montgomery was nervous.

Apart from his best friend, Titus, everyone had stopped talking to him years ago. Like his parents, they'd given up on him after Sarah left. Titus was the only one who didn't drift. Even the guys they hung out with—Calvin, Dante, and Miguel—were more Titus's friends than his, though nobody ever asked *Why are you inviting that loser?* he still felt it keenly, that sense of displacement. Of being the add-on, the guy nobody would include as their first choice.

Now he'd gotten invited to an actual party. Not poker night or beer with the guys. It had been so long that he'd settled into the awkwardness of not remembering how to talk to people. He'd be meeting Titus's girlfriend and all her friends, and he acutely didn't want to be *that guy* anymore. Not that he knew how to shake off the reputation—it was easier to wash out the scent of weed, and that skunky shit lingered. He liked being baked, maybe a little too much, but he could relate to those who hated the stink.

Thankfully, Titus didn't give him shit when he picked Trevor up, because he'd dug deep into his closet for an outfit that didn't say *Hey, I live in my parents' basement and my main hobbies are video games and quality Kush.* He kept tugging at the collar of his polo on the way over. It'd been years since he wore anything but a T-shirt.

"It'll be fine," Titus said.

"Easy for you to say. Your girlfriend flew to Arizona to get you back."

I'm such a fuckup. I can't believe you invited me to meet people who could be so important to you.

His knee jittered, and he wished he had something to take the edge off. Anxiety might eat him alive before the night ended. Drinking until everything went blurry sounded good, but he couldn't let himself do that either. Not when Titus trusted him to make a good impression on Danica's friends. Trev's palms went sweaty as they pulled up in front of the house. At least, he figured it must be the right place by the number of cars parked outside. After he swung out of the car, he rubbed his palms against his cargo shorts then followed Titus up the drive. In college, he'd attended house parties, so he shouldn't be this freaked, but it had been years.

Is it possible to forget how to socialize?

He froze by the door, overwhelmed by the laughter and the music, but Titus towed him into the mix, introducing him around. Trev immediately forgot all the names he heard, and he couldn't make eye contact with anyone either. He tried to control his breathing, but with every fiber of his being, he wanted to dash for the door and keep running, on and on, maybe until his heart exploded. *Because I'm such a tool, I can't even—*

"I'm Leanne. Want to be my third husband?" Those utterly unexpected words cut into his near panic attack with surgical precision, leaving him too stunned to be anxious. To mess with his head even more, they'd been spoken by the most beautiful woman he'd ever seen.

Bombshell. That was the only word for this curvaceous

redhead. She was gorgeous from head to toe, and she honestly seemed to be talking to him. If he hadn't made a point of coming to this shindig sober, he would've sworn he was high.

Trev blinked. *Nope, not hallucinating. She's still here.*

Before he even thought about it, he blurted, "I mean…maybe? Because I could get on board if you're looking for a low-key, no-ambition type to look after the house. I cook and clean, do most general maintenance as well. Ask Titus, I've got references."

Great, way to go. That's not how flirting works. You sound like you're genuinely applying for a job.

"As a handyman, not my third husband," Titus clarified.

The woman laughed, as she was likely meant to. She chatted a bit with Danica and Titus, then they moved off together, leaving Trev staring at the ridiculously beautiful redhead. Broad forehead, wide cheekbones, pointed chin, and she had big eyes that didn't know if they were blue or gray, framed by thick lashes. And her mouth—

Unexpectedly, she flashed him a wide, bright smile, indicating she intended to continue the conversation. *How does she have perfect teeth too?* Part of him couldn't believe she was even *talking* to him. If he'd spotted her at O'Reilly's, no way in hell would he have worked up the courage to approach. Trev couldn't even imagine that he was her type. Then she stepped closer, and he understood. Judging by the smell and the glint in her eyes, she'd been pregaming, so she was already working with beer goggles. A few drinks in, and he became a decent option. Disappointment deluged him, though he didn't let his smile falter.

At least I'm talking to someone, even if she's drunk.

"You didn't tell me your name, prospective third husband."

She stepped into his space and tilted her head, peering up at him through her lashes.

"Trevor. Friends call me Trev."

"Do you think we'll be friends?" There was no mistaking that flirtatious tone, the gentle brush of her hand over his bare forearm.

That innocuous touch felt better than it should have, reminding him just how long it had been. It was a little embarrassing how touch starved he felt. Trev paused, unsure what he was supposed to say. *If she's messing with me...*

Before he could respond, she went on, "I hope not."

She came over here to fuck with my head? That's so not on. He spoke through clenched teeth. "Oh yeah? Well—"

"Because you're totally my type, and it'll piss me off if you friend-zone me. I just wanted to put that out there first thing." Then her gaze legit wandered up and down his body, elevator-eyeing him in a way he'd never experienced.

I think I like it.

In the abstract, it wasn't respectful to objectify people, but it had been so damn long since anyone looked at Trev like he was worthwhile, let alone desirable, that a minor spark went through him, just from the way she was inspecting him. He stifled the urge to straighten his shoulders, like he was a horse she might decide to ride. *Wait, bad analogy.* Or considering how her regard intensified, maybe it was the right one after all.

"What do you think? Am I the kind of woman you find attractive? Shit, that was presumptuous, wasn't it? That's if you—"

"I do," he blurted. "Like women. I mean, frankly I'd consider anyone if our personalities clicked, but..." He took a breath, wishing he didn't have to do this. "Are you *seriously* trying to hook up with me right now?"

Leanne smirked, and it was such a cute expression that his breath caught. "What was your first clue, Surfer Boy?"

"I'm not a surfer. I mow lawns and I need a haircut."

"You really want me to call you Lawn Boy?" she asked in a skeptical tone.

"No, I'm pretty sure that's copyrighted."

She laughed. "Damn, you're funny. The cute ones rarely have the personality to match. Looks like this is my lucky night. Could be yours too if you're down."

Be a decent person. Be a decent person. He looped that thought a few times then took a breath. *I can't believe I have to do this.*

"Normally, I'd be all over that offer, but I suspect you've had too much to drink. I'd be an asshole if I went for it right now."

Leanne tilted her head. "You think I'm too wasted to decide that? I feel like that should be *my* call, but I respect your principles. If I drink nothing but water and I still want to do it in the bathroom in half an hour, how about it?"

Trev didn't even need to think about it. "Deal. Dance with me while we wait?"

CHAPTER 2

THOUGH LEANNE HAD HOOKED UP with a lot of people, nobody had ever attempted to protect her from herself.

She studied Trev with interest, taking a second look at him. He was cute for sure—shaggy, sun-streaked hair that made him seem younger than he probably was, if he was friends with Titus. That still meant he was four or five years younger than her, not that she cared. It wasn't like she'd been seriously proposing, though it was funny as hell when he listed his qualifications. Not the response she usually got when she dropped that line.

The players rolled with it, promising her the moon for a shot at getting in her pants. Serious people stammered and said it was too fast; hell, a few folks ran away, thinking she was the type to believe in love at first sight when the opposite was true. After everything she'd seen, Leanne had a hard time believing in love at all. Sex, though, sex was fun. Simple, even.

Currently, she was buzzed but not drunk. She wasn't about to argue with him, though. His caution struck her as adorable and kind of endearing. Normally, potential partners didn't worry about her; she wasn't the sort to make others feel protective.

"Sounds good," she said finally.

The music called for a bump and grind, and she moved on him with slow, explicit hip swivels. Laughing at his expression, she tried to twerk, but that wasn't happening. Vanessa took one look and started laughing.

"That is not remotely right. Here, watch me." Of everyone in the group, Vanessa was the most graceful. She could move between styles too, combining moves from hip-hop, modern, and ballet classes she'd taken as a child.

Leanne stood back. "I wouldn't even try to follow that. You're amazing."

"I know, but that doesn't mean you should stop trying," Vanessa said.

"Fine, I'll go again." Leanne almost got it the second time.

Trevor gave it his best too, but he had even less rhythm than she did. But when he stuck out his butt, she cracked up and slapped her own ass, then his. Vanessa beckoned Leanne toward the kitchen.

"I'll bring her right back," she called to Trev.

"No worries," he said easily.

"Everything good?" Leanne whispered, her gaze fixed on the witch hunter who was hovering unnervingly close to Clem.

Vanessa shook her head. "No idea. This is most nerve-racking party I've ever attended. I'm trying to act natural, but damn. Latest tea, the council is planning…something, but I can't get a read on what. Gladys is so cagey, she wouldn't even give me a hint."

The witch's council was the governing body that regulated the witch community, and it was made up of anonymous members to keep all judgments impartial. If witches didn't know who was on it, they couldn't lobby or push their own agendas. It was good that they seemed alert to the potential powder keg of a witch hunter in St. Claire, but the council might not act fast enough to protect everyone involved.

Worry nibbled away at her buzz. "Let's not fret about it tonight."

"Deal," said Vanessa.

Her friend got a drink and winked as she headed off to chat up an attractive, black-haired man who had been introduced earlier as Calvin Wu. Leanne spotted Trev still watching her, and she rejoined him. He was still her first choice for an entertaining interlude.

As she reached his side, the song changed to a slower tune, and she took it for granted that they'd keep dancing, just up close and personal this time. She looped her arms around his neck, not even pretending she meant to slow dance right. This was an excuse to rub against him, and from the flare in his hazel eyes, he knew it. Pretty eyes, she decided, understated, shimmering flecks of brown and green and gold, sort of tawny and deep, fringed with gold-tipped lashes. Close up, she could see he had long lashes, but they disappeared due to the lightness at the ends.

"Wouldn't you rather find someone else to talk to?" he asked.

"Like who? You're the only one in my world right now." She rubbed her nose against his, deciding he would enjoy careful moves rather than overt ones.

He grinned, seeming reluctantly amused. "Wow, that's a great line. How often does it work?"

"Eight out of ten lovers recommend," she said, winking.

"Seriously, though. There's a room full of people, and I happen to know that both Calvin and Dante are currently single. I don't understand why you went right for *me*."

"You need to work on your self-esteem." Leanne kept her tone gentle because she could tell he was genuinely puzzled, and her heart twinged. Hard. Odd, ordinarily her emotions didn't engage when she was trying to hook up with someone. "But to answer your question, I like your smile. And your hair. Your eyes are a little sad, but that means I'll enjoy making them sparkle. Doesn't hurt that you have an *excellent* ass."

He swallowed, his throat working visibly. "You get right to the point, huh?"

"Candor gets me what I want faster."

"And you want *me*?" His tone caught her attention.

On any other night, she'd give a flirty response or say something like "For an hour or two," but the way he was looking at her, full of desperate yearning and hope, made her pause. Then she simply said, "Yes."

No qualifiers. *So unlike me.*

But she didn't back off the statement. It was true, even without making any promises. Tonight, she did want him. And she chose not to think about how she was on course to repeat her mother's mistakes. If she wasn't careful, she'd end up alone, just like Junie. Hell, Leanne's situation might be worse since she wouldn't even have a kid to pester later on. She'd never trusted *anyone* enough to reproduce with them.

Why am I even thinking about this crap? Bathroom hookup, remember? You're here for a good time, not for a long time.

Trev skimmed his hands down to her hips. "It hasn't quite

been half an hour, but you don't seem impaired. You really think we should—"

"Definitely." She grabbed his hand and towed him toward the downstairs bathroom before doubts could get the best of her.

What are the odds? She'd picked this one because he looked the most like a fuckboy out of everyone else in the room, but instead, he was turning out to be unexpectedly sweet and sensitive. Maybe they'd just end up making out a little, but whatever. She needed spontaneity and to stop thinking for a while.

Thankfully, there was nobody in the half bath, and there was another bathroom upstairs if someone had to go. She flipped the light on and locked the door behind them. Trev eyed her like he didn't know what to expect. *Looks like I'll be driving tonight.* Leanne didn't mind that either. She nudged him against the door, pressing her body to his.

With her heels on, he only had a few inches on her, so it was simple to cup his face, tilting his head for a kiss. His lips were soft but slightly chapped, and he breathed through his nose like he didn't even know how to kiss. *It's been a while.* For some reason, that sent a bittersweet feeling through her, leaving her sad and satisfied at the same time.

Eventually, he relaxed and wrapped his arms around her, making a quiet sound into her mouth. She teased her tongue against his. Trev tasted like mint toothpaste since he hadn't even taken a single drink before she'd decided to have her way with him. He ran his hands over her back as they kissed, shaping her body in slow, luxuriant strokes. The pace didn't feel like a frenzied quickie, more like he wanted to take his time.

Here, though? In the bathroom?

Everything was getting scrambled. She bit his lower lip, drawing a moan from him, and when he shifted his hips, his stiff cock nudged her. Trev tried to jerk away, but she chased that contact, glorying in the confirmation that he was into this, even if it wasn't happening like she'd expected. Leanne had figured he'd have his hands in her panties by now, but he seemed so tentative that she had to break the kiss to ask.

"Um. You've done this before, right?"

"Hooked up in the bathroom at a party? Never."

She laughed softly. "Not what I'm asking. This can't be your first time."

Quickly, Trev shook his head. "Am I that out of practice?"

"It wasn't a complaint."

"I'm still having a hard time processing that this is actually happening," he confessed. "I'm not the guy, you know? I'm the sidekick. I can't believe someone like you even looked twice at me, let alone wants this. My body is on board, but my head is confused."

"If you're not ready or you have doubts…"

Dammit, it sucked, but she had to let him change his mind. She stepped back, but Trev followed, his eyes catching fire. In this light, they glimmered like topaz. To her astonishment, he lifted her onto the sink.

"I didn't say 'stop.' I *do* want this, Leanne. Shit, that's probably not even the right word. 'Need' is closer, if I can say that without weirding you out."

"Need is fantastic," she whispered, just before he kissed her again.

This is happening.

Trev touched her just so she wouldn't see his hands shaking, and once he felt her warmth on his palms, his nerves steadied. Once, he'd been careless, quick to act, fast to forget, and it didn't matter as long as it was fun. Maybe he could relive those moments of freedom, take a taste of what this woman offered. Her choice still didn't make sense to him, but he didn't care.

Her mouth was sweet and lush with a fruity tang. Mango? And tequila. She sank her hands into his hair and tugged as he kissed her neck. Her head fell back, her riotously red hair spilling down her back as she closed her eyes. Their earlier kisses hadn't smudged her lipstick, a magic he couldn't begin to fathom. Leanne breathed faster as he ran his teeth over her throat, and she wrapped her legs around his hips, drawing him closer still.

"Fuck. I don't have a condom."

He'd stopped carrying them around years ago. Keeping one in the wallet was ridiculous and optimistic, a relic of the high school boy who'd thought sex could happen anywhere, anytime.

She laughed lightly and opened her purse. It was a small clutch, only big enough to hold her phone, lipstick, some cash, and a handful of condoms. "I come prepared."

"Was that a pun? Wait, maybe don't answer that. It might diminish the mood."

"Who says banter has no place in the bathroom?"

"Uh, pretty much everyone." He hesitated. "There's not a lot of room, and—"

"Let's cut to the chase. I'm in the mood to fuck, and I want to get on your dick. It doesn't have to be more complicated."

The sheer honesty of her words settled in his cock, and suddenly that was all he wanted too—to get out of his head and live in the moment. A gorgeous woman asking to fuck? *Yes, please.* Confidence kicked in. Once upon a time, he was good at this. Before Sarah, multiple people used to hit him up for booty calls when there were *lots* of other options.

"Lift your ass," he said.

She complied without a flicker of hesitation, and oh yeah, he liked that. Trev rolled her skirt up, grazing her thighs with each careful motion. Her skin was incredibly smooth, lightly tanned, and she practically burned his fingers the higher they went. The heat from her sex was palpable, her panties already wet with excitement. He traced up the center, watching her face the whole time. Leanne's eyes went hooded, and she let out a shivering breath.

"That's it," she whispered.

He pulled them off entirely and tossed them over his shoulder then shucked his bottoms. There evidently wasn't a shy bone in Leanne's body; that would change when Trev started fucking her. With eyes round as saucers, she stared at his cock until he shifted uneasily.

"What?"

"Holy shit. I'm pretty sure you're legally obligated to advise potential partners that you're bigger than a bread box beforehand."

"Oh my God." Heat rushed to his face so fast that he almost passed out from having his blood flow divided so severely.

"You'll just say anything!" In a softer tone, he added, "It's not *that* big."

But honestly, his cock had an ego, because it swelled more beneath her admiring gaze. He squeezed his eyes shut, trying to get a handle on his emotions. Embarrassment warred with...pride? Yeah, fuck. It was ridiculous how much he wanted to make this good for her. Memorable, even, in the way he never was.

"That thing should have its own zip code," she said decisively. "Take it easy on me, okay? I'm not exactly new at this, but you're packing more than I'm used to."

With her avid eyes locked on his junk, it took him two tries to get the condom on, and then he nudged forward, tilting her body to meet his first thrust. Taking Leanne at her word, he pushed in slow and careful, pausing at the halfway point when she started to squirm. He leaned in for a kiss, and she nuzzled her mouth into his with a little purr, her tongue swirling around his until his heart kicked in his chest.

She wants this. I want her. It's all good.

"How am I doing?"

"You want a Yelp review or what?" She grinned and nipped his lower lip.

He'd never laughed so much during sex, yet it didn't even seem strange. *Oh fuck, yes.* Once he pushed all the way in, he closed his eyes, trying to get a grip on the unexpected intensity. Trev forgot they were at a party, forgot everything but the woman wrapped around him. She held on while he fucked her, and he moaned because it felt so damn good.

Sometimes they kissed while they fucked, but mostly, he buried his face in her shoulder, biting down to keep from yelling while she rolled her hips against him. If he went as hard as he wanted to, he might break the sink and the mirror, and hell if he wanted to be remembered as the dude who wrecked the downstairs bathroom at this party.

Finally, she whispered, "I'm getting close," and came all over his cock.

The tight clutch of her pussy carried him over, and he filled the condom in panting spurts. His head went gloriously clear—no thoughts, no anxiety, nothing but the endless pleasure of her making him whole. When the orgasm glow faded a little, so did some of that euphoria. What an absurd thing to imagine about a total stranger.

When he was sure he could manage without falling over, he drew back and pulled out. At least he could still deal with a condom neatly. Leanne hopped off the sink, and she wobbled a little. Trev took serious pleasure in that as he steadied her.

"You okay?"

"I'm awesome."

It should've been awkward as hell as they did their best to tidy up in that small space, but somehow it wasn't. He kept waiting for the punch line or for her to dismiss him, but by the time he buttoned up his shorts, she was wearing a thoughtful look.

"Something on your mind?"

"Actually, yeah. We could stay here and drink, but honestly, I'm not feeling it. I chatted with my girls enough before you got here. I thought a quickie would be enough to take the edge off, but as it turns out, I want more."

"This is the classic 'let's get out of here' maneuver, then."

She lifted a shoulder, not denying it. "Basically, yeah. Did you drive?"

Trev shook his head. "I rode with Titus."

"I had a few margaritas with my mom before I came over, so I got a rideshare. We could pick my car up at my place and get a room somewhere. If you're interested."

"You live with your mom?" That surprising revelation made him feel marginally better about his own situation.

Until she shook her head. "She dropped in unexpectedly, wanting to party. Junie is what people call a 'free spirit.' By which I mean, she loves inconveniencing me with her whims."

Relatable. While Leanne looked perfect, her family situation was no better than his, just difficult in a different way. Once he processed that insight, it was easier for Trev to believe she truly wanted to spend the night with him. As he pushed open the bathroom door, a handful of partygoers scattered. "Were they listening to us?" he wondered aloud.

"Ignore them," Leanne advised. "They're probably just jealous. Are you ordering us a ride, or should I?"

"I'm on it." Trev set his hand on her lower back as he eased them through the living room. He flashed a grin at Titus and waved.

If this is my lucky night, I might as well make the most of it.

CHAPTER 3

LEANNE DIDN'T KNOW THE RIDESHARE driver, thankfully.

One pitfall of living in St. Claire was she often got picked up by somebody's grandpa and then had to listen to a lecture on her questionable life choices. This time, however, she sat in the back with Trev and waited out the ride to her condo. The woman dropped them off at the curb on the other side of the gate, and Leanne's car keys lived in her purse, so she didn't have to go upstairs and face Junie, who would doubtless be upset that she was choosing to spend the night somewhere else.

Once the driver took off, she tossed the key fob to Trev. "You haven't had anything to drink, right?"

"Yep. You didn't give me the chance."

"That's good for us. You're driving." She led the way, waving to the night guard as they walked past the security hut. He lifted a hand in turn as she made for her car, a cute convertible that was fairly inconvenient during fall and winter. "Here we are."

"Sweet ride," he said, pressing the button to unlock the doors. She stared at him hard, but the glow from the parking lights didn't reveal any hint of sarcasm. So she smiled and said, "Thanks," as she got in on the passenger side.

"Where to?"

"Let's head to the Holiday Inn Express." Not exactly a posh night out, but it was the closest spot she could think of that got a lot of traffic from travelers. Less likely that she'd be recognized.

"I know where it is."

Leanne handed him her pass card, the one that allowed her to come and go freely from the gated community, and then he set out, driving with relaxed proficiency. Now that they were alone, she wondered what the hell she was doing. This qualified as high-risk behavior, going off alone in the middle of the night with someone she'd just met. Yet she didn't tell him to turn around, because whatever awaited her in the hotel room with Trev, it had to be better than dealing with her mother after she'd drunk all those margaritas on her own.

I hope she doesn't puke in my favorite purse. Again.

That prospect was almost enough to make her tell him to stop the car, but then she imagined the cleanup and shook her head silently. *No way. Stay in the moment.*

"You're quiet," Trev said.

"So are you. Worried I'll strip you naked, tie you up, and rob you?"

He paused, aiming a smiling look in her direction. "Well, I *wasn't*. You should know, I don't have any cash on me, and my card is pretty much maxed out."

"Card, singular?"

"Is that a problem?" Now he sounded defensive, eyes fixed hard on the long, dark road ahead of them.

"No, I make good money. I can be your sugar mama tonight."

He laughed. "This was your idea anyway, remember? It's only fair."

"True enough." She liked that he didn't seem to mind her being more successful, at least in the eyes of the world. "We're here," she added. "If you want, you can park the car while I take care of registration."

Nodding, Trev dropped her off at the front door and circled out of sight, leaving Leanne to stride in briskly. The lobby was decorated in earth tones, and the designer had clearly gone for a modern lodge feel, though there was no fireplace and all the furniture looked like it had come from the same store. Nobody could ever forget such a loud carpet, however.

She smiled at the woman working the desk. "Do you have a room? King bed, nonsmoking."

"We certainly do." The night clerk summarized the costs and fees; Leanne nodded through the recitation. "Then may I have your credit card and ID?"

That was easy. Leanne slid the cards across and waited. Two minutes later, the clerk had forms for her to sign. She filled out the info on the car she was parking in the lot, signed in two places, and she was accepting the keys when Trevor strode in. The woman smirked a bit when she saw they had no baggage, but Leanne maintained a neutral expression.

"Thanks for your help."

"Certainly! The elevator is that way. You're on the third floor.

The pool is closed. Breakfast is included, and it's in the lounge starting at 6:00 a.m. Checkout is at noon. Have a nice night, and please enjoy your stay."

Linking her arm with Trev, Leanne sauntered down the hall and pressed the call button. As the elevator dinged and the doors opened, she whispered, "Pretty sure she thinks we're cheating on our partners."

He stepped inside without looking back. "Gotta admit, I don't care."

"Honestly? Same."

Their ascent was slow and clunky, but they got there eventually, and Leanne found their room at the end of the hall. Inside, it was about what one would expect from a place that specialized in attracting weary highway drivers, but the room was clean, and the bed looked inviting. There was also a desk, a coffee table, a small sofa, and weirdly, a massive whirlpool tub in the corner, outside the bathroom.

"Should we risk it?" she wondered aloud.

"Probably not. I'm game for a shower, though, if we both fit."

"You're assuming I want to shower with you."

Trev smiled. "I guess I am. We can do it separately, but I figured you wanted to keep rolling. Otherwise, you'd have slapped my ass and sent me on my way at the party."

"True enough." She wasn't one for delaying gratification, so she unbuttoned her skirt then her blouse. Soon she stood in her lingerie and gave him the look over one shoulder before sashaying into the bathroom.

He followed her a moment later as she tinkered with the faucet to find the perfect temperature. The bathroom was simple and white, clean, and the tub-shower combo ought to hold the two of them. If they were careful. Leanne wasn't great at being careful.

Trev swept her hair to the side and kissed her shoulder, a tender gesture that surprised her. Her breathing kicked up a notch, and her confident smile faltered, but since he couldn't see her face from this angle, it would be fine. She closed her eyes, focused on showing the fun woman with perfect armor around her heart. Then she turned and wrapped her arms around his neck as the water warmed.

He kissed her, one hand on her waist, the other gently skimming down her spine. This didn't feel like a one-nighter—he took his time, with delicate pecks slowly deepening into the hungry swirl of his tongue, like he had nothing better to do than kiss her for the rest of his life. That thought shocked her enough that she stiffened in his hold, and he pulled back to regard her with an uncertain look.

"You okay?"

What's wrong with me? Don't make this weird.

She forced a smile, grateful he didn't know her well enough to recognize how off she was tonight. "I'm great. Get naked."

"You don't have to ask me twice."

Trev couldn't shake the idea that there was something fragile about Leanne.

He knew next to nothing about this woman, apart from the fact that she was friends with Danica, the woman Titus was dating.

Twice, he almost said they didn't have to do this, but she seemed to *want* to, even if she had some personal stuff going on, possibly related to her mom's unexpected visit. These days, he rarely even spoke to his parents despite them living right upstairs, and when they did have a conversation, it was just this pointed bullshit, telling him how awesome his older brother, Tanner, was doing. To cover a rush of thoughts he'd rather not deal with, he stepped into the tub and extended a hand to help her in.

She cocked her head and smiled. "You're sweet. I could get used to this."

Once they got situated, he made sure they weren't leaking water out the sides of the curtain, then he lathered up his hands. "Wash your back?"

"Please." She turned away, revealing the smooth slope of her back and the lush curves of her ass.

He'd never been with anyone so unabashedly sexual and glamorous. Somehow, her makeup didn't run, even when she tipped her face up under the silvery stream of the shower. *Maybe she has a permanent tint done on her lips and eyeliner tattooed on?* Whatever the case, with the water darkening her hair to deep crimson and her features glazed with water, she looked like a siren, aching perfection that came with a curse and would end with him drowning in her depths. Mentally, Trev shrugged, gently circling his soapy hands on her slick skin.

I'm basically okay with that.

After he washed her everywhere, she returned the favor. A hotel meant unlimited hot water, and he spent ages caressing her long after the soap rinsed away. Eventually, he grabbed a couple of towels and wrapped her up in the first then carelessly pulled the other around his waist. This time Leanne got out first and helped him, and he restrained the urge to pinch himself.

This isn't a dream, right? It's gonna suck if I wake up in the basement alone.

"I shouldn't have gotten my hair wet," she said, frowning at her reflection in the steamed-up mirror. "It'll be a nightmare to deal with tomorrow."

Nah, my imagination isn't good enough to add details like that.

"Same. My hair will be a bush in the morning, and I don't even have a comb."

She smiled, turning away from her own image to lick a stray drop of water from his shoulder. "You'll be cute anyway."

"Glad you think so."

He had a quiet idea about sweeping her off her feet, but he didn't trust himself on slippery tiles, so he waited until she left the bathroom, and then he swooped, carrying her to bed like a bride. But he didn't stop there, and they bounced onto the bed together, ending up in an untidy sprawl atop the white comforter.

Leanne pulled back enough to scramble beneath the covers because the air con was set to chill. He burrowed in after her and chucked his towel; she did the same. The lights were on low, and he rolled onto his side to gaze into her eyes, content to let her lead. Everything about tonight had been her idea, after all, and he hadn't been disappointed once. In fact, this was the best night he'd had since—

No, don't do it. Don't. You're happy right now, for fuck's sake.

But his brain refused to listen and completed the thought anyway. *Since Sarah dumped me for good.* Sometimes Trev imagined there was an enemy living in his head, one who gloried in reminding him of painful memories every time he inched closer to not hating himself, every time the misery abated.

Leanne must've noticed something in his expression because her brows drew together, and she touched his cheek lightly. "You okay?"

He'd answered that question so many times. Breezily, lying through his teeth. *Yeah, I'm good. No worries. Everything's fine.*

But, for some reason, he couldn't be that guy tonight. Not with her. The simple deception wouldn't come, even though he knew the script by heart. It was all about reassuring other people, setting them at ease, because if he told the truth, they'd be scared shitless of what he might do.

"No," he said. "I'm not. I haven't been in a really long time, and I don't know why I'm telling you this, because it's nothing to do with you."

"You want to talk about it?" The offer surprised him. "Sometimes it's easier to open up to a stranger than someone you've known your whole life. I don't have any preconceptions about who you're supposed to be."

"You wanted to go for round two, not listen to my problems," Trev said softly.

"Eh, you're not a fuck machine. I'm not normally anyone's first choice for serious topics, but what can I say? It's been a weird night. Maybe it would do both of us good to step outside our usual roles."

If you dump your issues on her, you'll never see her again. Nobody would be interested if they knew—

Trev decided to nutshell it. "Basically, my life's been in a holding pattern since college, and I never got over my last breakup. I'm not happy, but I pretend otherwise. In short, I'm a colossal waste of oxygen, and my parents were right to give up on me."

"Bullshit," she said. "The last part anyway. I just met you, but I *know* you're a good friend to Titus. And you're...gentle. Not once tonight have you made me feel like you only care about getting sex. Honestly, you're so nice that it's throwing me a little."

For a minute, he thought he might cry—*beyond* embarrassing. He closed his eyes briefly before responding, "Wow. Well, honestly, I was just so happy to be wanted...the whole night's been like winning the lottery. The sex was fantastic, but I'm just...enjoying you. As much as I can before you realize you can do better."

She smiled at him. "What if I never realize that? Will you date me?"

"Are you seriously asking?" Trev monitored her expression carefully, wondering if this was a joke.

"If I am?"

"Then yeah. I'd definitely see you again."

"I'll get your number in the morning. Would you hate me if I said I'm tired? I was all for going again, but the shower made me sleepy, and I have to be up early."

Trev laughed at the amazing irony. "So you got us to hotel room to...cuddle?"

"Shut up," she said. "Turn over. I'll be the big spoon."

Obediently, he rolled onto his other side, facing away, and she curled into his back. The feeling was...indescribable. Until this moment, he hadn't realized how much he missed the warmth of someone snuggled up against him. When Leanne slid her arm around him, he put his hand over hers.

"I love this," he mumbled.

"It's not too late," she said unexpectedly.

"What's not?"

"To make some changes." It seemed like she'd been contemplating his confession. "First, ask yourself what you want. That can be hard to figure out. Once you know, little steps will get you there eventually. Don't give up, Trev. You can do anything you want."

Nobody had *ever* said that to him. Not ever.

He fell asleep smiling.

CHAPTER 4

IN THE MORNING, LEANNE WOKE up in Trev's arms.

They had swapped positions at some point in the night, and he was curled around her naturally, his face buried in the bird's nest her hair had become. Her phone was on the bedside table with 30 percent left on the battery. She had eight missed calls from Junie and a dozen smart-ass comments in the coven group chat, and she'd managed to stir before her alarm. Ever so carefully, she rolled out from under his arm and got dressed. She put her panties in her purse and wrangled her hair into a braid, fastened with the emergency hair band she kept in her bag. Her Fresh Face spell was starting to fade, cracking at the edges, so she carefully locked the door and whispered the words while the energy gathered before flowing outward over her skin in a shimmering ripple.

There, I'm gorgeous again.

Leanne rinsed her mouth with water then used the mouthwash the hotel provided. *Can't wait to brush my teeth.*

In hindsight, she couldn't believe they'd gotten a room to cuddle and talk. *I'm never telling anyone. I'd never live it down.* Quietly, she moved back to the bed, her heels in hand.

As she gazed down at Trev's sleeping face, she considered leaving him to make his own way home. But coming here had been her idea, and it would be shitty to abandon him when she knew he was financially challenged—by his own admission. So he'd either have to pay for a ride he might not be able to afford or call someone, which entailed admitting she'd left him stranded. *I don't want to screw him over.*

So she perched beside him on the bed and woke him by touching his cheek. "Morning. Did you sleep well?"

Before he even opened his eyes, he gave her a sleepy smile, so much effortless sweetness that it wreaked havoc on her insides. *I'm hungry, that's all.*

"Surprisingly, yeah. Better than I have in years. You're great in bed." Suddenly, he snapped alert. "I mean, you're great to share a bed with."

"I'll take either," she said lightly, trying not to reveal how awkward this felt. Leanne rarely spent the night with people, and she couldn't recall the last time she'd had a conversation the morning after. "Get dressed. I'll drive you home."

It took all of five minutes for Trev to put himself together. Soon, they headed out—with a brief pit stop for Leanne to check out of the room—and then he gave her his address. Mentally, she charted the route. Taking Trev home meant she'd have minimal time to get to her condo and tidy up before work. *Hopefully Junie doesn't delay me further.* While she couldn't put off finding out why her mom was here forever, she doubted the conversation would go anywhere good.

The last time Junie showed up unannounced, she'd proposed

moving in with Leanne. "It'll be fun," she'd said. "Just like having a roommate! Think about it anyway. I miss you and we're both single, so…"

A cold shudder ran through her. She'd lived through the joy of listening to her mother's active love life through the walls, and she had no intention of experiencing it again. It wasn't that she opposed Junie doing as she wished; Leanne just didn't want to hear it. And the converse was also true: living with her mom meant she couldn't bring people home as she pleased. Silently, she shook her head.

"Arguing with yourself mentally?" Trev asked.

The question surprised her. He was sharper than he initially seemed, quietly paying attention to every detail. She forced a smile.

"Mother-daughter stuff. It'll be fine."

He didn't press the issue, and she drove the rest of the way in silence. He lived relatively near Danica and Clem, in a similar neighborhood, though the lots were a little bigger and farther from downtown St. Claire. She pulled into the drive, but she didn't go all the way to the house.

Trev turned to her with a tentative smile. "This is it, I guess. Not sure if I'm supposed to ask, so I'll make it a statement instead. I'd like to see you again. You said something about swapping numbers, but I understand if you're not into it, if this was a one-time thing or whatever."

Normally, she'd flash a smile and say "This was fun" and that would be the end. But he so clearly expected she had no use for him that she couldn't stick to the usual script. "Give me your phone." Leanne held out her hand imperiously.

Wearing a baffled expression, he unlocked it and passed it over. Silently, she created a new contact and keyed in her number. His tense posture eased when she returned it.

"Taking this as permission to call you. Thanks for an amazing night."

Before she could respond, he kissed her cheek and hopped out of the car, sauntering toward the house with a certain confidence in his step. Hard to believe getting her number boosted his mood so much, but she found herself smiling as she backed out of the drive. *Crap, look at the time.* She sped over to the condo and crept inside like a thief. Fortune favored her: Junie was asleep in the guest room, freeing Leanne to freshen up and change her clothes. She was in and out in fifteen minutes.

That got her to work with a few minutes to spare. She greeted everyone on the way in, ignoring the looks. Nobody had ever seen her hair in a braid, but there had been no time to fix it, and spells could only go so far. There was a difference between a good glamour and an outright illusion. With a sigh, she settled at her desk and dove right into her to-do list.

Sadly, that bright start to the day didn't last long. Mayor Anderson called her into his office, and she strode in ready to fight. If this was about the meeting with the community center, she'd love to remind him that attending such events in his stead wasn't even part of her job description. Writing speeches and press releases, handling social media, controlling the way he appeared in the media—yes, all of that. But she wasn't the deputy mayor, and she wasn't even his chief of staff. Leanne was sick of filling in and being used as a convenience. She'd taken it up until now because it wasn't like she could easily find another job like this; it would entail moving, most likely, and she was happy here.

Anderson kept her waiting, shuffling his papers around, and she folded her arms, determined not to lose this fight before it ever began. Finally, he glanced up from the busywork and indicated the chair opposite his desk. "Have a seat."

"Will this take long? I have a meeting in twenty minutes."

With a journalist. And I'd love to tell the truth about you. But I won't. Like everyone else, she'd bought into Anderson's progressive bullshit, but as it turned out, he only cared about reaping the benefits of office and upholding the status quo. He'd only kept one of his election promises, and it wasn't to the people who mattered. More than once, she'd considered hexing him, but so far, Danica had talked her out of it.

"I got an email from the community center. You gave them hope that we'll revisit the budget? What were you thinking?"

You can find the money; you just don't want to.

"If you don't like the way I respond in those situations, don't put me in them. It's simple. Frankly, you should be talking to Deputy Mayor Dudley or your chief of staff. They're the ones who off-loaded their responsibilities onto me. I won't be so willing to assist in the future if this is how you react to me going above and beyond."

She straightened her shoulders and strode out without looking back.

———

Trev had never been more grateful to have his own entrance; he came in through the back door of the garage then went straight down the steps into what qualified as home.

Dealing with his parents while doing the walk of shame? It didn't bear thinking about. Except this didn't really fit the bill. For once, he didn't feel shitty about how the night turned out. He had Leanne's number, even if he didn't know her last name or what she did for a living. Better, he knew how she tasted, he'd seen her face when she came, and he understood she had a complicated relationship with her mother.

That was a lot to unpack from a single night.

It was too soon to text her, and for once, he had no desire to sleep until noon. In fact, he couldn't recall the last time he was up this early. Sometimes when he helped Titus out, he kept weird hours because Titus's dog, Doris, liked her breakfast early, and she didn't eat as well with the automatic dish. But otherwise? He lived like a vampire, staying awake through the night trying to keep his brain busy so it wouldn't hound him. With varying degrees of success.

Even his "apartment" was depressing. His parents had intended to remodel the basement completely, but when they figured out he'd be staying there indefinitely, they just sort of... stopped working on it. Because why bother, right? It didn't matter if the floor was painted cement or if pipes showed here and there. All his furniture had been banished from the nicer part of the house—an old brown plaid love seat, a clunky TV his grandfather had bought, resin side tables, and a two-chair dinette set he rarely used. The bathroom was unfinished too, wide open to the laundry area, and the kitchenette was a hot plate and a mini fridge.

"You won't bother cooking for yourself, what do you need a proper kitchen for? If you want to eat with us, come upstairs," his mom had said.

In fact, he *did* like cooking. Not that anyone was interested. His dad only grunted, ignoring him in favor of a hunting and fishing magazine. That was another way that Trev couldn't compete with Tanner. His relatives saw nothing wrong with shooting animals, but the one time he went along, he'd hurled at seeing the deer thrashing on her side, eyes wide and terrified. Shit, that memory haunted him to this day, along with the awful noises she'd made. Tanner slit the doe's throat, finishing her off without hesitation, and their old man clapped him on the shoulder and spent the next month bragging to all his buddies what a natural hunter his oldest boy was. Nobody was asking Trev, but he privately thought it was fucking worrisome how fast Tanner was with a knife. But he *was* a surgeon, after all.

God, my family sucks.

He showered, rinsing a few silverfish down the drain in the process. Damn, he hated those things, but nothing ever seemed to get rid of them. His parents were blaming him for it, but that was nothing new. Basements were damp, and only a full remodel with weatherproofing could keep them out permanently.

As he stepped out of the shower, he contemplated what Leanne had said. *Ask yourself what you want. You can do anything...* He made a bowl of cereal and ate it on the sofa while scrolling news articles on his phone. Normally, he'd smoke a little weed, take a nap, and play some video games, but after last night, he wished he had something else to do. Like, practically anything.

He'd never admit it, but he looked forward to Titus messaging him with some random chore he needed done. Watch Doris for a few days? Absolutely. Spend all day painting his stepsister's bedroom? No problem.

And when he came home?

"Don't you have any pride?" his old man had demanded once. "When are you planning to stop leeching off your friends? We thought you'd get sick of living in our basement eventually and pull yourself together. Jesus, I can't stand looking at you."

"Good talk." He'd kept a smile on his face the whole time, knowing his insouciance pissed his father off something fierce.

Wade Montgomery had high standards, and he rarely let a chance slip by to tell Trev how far short he fell. Trev's mom, Barb, usually tried to keep the peace, but not in a way that included arguing with her husband. She just wanted everyone to be polite, no matter how horrible the underlying sentiment might be.

But here it was, 10:00 a.m. on a weekday morning, and he had nowhere to be. He killed some time texting with Titus. It was cool picturing the guy taking a break at the bakery. Sometimes he imagined being that dedicated to his work—that he'd get up early every day, but he knew himself well enough to realize it was a fantasy, not his thing at all.

Titus: You good?

Trev: Always am.

That's a fun-sized lie. One he couldn't quite believe he'd admitted to Leanne, and he'd done it without being chemically enhanced too. She had the magic touch—just enough interest, not enough for it to feel like pressure—and all his depressing secrets came tumbling out, like a closet where someone hastily crammed all their junk.

Titus: Glad to hear it. You didn't stick around long last night. Just a heads-up...

Trev: Yeah?

Titus: Pretty much everyone knows you two hooked up.

Trev: I had one job and I did it well.

Titus: DUDE.

Trev: It's not bragging if it's true.

Titus: I'm out.

Trev plugged in his phone and fell into a multiplayer session. He didn't wear a headset because he had zero interest in listening to the bullshit other players spewed. Most of these missions, he could run solo and with his eyes closed. It wasn't worth instructing people he'd never play with again. He had a regular group that met up once a month on a different platform, and he'd never admit it, but he looked forward to hanging out with those faceless strangers.

I wonder if Leanne would think I'm a total loser.

Making up his mind, he decided to text her tomorrow and ask if she was interested in seeing him again. No risk, no reward, right?

Annoyingly, that sounded like the kind of thing his dad would say, but even a broken clock was right twice a day.

CHAPTER 5

THERE WOULD BE A RECKONING for the way Leanne had spoken to the mayor.

Mayor Anderson wasn't the type to forget a slight. He could be as petty as an elementary school kid, and he'd work out some way to make her sorry for pointing out a few problems. But she refused to worry about that today, instead focusing on her actual work. At the end of the day, she drove home, halfway hoping Junie would've succumbed to yet another whim and gone off to hike in the Adirondacks or something.

No such luck.

When Leanne let herself in the condo, Junie was sprawled on the sofa, the wreckage of a day spent lounging spread around her in the form of chip packets and chocolate wrappers. If Leanne knew her mom, she hadn't fixed herself a decent meal all day. That gave her flashbacks to childhood; she'd been the only kid she knew who got excited to have salad and vegetables since they were a rare treat.

"Have you been watching daytime TV all afternoon?" she asked.

Junie grinned. "You know me so well. By the way, I totally

heard you sneaking in this morning, I just chose not to give you grief over it."

And chose not to leave your cozy bed.

"Thanks. I appreciate that."

"You must've had a great time last night. Tell me all about it!" Junie curled onto her side, seeming to expect the kind of details Leanne would provide her coven sisters. In fact, it was a little strange that she hadn't already shared the story about their bathroom hookup in the group chat. It was kind of her thing, taking great delight in oversharing.

"I'd rather hear why you turned up out of the blue. Is everything okay?"

So help me, if she's invested in another pyramid scheme. Junie's last job had involved more MLM than actual work, and it had been expensive as hell to extricate Mom from her own trusting nature. Sometimes her mother frustrated her so much that—suddenly, her attention sharpened, because Junie was answering the question.

No. Oh no.

"—because it's time we revisited the idea of moving in together. I don't have much, so you wouldn't have to get rid of any furniture to make space for me. And you have the guest room all ready to go. It would be so much fun! I could even join your coven. I want us to be closer, LeLe, and this is definitely the way to make that happen."

Leanne's mouth compressed. "First, don't call me LeLe. Next...." She took a breath, fighting to keep her emotions in check.

Words clawed at her brain, desperate to escape. *You don't get to just show up in the middle of the life I built and expect me to accommodate you. Our entire lives, you did exactly what you wanted, and now that you're lonely, you expect me to give in again and make room for you.* But instead of speaking the truth— ironic because she was known for pulling no punches in other aspects of her life—the most ridiculous lie of all time popped out.

"That would be amazing, but unfortunately, my boyfriend will be moving in soon, and it would be awkward taking the next step with you living with us."

Junie stared at her in astonishment. "I had no idea you were even seeing anyone seriously. Oh, I'm so happy for you! What's his name? What's he like?"

Before Leanne could answer, her phone rang. That number wasn't in her contacts, but she fully intended to confuse the hell out of the telemarketer on the other end of the line. She faked a brilliant smile, gazing at her phone with what she hoped was a sufficiently gooey expression.

"Hey, sweetheart. I missed you."

There was a brief pause. Then a familiar voice said, "Uh, really?"

Trev. This was a lot better than a random sales call. "Definitely. I'm glad you called. I was just telling my mother about you."

Please don't hang up. I'm not normally like this.

Another pause, longer this time. "Seriously? That's...I don't even know what to say."

Leanne laughed as if he'd made a joke. "Don't worry, she'll love you."

He made a strange noise. "Wait, are you...? Oh. You're using me as a ruse, right?"

"You're so smart," she said.

"Then I'm glad I called. Should I push my luck by asking you out, or do you just need to fake a conversation with me for a while longer?"

"I'd love that. If you want, you can come for dinner tonight. It's short notice, but I'm worth canceling your plans."

Trev chuckled. "You know damn well I don't have any. Text me your address. I'm not a hundred percent sure I can find the place again otherwise. I'll be there whenever you want me."

"How's seven? I need time to sort out the menu."

"See you then. Babe."

When Leanne turned, she found Junie studying her with overt fascination, one hand pressed to her heart. "Your man will just drop everything for you? I love him already. I can't believe you finally met the one! Now that I look at you closer, you do seem to be glowing."

Leanne stifled a smile. Her mom had the ability to see whatever she wanted. Those rose-colored glasses would be admirable if they didn't cause Leanne so much trouble.

"Like a radioactive spider," she said.

"None of that. You're not allowed to be cynical. Oh, look at this place! I need to tidy up before he gets here. Are you cooking or—"

"I'll order takeout," Leanne cut in.

She'd never promised Trev a home-cooked meal, though she did mention dinner. Food was food, right? Quickly, she requisitioned a few dishes from her favorite delivery app then helped Junie clean up the condo. Her mother even made the bed in the guest room, which showed how desperate she was to make a good impression on Leanne's man. While her mother worked, she texted her address to Trev. While he'd driven to her place the night before, everything looked a bit different at night, and he didn't know the unit number. She also added, I may have said we're serious about each other and considering cohabitation. I will owe you so big if you save me from my mother and play along.

"You should change," Junie said eventually. "Not that your work clothes aren't…respectable, but you want to look pretty for…" She hesitated. "I don't think you ever told me his name. Or anything about him."

"His name is Trevor. And yes, I'll go get ready." That effectively ended the gentle interrogation, a necessity since she didn't know shit about Trev.

She wasn't about to admit she'd met her "serious boyfriend" once and that he was walking into this situation as a favor. Hopefully, he wouldn't mind playing his part in this ridiculous drama, even if Junie grilled him like a choice sirloin. Her babbling could overwhelm a person quick, if they weren't used to her conversational style.

He hasn't answered. Did he see the text?

Fighting a wave of misgiving because it felt like this white lie would rapidly spiral out of control, Leanne slipped on a little black dress from her "dress to kill" closet. She even took the time to sort her hair, getting ready as if this was, indeed, a date with the love of her life. Finally, she closed her eyes and focused, drawing threads of glamour toward her so she'd seem wreathed in beauty. Frankly, the spell work was over the top for the occasion, but for reasons she couldn't articulate even to herself, she wanted to take his breath away.

Leanne winked and blew a kiss to her reflection.

Trev filled his gas tank on the way to Leanne's place.

Thankfully, he'd done some work for Titus recently, pet sitting and painting, so he had some cash on hand, though he hadn't brought it with him to the party. Since he didn't contribute to household expenses—a fact he wasn't proud of, whatever his old man said— any income lasted him a long time. He'd dressed carefully in a pair of navy Dockers and a blue-and-white striped button-down, clothes his mother had bought back when she still held out hope of him getting a day job. And it wasn't that he hadn't *tried*. He'd interviewed until failure made him nauseous every time he'd put on his professional clothes and tried again.

Maybe the problem lay with Trev, just like his parents said. Sometimes he made it to the second round, but he never got that final callback. No matter what he was trying to do, he always fell a little short. And at this point, his resume was essentially useless because no company would be satisfied with his explanation for why he'd been underemployed for almost ten years.

Stop thinking about it.

Leanne had left word at the gate, so the guard waved him through. There were assigned spaces for visitors, well away from the building. If he had been thinking straight, he would have brought... something, but he'd rushed right over, more concerned about being on time than making a good impression. And hell, he didn't even know what he should get anyway. Wine or flowers, maybe? He'd flubbed meeting Sarah's parents. *They freaking hated me.*

Don't think about that either.

He took the elevator to the top floor. Leanne's text directed him to 407, and he took a moment to gather his courage. *Why am I so nervous? This is a good deed. I'm not meeting her mom for real. It's more like I'm helping out a friend.* A singularly unhelpful voice added, *A friend you banged in someone else's bathroom.*

Trev rapped on the door before he could chicken out. There was no telling how this dinner would go, but he was strangely game for it. His life had become endlessly the same, minutiae and monotony with no hope for change, but now, now he dared to imagine something different, at least in the hidden corners of his brain. The full vision of what he wanted his life to resemble wouldn't coalesce, but before now, he couldn't even conceive climbing out of the miserable hole he called "home."

Leanne answered quickly, and her gaze skimmed him up and down intimately, a look he recognized as her unique style. He straightened a little, tugging at his shirt. "Will I do? Is there anything particular I should know?"

"Just go along with whatever I say," she whispered.

He smothered a laugh. "Yeah, okay. I played a tree in the school play in elementary school, you know. I'm sure I've got this."

She took his hand unexpectedly, sending delicious sparks all the way up to his elbow. It could be the fact that he wasn't used to being touched anymore, but it was impossible to deny it felt amazing. He shifted it from a peremptory touch to an intimate one, lacing their fingers together. Leanne paused to smile at him, and...wow. His head spun a little. He'd known she was gorgeous, but she was beautiful in a timeless way. Like Marilyn or Rita at their height, almost too glamorous to be with someone who wasn't a celebrity or professional athlete.

Panic fluttered inside him. *This will never work. Her mom will never believe she'd settle for someone like me.* Yet it was too late to flee. Leanne towed him into her condo, and for a moment, he glanced around in awe. The place was lovely, exactly the sort of home he'd want if he could afford something on his own. Open floor plan so the kitchen overlooked the living room, connected via breakfast bar. Near the kitchen, she had a four-seat glass dining table. There was a half bath by the front door, and a hallway led out the other side of the living room, presumably to the bedrooms.

The decor was elegant and modern, done primarily in white and gray with red accents. He loved how bright and spacious it was, but he tried not to show his admiration. He'd already figured out he was pretending to be her man for some reason, so it stood to reason that he would've been here before. Trev turned to the older woman currently making no secret about giving him a head-to-toe inspection.

He extended his hand. "Trevor Montgomery. It's nice to finally meet you. Leanne's told me so much about you."

When she nudged him, he only smiled. It wasn't exactly a lie since she told him last night that her mom was a free spirit who enjoyed making trouble. Well, those might not have been Leanne's exact words, but near enough.

"Junie Vanderpol. I can't wait to get to you know better." She smiled then took his hand, which was a relief since he'd been holding it out for a while. To his surprise, Leanne's mom pulled him into a hug. He returned the embrace in confusion, as she went on, "I can tell you really cherish her. I have a knack for reading people."

Trev blinked. But he didn't deny the claim. Leanne rolled her eyes, beckoning him toward the table, where food in Styrofoam containers had been set out.

"Sure you do," Leanne muttered. "That's why you've been married six times."

Holy shit. Getting married that often showed peerless optimism if nothing else.

"Hey." The older woman sounded hurt. "You know my abilities don't work when I try to use them for my own benefit."

"Junie," Leanne said in a warning tone.

Trev had the feeling he was missing some important context here. "Are you a psychic, then?" he asked, trying to be polite.

Junie smiled. "Something like that."

Leanne pushed the chair beside her with one foot while setting down plates and cutlery. Trev helped her set the table and received a grateful smile in return. *Yeah, I could get used to this, even if she's using me.*

In honor of their ruse, she'd ordered Chinese food from one of Trev's favorite restaurants: noodles, kung pao chicken, broccoli beef, fried rice, steamed dumplings, spring rolls, and egg drop soup. Basically, it was all his favorites, and if he didn't know better, he'd swear she'd done some research, maybe even asked Titus what he liked.

"You remembered my order," he teased. "Thanks, babe."

Leanne cast him a narrow look, but then she smiled. "How could I forget? Eat up, everything tastes better when it's hot."

He took a big bite of kung pao as Junie said, "Tell me about yourself, Trevor."

"Let him eat," Leanne answered at once.

Her mom sighed. "Fair enough, I can be patient."

That earned him some breathing room, and while everything might go sideways after dinner, he enjoyed every bite. He didn't often get to eat with people unaware of his reputation, and there was a certain freedom in not being *that* Trevor, at least for a little while. Right now, he was helping Leanne out, and it had been a long time since he felt...*useful,* let alone valuable.

As Trev finished his soup, Junie asked, "When are you moving in together?"

CHAPTER 6

THAT WAS ABRUPT, EVEN FOR Junie.

Maybe she suspects something? In all fairness, Leanne couldn't expect Trev to play along with this. He might not have even seen the text yet; she hadn't gotten the chance to confirm. They'd known each other for like a day, and he had zero reason to go this far backing her up. But for some wild reason, his smile didn't falter. He ate a little egg drop soup and kept his focus on Leanne.

"It's not up to me, really. Leanne's in the driver's seat, and I'm good with whatever makes her happy."

Wow. That was smooth as hell, and it made Junie go goofy-eyed. There was nothing she loved more than a man who seemed eager to please. Unfortunately, she wasn't very good at discerning when it was real and when it was a pretense held up just long to get what they wanted from her, whatever that happened to be.

"You're so sweet," Junie gushed. "I see how you swept Leanne off her feet."

Trev smirked and raised a brow; Leanne tilted her head and jerked her chin. It was a more complete conversation in a look than she'd had with people after dating for months. Whether she liked it or not, she owed him. The debt would be compounded if Junie gave up on the idea of moving in and decided to travel onward, like she usually did.

"I'm just being myself," he said.

After dinner, she tried to give him an excuse to leave, but Junie wouldn't hear of it. She grabbed Trev's arm and guided him to the sofa. "We still haven't had the chat I was promised before. I have so many questions!"

"He's self-employed and never been married," Leanne cut in sharply. "Thirty-three, and he's got all his hair and teeth. No pets, no dependents. Do you need to ask anything else?"

Junie blinked. "That's...thorough."

Trev grinned, nodding along, so she guessed she'd gotten the details right. She'd been pretty sure of Titus's age, based on Danica's gushing, and she thought she recalled Danica saying Trev and Titus had gone to high school together. Which should make them around the same age. Normally, she didn't go out with younger people. Stepdad number three had been closer to her age than Junie's, and that didn't work out great for anyone involved.

"Give him a break. I sprang meeting you on him out of the blue."

Junie sighed. "That's true. I didn't give you any notice about this visit. It...never occurred to me that I might be interrupting a serious relationship. I'm so surprised. In a good way," she hastened to add.

Frustration pecked away inside Leanne like a murder of crows. If she could get away with it, she'd cast an aversion spell on her mother, but since they were both witches, Junie would notice as soon as she skedaddled for no reason, and then there would be hurt feelings in the mix. *Why did you resort to underhanded tactics? You could simply tell me how you feel.* But it wasn't that easy.

What am I supposed to say? Thanks for giving me life, but I don't enjoy hanging out with you. I'm also haunted by the prospect of turning into you—do not want.

"Why don't we compromise and watch a movie?" Trev suggested.

Junie gazed at him with transparent appreciation. "That's a great idea. I don't mean to be intrusive, but I want to spend time with both of you now that I'm here."

"What's your favorite type of film?" he asked.

That was a more cunning question than it seemed because Junie had a lot of opinions about rom-coms, and she rambled on while Leanne put away the leftovers and stacked the dirty plates in the dishwasher. Trev came in to help without being asked, rinsing the glasses and cutlery before handing them over. Junie was still talking about *10 Things I Hate About You* and finally finished her lecture with, "They don't make movies like that anymore."

"I don't know," Leanne said. "Streaming services are bringing it."

They settled on a rom-com none of them had seen, and Trev sat between Leanne and Junie on the couch. Stretching his arm out along the back of the sofa, he offered Leanne a cuddle with a crook of his elbow. She surprised herself by leaning against him. This was the first time in recent memory when she'd literally Netflix'd and chilled instead of using it as a euphemism.

Once the movie ended, she scrolled through More Like This until they found something else. It was surprisingly not a terrible evening, pretty relaxing all told.

But it was late when they wrapped up. Junie yawned and stretched as she rose, bestowing a benevolent smile. "Don't let me keep you. I'm sure you usually stay over, and I'm a heavy sleeper. Just carry on like I'm not even here. I'll stay for a few days and then…figure out my next move. I'm just so thrilled things are finally on track in LeLe's private life. She's got it all together career-wise, but—"

"Good night," Leanne cut in.

Junie waved and headed into the guest room, leaving Leanne to face Trev. He was smiling slightly, still sprawled on the couch. She'd never met anyone so easygoing in her entire life. By now, he ought to be demanding explanations as to why she'd dragged him into all this, but instead, he was just…waiting. For what, she had no idea.

"So that happened," he finally said. "Guess I should sneak out before she decides to read us a bedtime story."

"You could stay."

Trev stared at her, evidently as stunned to receive that offer as she was to be making it. Hastily, she added, "If you're seriously okay with helping me out, it would sell the lie. Do you have anything pressing to do first thing tomorrow?"

"I can rearrange my schedule."

"Then let me get you a toothbrush," Leanne whispered. She'd bought a value pack and hadn't worked through them all yet, so she gave Trev the blue one, along with a washcloth and towel. "Do you usually shower at night?"

"I did before I came over."

"Then you can use the bathroom first."

It was weird as hell hearing him move around in her en suite while she changed into a nightgown. This reminded her of being married the second time. Her first husband, Garrett, had hardly even been home, while the sequel husband, Malcolm, tried to force a functional relationship, but the more he pushed, the more uncomfortable Leanne became. He had been so determined that they made sense together, as if logic alone could create a lasting bond. But then, of course, leaving proved so easy for him in the end: another rational decision, a foregone conclusion. *I could spend years in therapy figuring out my emotional damage.*

When Trev came out, she had the bed turned down. A queen seemed like a ridiculous luxury for sleeping on her own, but now she was glad for her foresight. The mattress was new, so nobody but her had ever slept in this bed. It had seemed like an auspicious decision, sweeping out the old to make way for the new. He'd stripped down to his boxers, and she bit her lip. Tonight, she'd had nothing to drink whatsoever, and he still looked damn fine. Not cut, but his arms were thick, and his shoulders were surprisingly broad, probably from when he did lawn care.

"This okay?" he asked, cutting into her vaguely steamy thoughts. He gestured to his attire or lack thereof.

Leanne shrugged. "It's fine. We've already slept together naked."

"Glad I'm not the only one still thinking about that. I'll get cozy. Come to bed whenever you're ready."

Why does that sound so damn inviting?

———————

The next morning, Trev woke to find Leanne already gone.

Using some arcane sorcery, she'd slipped out from under his

arm—he'd stirred at some point in the night spooning her—and gotten ready without bothering him. It was weird as hell waking up in a strange place; he could hear Junie moving around, and he braced himself for the most awkward morning after ever.

Except they hadn't done anything but sleep, too aware of Junie in the guest room. Plus, Trev wasn't even sure what was going on. It didn't seem accurate to say they were dating, but since they'd hooked up, this wasn't a friendly favor either. However it happened, he'd basically agreed to act like Leanne's boyfriend, one serious enough to be talking about cohabitation. He stretched, sliding his hand across the wrinkled white sheet. It was high-quality cotton, so smooth, it felt incredible. Everything about the room was luxe and high-end. The furniture was light, and there weren't many colors; this style might be considered Scandinavian.

Mentally shrugging, he cleaned up in the bathroom and got dressed then made Leanne's bed. Just good manners when he was the last one out of it. Junie was eating Corn Pops from a big yellow bowl with her legs folded like a little kid, watching some court TV show. Former roommates were arguing about who had to pay for damages after the tub overflowed.

"Good morning," she chirped brightly. "Want some cereal?"

"Sure."

He served himself and joined her on the sofa, as it seemed rude to eat by himself at the bar or the table. Though he got along with most people, he didn't feel comfortable with many. Leanne's mom was a rare exception. She didn't ask any questions, just chatted casually about the case and added a few wild anecdotes about problems she'd had with various roommates.

"If you tell me when, I can help you move," she said suddenly.

Trev blinked. He'd gotten too relaxed, apparently, and now she was launching the sneak attack when his guard was down. He had no idea what to say. If he deferred to Leanne again, Junie would probably suspect something was up. It wasn't normal for someone to have absolutely no preferences or ideas of their own.

So he replied, "So nice of you to offer, but I have burly guys for that. Thanks for breakfast, I need to take off now."

Before you ask me how long we've been dating or when her birthday is.

"Oh, I didn't do anything. It was so nice meeting you." She hesitated, padding after him when he went to the kitchen to rinse his bowl and spoon and put them in the dishwasher. "I hope you'll take care of my baby. She acts like she doesn't need anyone, but it's a front, you know? Once you get through her defenses, there's nobody sweeter or more loyal."

"Right," he said, feeling like the biggest asshole in creation.

"Take care!" At the front door, Junie hugged Trev, surprising the hell out of him.

As he drove home on automatic, he imagined what it would be like really dating someone like Leanne, so put together, working a professional job—smart, successful, beautiful. He laughed softly, shaking his head. *Yeah, right. What would I bring to the table?* That wasn't just him being hard on himself. She didn't even have a yard for him to mow, so she didn't need the maintenance skills he'd mentioned the night they met. Being willing to remove spiders—and frankly, he was sort of scared of them anyway—get things on high shelves, and change light bulbs in the ceiling didn't seem like enough.

At home, he headed in without seeing either of his parents. Part of him wondered if they'd even notice if he stopped coming back. Hell, his old man might be pleased he was finally moving out, even without asking where he was headed. They'd told him Tanner was coming home this weekend, bringing the wife and kids too.

That'll be fun. I wonder… No, I can't ask her to do that.

He paused, staring into his mini fridge despite not being hungry. But why not? It would be fair to ask Leanne to come to the family dinner and get him off the hopeless hook. If she could benefit from this pretense, so could he. Trev chewed his lip, trying to decide if he had the balls to ask for this favor in return.

Just then, his phone beeped, making him juggle it. He opened his messages to find one from Leanne. Smirking, he changed her contact to "My Honey," knowing she'd likely hate it. Though he hadn't known her long, she didn't seem like the gushy, sticky-sweet type. Trev tapped on the message notification and read.

Leanne: We should talk.

Huh. That's not ominous at all.

Trev: Name the time and place.

She sent him a pin on the map for a restaurant near the old courthouse. Apparently, Leanne's office was a few streets over in the new government building. With a shrug, he agreed to be there in three hours and killed the rest of that time doing a Twitch stream. He'd hoped to get some followers and maybe spin his hobby into something more, but it seemed like that wasn't his thing either. Currently, he had fifty-eight followers—wild that some people had millions.

Trev couldn't believe it, but for the second day in a row, he went looking for a decent outfit and got himself ready to go out. He even tried to style his hair, though that didn't go well. *Maybe I'll get a trim.* The layers were beyond grown out, and in all honesty, he couldn't recall the last time he'd done more than shear it off himself when it got too long to see.

That's probably not a good sign.

At the appointed time, he headed out, but finding a place to park on the square ate into his head start, and walking the two blocks to the restaurant she'd suggested took a bit as well. When he arrived, Leanne was already waiting for him. She lifted a hand as he stepped in. It was a small Mexican place with only eight tables, and the food was fantastic. He'd eaten here a few times with the guys since Miguel knew the family that ran the place.

"What's up?" he asked.

He didn't say she looked great, although she did, because he hadn't gotten date vibes from her terse text. As soon as he sat down, she said, "I heard you had breakfast with my mom."

"Was I not supposed to?"

"She *loves* you," Leanne snapped.

"Uh, sorry…" He really wasn't following.

This is what she wanted, right?

"It's a little bit of a problem because now she's talking about renting an apartment in town or answering a roommate ad here. She wants to stick around for our wedding."

"Oh shit," Trev said. "Dinner is one thing. But we can't get married as a…" The word escaped him for a bit, then he snapped his fingers when it came to him. "As a ploy."

She grinned. "That's *exactly* what I wanted to talk to you about. Why can't we?"

CHAPTER 7

LEANNE LAUGHED AT TREV'S EXPRESSION.

If she'd shared her idea with any of her coven sisters, they'd stage an intervention and maybe do a spell to rid her of unwholesome influences. That was why she was keeping quiet, talking to Trev first. Articulating her thoughts would help him understand her intentions and maybe he could get on board. Then again, a photo-op marriage might seem like a *terrible* idea for someone who hadn't already done it twice.

"Just so you know, I'm totally ordering the biggest burrito they have and you're paying for it. You owe me for dragging me over here to screw with me," he said.

He thinks I'm joking.

"Let's order, and then...just keep an open mind, all right? That's all I'm asking."

The server came over with chips and salsa, and as promised, Trev ordered a jumbo burrito. Leanne went with chicken enchiladas with green sauce. Once they were alone, she laid out her case.

"People get married for all kinds of reasons. As I see it, we both benefit from this. You said you're good at basic maintenance—what about cooking and housekeeping?"

Trev eyed her skeptically. "You don't have to marry me. Just hire a housekeeper."

"If we get married, you'll be eligible for my insurance and get out of your parents' house. There's really no downside for you. I just expect you to handle all the domestic crap I don't have time for or care about. Can you cook?"

"I can, actually." A flicker of something darkened his hazel eyes. "I mean, I'm not Ina Garten, but I can follow a recipe."

Leanne regarded him, surprise welling up within her. "I'm impressed you know who the Barefoot Contessa is."

"My mom loves her books."

"Makes sense."

Trev said, "You've laid out the benefits for me, but I don't see what you get out of this. Other than fooling your mom, but this seems excessive."

She bit her lip, wondering if she dared confess what she was really after. Getting Junie off her back was an excellent bonus but... "Very astute. There's another reason I need to get married. But this is important, I can't leave it to chance and random emotions."

He folded his arms, sitting back in his chair while eyeing her with an expectant air. "I'm listening. Convince me."

Briefly, she pressed her lips together, unable to believe Trevor Montgomery—a mundane she'd just met—would be the first person to hear her innermost ambition, one she'd nurtured for a long time in secret without having the courage to go for broke. "You know I work for the city, right?"

"Yeah. To be honest, I'm not clear on what you *do* exactly, but I got that much."

"I'm the director of communications for the mayor's office. I got into it because I wanted to make a difference, but mostly I watch while they take credit for my work. Dan Rutherford on the city council is the *worst*. He was talking to my boobs earlier in the week while putting the moves on me.

"And if that's not enough fun, he's buddied up with my boss. Their cronyism is costing the city. In fact, I suspect they're skimming. So...I've thought about this long and hard, and my best option is to run for office myself in the next election."

"Holy shit," Trev said.

"I'll run for city council to get my foot in the door. The election's coming up in November, and I should really have started this earlier. That's why I can't wait around for a normal relationship to give me the right...look for the voters."

"Wait, if I understand where you're headed with this, you think getting married will help your image. And you picked *me* for that?" He laughed, throwing his head back in a move that resulted in an adorable hair toss.

Not that she had a soft spot for surfer-looking types or anything. It was just that he was convenient, and he'd slot right into her plans, serving the purpose on multiple fronts. *I just need to convince him of that.*

"Serendipity," she said. "I didn't choose you, per se, but you'd be perfect. We flip the traditional First Lady role, and you're the man behind the woman, keeping house and supporting me. The optics are fantastic, I come off looking more stable—trust me, they'll spin the hell out of my two divorces otherwise—and you get to reinvent yourself as the icon who helps me make history."

"I don't want to be an icon."

She sighed. "It's just a word. Think about this, then. If we get married, your parents won't be on your back all the time. You'll have your own place and the space to figure out what you want from life. I'll help you, whatever you decide to do. If you'd rather take it slow, you can sleep in the guest room. I'm not opposed to sharing the bed with you, though. We've already proved we're compatible."

For the first time, Trev smiled. "That's true enough."

At that point, the server came over with their food and arranged the dishes on the table. "Careful, the plates are hot. Can I get you anything else?"

"We're fine," Leanne said.

Trev had nothing to add, apparently. She dug into her enchiladas, letting him mull over what she'd said. It was important to know when to push and when to provide breathing room. Now it was time for the latter.

Finally, he murmured, "What if you meet someone you actually want to be with?"

"What if *you* do?" she countered.

He laid down his fork with a sober mien. "Let's not pretend I'm a catch. Don't do that."

"Look, I realize you have self-esteem issues, and we'll work on that. Understand that you fit uniquely into the life I'm trying to build. Do you think it's easy to find a guy who'd even contemplate being a househusband and taking the back seat while I launch a political career?"

He blinked. "I didn't even consider that."

"Then start. As it happens, I have a Trev Montgomery–shaped hole in my life, and I'm trying to get you to fill it." After the words came out, she heard the filth, but she didn't back off what she'd said. Instead, she followed it with a wink. "I know how I come across, and it won't poll well with voters unless you mitigate my image. In a regular relationship, all kinds of things can go sideways. I need someone who will stick around, period."

He was silent for several long moments, staring at his burrito. "Well, historically, I'm not the one who leaves, even when things go really, really wrong."

"That's why you're my man," she said. "Sure, it helps that you were willing to step in with Junie, no questions asked. But logic suggests that if we do this, I can have the life I've always secretly wanted."

"You didn't answer my question," he said.

"About meeting someone else?" She sighed quietly. "Okay, all cards on the table. I don't look for relationships anymore. I have sex with people, but I haven't tried to find a partner since Malcolm left, and I have no plans to start. I care about getting into politics. That's it."

He studied her for a long moment. "I'm not looking either, but we should have an understanding in place before we get carried away."

"Then...we agree to keep communication open, and if at some point you meet someone special, tell me. We'll cross that bridge when we come to it. I promise I won't cheat, and I'm open to keeping things flexible. I can keep listing benefits, but...what do you say, Trev?"

A smile broke over his face, crinkling his eyes. "I might be out of my mind, or maybe you're just that good at talking, but this… sort of makes sense? Whatever, point is, you'll be a great politician and I…would be *honored* to be your third husband."

Trev was so startled when Leanne launched out of her chair toward him that he almost tipped his over.

Thankfully, she caught him and bestowed an amazing kiss while the older couple at the back of the restaurant looked on with disapproval. Until she pumped the air with her fist and crowed, "Yes! He said yes! We're getting married!"

At once, the censure melted into congratulations, and the owner of Pablo's, whose name was Enrique, amusingly enough, sent them free flan in honor of such an auspicious occasion. Trev still couldn't believe he'd agreed to this, but even as he went over the terms in his head, nothing about the agreement worked out badly for him. She was willing to sleep beside him and have sex, and he got free health insurance, plus time to get his shit together. In return, he just had to cook and clean. At least he'd have something to do with his day now.

Later, there would probably be photo ops, but she needed to get the backstory in place first. In a way, he admired how methodical she was being, chasing her goals with a single-minded capability that he envied. When she surprised him by offering a bite of flan, he ate it without hesitation, and the elderly couple made "aww" noises. PDA was more acceptable in newly engaged couples, he supposed.

Wonder if Sarah will think I did this in reaction to her wedding invitation.

"What will your friends say?" he asked.

"Oh, they'll all think it's a reckless, terrible idea—that I've fallen into an ill-advised infatuation and that our relationship is destined to crash and burn."

"Whoa. Will they say that to your face?"

Leanne laughed and shook her head. "Not a chance. They'll pretend to be supportive, not realizing I can tell the difference, and be braced to pick up the pieces when it all goes horribly wrong. At least, that's how it always was before."

"What's different?"

"You are," she said with a cheeky grin.

"Seriously."

"I have disparate goals this time. In marrying you, I want to realize my political dreams. I'm hoping we'll become friends who cooperate well as housemates and who also enjoy having sex with each other. That's the extent of my ambition on the home front."

In all honesty, it didn't sound bad to Trev at all. When she put it that way, he could fully get behind being her husband. If she wasn't expecting some deathless, perfect love, there was little chance he could fuck it up. Companionship? No problem. Good sex? Awesome.

"This is a better deal than I ever thought I'd get," he said then.

"I'm glad you came around to my way of thinking. I've been married twice before, and each time, I thought I'd met the one. I don't believe in that anymore, but that doesn't mean I want to grow old alone."

"Like your mom."

Her eyes flashed, and she bit her lip, restraining her initial response. "Correct. When we start the next stage and you're doing appearances with me, I'll rely on your judgment."

"You think I can help you? I mean, not just as a prop or set dressing, but you're interested in my opinions too?" Surely, he'd stepped into a portal into an alternate reality at some point, because it felt so good hearing this that he couldn't stand it.

Leanne's bright smile took his breath away. "Definitely. We're a team now, so I need you to stop questioning my acuity. I picked you, and that means you're a valuable campaign asset." She winked again and paid the bill before he could even think about getting his wallet.

It was wild. He'd never been with anyone who cared so little about his monetary situation. The idea that he could possess worth unrelated to his earning power was so foreign that he hadn't adapted to her style yet. Hurriedly, Trev got up and rushed out the door after her.

"Thanks for lunch."

"You drove, right?" He nodded, and she kissed his cheek then gave his butt a pat. "We'll talk more later about the logistics. I'd start packing your stuff, though. The sooner you move in, the faster Junie will be out."

While Leanne's mom seemed nicer than his parents, he understood not wanting to live under the same roof. He'd been withering for years without having the wherewithal to remove himself from that situation. Until the solution appeared like magic in the form of an irresistible redhead sweeping him off his feet.

Since he was on the square already and there was time on his meter, he walked over to Sugar Daddy's instead of going straight home. Downtown St. Claire was charming, though he rarely took advantage of the cool stuff they had going on. There would be a food festival soon, with restaurants offering samples at stalls all around the old courthouse, and he'd heard the city would be starting a community garden next year. Absently, he cataloged the minor changes: the hardware store had repainted the trim, and the Realtor had a new sign.

Hopefully, Titus had time to talk. Trev needed to tell someone, and Titus had been a loyal friend for most of their lives. Trev could admit he hadn't made it easy the past few years. Maya was working the front counter as usual; she greeted him with a squeezy hug.

He patted her back in fraternal fashion. "All good, little Winnaker?"

"Why are you still calling me that?" she demanded.

"Habit. Can the big man come out and play?"

"I'll ask." She went to the galley door that led to the kitchen and cracked it enough to call, "Titus! Trev's here. Do you have a minute?"

"Make him a coffee, and tell him I'll be out in five," Titus yelled back.

"I got that," Trev said, taking a seat at the table farthest from the door.

The bakery was truly remarkable, a monument to a dream Titus had realized, thankfully before his mother passed away. Everything about the place was adorable, from the mint chocolate chip interior design to the white wrought iron tables. And the smell—he inhaled deeply to appreciate the mixed deliciousness of butter, caramel, coffee, chocolate, and cinnamon.

A minute later, Maya brought the drink to him. "Flat white. Did I get it right?"

He sipped. "It's perfect. What do I owe you?"

"Please. I don't know why you bother offering. Titus wouldn't take your money even if you ate everything in the pastry case." She smiled to soften the disparaging words. "You're family, you jerk."

"You love me."

They bickered playfully until more customers came and demanded Maya's attention. He nursed his drink until Titus came out, all geared up in baker's togs. Taking the seat opposite Trev, he said, "This is rare. What's up?"

"Before I tell you, you have to promise you won't try to talk me out of this."

Titus rubbed a hand down his jaw, something he did when he was unsettled. "Uh-oh. That's a worrying start, you know that, right? Please tell me you aren't joining the armed forces. I can help you find a day job."

"Do you promise?" Trev persisted.

"Fine, hit me with it. I'm braced." His friend gripped the edge of the table in a dramatic show of being prepared.

He rolled his eyes. No question, Titus was undeniably happier since he'd been with Danica, ups and downs aside.

But what's the best way to frame this announcement? No way could he make it sound as reasonable and plausible as Leanne had managed, so there was probably no point in going at it from that angle, and he suspected she wouldn't try to persuade her friends that their decision made sense either.

One impulsive, reckless romance, coming up.

"Remember the line Leanne served me at the party?"

Titus drummed his fingers on the table, evidently thinking hard. "Unless I'm mistaken, she asked you to be her third husband. Funny opener, I'll grant you that."

"Yeah, well, we've been hanging out a lot since then. Like, every day, and it turns out we make sense together. I'm moving in with her as soon as we can make it happen."

That's probably enough for now. Otherwise, Titus would absolutely tell Danica, and *she* might share the news with all Leanne's mutual friends. And Trev didn't know how she wanted to disperse the message. Maybe it would be better to wife her up quickly and quietly then come back with a huge surprise announcement.

Mouth half-open in shock, Titus stared for several long moments. "Are you serious?"

"Absolutely. I know it's fast, but—"

"Are you sure this isn't just...?" His friend paused, likely looking for the least hurtful way to phrase his doubts. "A reaction to Sarah sending you her wedding invite?"

Ouch. Fair question, though.

"I won't lie, that messed me up. But that's separate from what's going on with Leanne. I know it's fast, but I wish you'd be happy for me." Asking for unconditional support didn't come easy, and he kept the smile fixed in place, waiting to hear what a dickhead move this was.

To his relief, Titus got up and gave him a huge hug, lifting him off his feet. "This is *huge*. And yeah, it's fast, like you said, but I'm happy for you."

He grinned. "So that's a 'congrats,' then?"

The other man drew back to arm's length. "For sure. You make a cute couple. What kind of cake do you want for the house-warming get-together?"

After pretending to think for a minute, Trev shook his head with mock reproach. "Can't believe you even asked me that, dude."

"Vanilla raspberry cream cake?"

"Always." Then he reconsidered, realizing he now had some-one to consult for matters like this. "Wait. Let me make sure it's good with Leanne. I'll confirm later. And…yeah. That's it, pretty much. Thanks."

"For what?"

"Being on my side."

Titus smiled and hugged him again. "Always."

CHAPTER 8

LEANNE WASN'T READY TO DEBUT her idea at the next coven meeting, which was why she'd invited Vanessa and Margie out for drinks after work.

Yeah, Junie was waiting at home, but that was *her* problem. Leanne had spent countless nights alone growing up, waiting for Junie to remember that she'd promised to do something with her daughter. Without fail, her mother had chosen whatever man popped up as a distraction, so this didn't bother her in the slightest. *At least I'm with friends, not ditching her for a hookup.*

"What's up?" Margie asked, as Leanne ordered a bottle of wine.

She'd chosen Heart of Artichoke, an upscale vegetarian place, mostly because she didn't want to run into Dan Rutherford or any of his cronies. Their group preferred to dine at steak houses and expense as many meals as possible, even on the slimmest pretext of calling it a business dinner. Sophie from accounting had given her *all* the gossip a few months back.

Before she answered, she let the server pour, then she took a fortifying sip. Setting down her glass, she launched into the short version of her plan. To their credit, both Vanessa and Margie listened to every word she had to say without interjecting or passing judgment.

Vanessa reacted first. "Are you out of your damn mind?"

Leanne laughed. Vanessa could always be counted on for complete honesty. The dark-skinned witch regarded her with one brow raised and sampled her own wine, waiting to hear if she'd add anything.

Leanne shrugged. "It makes sense to me."

"You're the only one," Vanessa muttered.

Margie said, "You've given up on love, then?"

That shouldn't sting so much when it was essentially true. She tried to feign indifference. "More accurate to say it's given up on me. Romance isn't for everyone, you know? These days, I want something else far more."

"To rub Dan Rutherford's face in the dirt," Vanessa guessed.

"Figuratively, but *yes*. Do you know how many times I've caught that asshole staring at my butt or my boobs?"

"If only pervy looks were actionable," Margie said wistfully.

"Every time our paths cross, my skin crawls. Recently, he more or less told me I'm best suited to be his arm candy."

"That son of a bitch," Vanessa bit out.

"Rutherford always votes for whatever the mayor suggests and shuts down council members with a different point of view. He's the reason nothing ever changes around here!"

Still frowning, Vanessa shook her head. "Say that's true, I still don't see how shacking up with some low-achieving white boy will help."

Leanne could say to them what she couldn't to Trev. "He'll make me relatable, more appealing to the lowest common denominator. Voters like him will picture themselves in his shoes. 'He got an attractive, successful woman. Why can't I?' And it increases my appeal to a demographic who otherwise would *never* vote for me."

Margie drank some of the wine and sampled the appetizer platter that had arrived while they were talking. "People who play devil's advocate are annoying, but I feel like I should anyway. Are you *sure* about that? Men who aren't inclined to vote for you aren't likely to change their minds because you pair up with Titus's friend."

Leanne sighed. "It's impossible to be sure of these things, but precedent indicates that I'll appear more stable and more in tune with family values if I'm married. And I guarantee Rutherford will go after my private life. Hell, in the last election, he dug up his opponent's personal bankruptcy."

"What a dick." Vanessa stabbed a stuffed mushroom with an extra-vicious fork maneuver. "The more I hear about him, the more I think we should hex him."

Leanne snickered and helped herself to the appetizer platter. "Don't tempt me."

Once Margie processed the new information, she nodded with a pensive air. "When you put it that way, the strategy is sound, but...isn't it sort of hurtful? You're using Trevor."

That gave her a minor twinge, and she protested, "More like we're using each other. Right now, the man lives with his parents. He doesn't have a job. I'm giving him a purpose. People get together for all kinds of reasons, right? How is this worse than dating someone because they're rich or they have a nice rack?"

"That's not okay either," Vanessa said sharply.

"I haven't lied to the man," she pointed out.

Since Margie tended to try and see the good in any situation—and that was why Leanne had invited her—she said uncertainly, "Well, it's...practical. If neither of you have any illusions about why you're together..."

"Put aside traditional crap for a minute. Just think about whether this will work or not, as a *strategy*," Leanne added, seeing more objections building in their concerned faces.

Both Margie and Vanessa paused, eating some hummus as they reflected. Finally, Margie said, "Honestly, I think it might. You understand male voters pretty well, and picking someone who resonates like—"

"'One of us,'" Vanessa quipped, making air quotes.

"Could be the edge you need," Margie finished.

Leanne sat back, satisfied with their response. "I think so too. For now, you're the only ones I'm telling. Priya and Kerry are too committed to each other to understand how I could do this. They got their happy ending, and that's cool."

"Not everyone is so lucky," Margie said softly.

Vanessa added, "Danica seems pretty set on the CinnaMan too. And I hate to say it, but I'm pretty sure Clem isn't just 'distracting' that witch hunter."

Wincing, Margie nodded emphatically. "You see it too? I don't know if Clem's admitted how she feels even to herself, but that's next-level complicated."

"I wish she talked to us more," Leanne said. "But you know how she is. If we offer help, she'll say she's fine and get mad at us for meddling."

Nodding, Vanessa served herself some stuffed grape leaves. "I think she confides in Ethel. Clem has a hard time leaning on people because of her mom and dad." She leveled a pointed look at Leanne. "You should understand *that*."

"Fair," she admitted.

With anyone else, she might take offense, but Vanessa was right. She had a few things in common with Clem as a result of parental failures, but while Clem tried to do—and control—*everything*, Leanne did what she wanted. Except at work, where sometimes they backed her into corners and got her to volunteer for shit outside her lane. She couldn't change policy or push for any improvements. Taking orders from people she knew were incompetent sucked, and Dan Rutherford treated her like she was nothing more than T & A, an attitude she often found reflected in the mayor and deputy mayor as well.

"I think we're getting off track," Margie pointed out.

While Leanne enjoyed gossip in general, she did regret talking about other members of the coven behind their backs, so she accepted the reproof. Vanessa mimed zipping her lips as Margie went to the restroom, and Leanne laughed.

The other witch leaned forward. "Tell me straight up—there's something special about this dude, or you wouldn't be ready to move him into your condo." Vanessa held up a hand. "Don't even play. You can front for Margie about your mom and the city council election, but I refuse to believe you'd consider this if there was nothing else in it for you."

Biting her lip, she considered for all of two seconds before admitting, "I do like him. And the sex was good."

"Good? Really? We heard you in the bathroom. I'm just putting that out there."

"Surprisingly awesome," she muttered.

Vanessa smirked. "There it is. For what it's worth, you have my stamp of approval. If you can get some and get the job done, why wouldn't you? We've got your back when the time comes. What are we looking at, logistically speaking?"

"I can work for another month or so, but after that, I need to give notice and start campaigning for city council. Really, I should do it sooner, but I need to collect a couple more paychecks while I still can."

"You won't earn enough as a council member," Vanessa cautioned.

"I'm aware, but I can't keep working for the mayor either. Rutherford's been seated forever, and he plays golf with my boss. Dunno if this qualifies as a conflict of interest, but Anderson would definitely snoop and try to keep me too busy to challenge his buddy."

After sipping her wine, Vanessa said, "Try to lock in young voters along with the seniors. I think I read both those age groups tend to vote in a block."

She nodded. "See, this is why we're friends. I was planning to go for the lower and upper age brackets. But would it be unethical to use certain...advantages?"

Leanne spoke volumes with her eyes. Clem and Danica could do all kinds of fun things on the internet to ensure her message went viral. Leanne herself could influence crowds using magic, and Ethel could help with divinations to determine which speaking engagements would prove most beneficial in winning hearts and minds.

The other witch laughed as Margie walked up. "What's so funny?"

Vanessa said, "Leanne's wondering if she should run a regular campaign."

Using that word wouldn't set off any alarm bells, but Margie got the gist. She smiled too. "Why would you do that? I say use every advantage at your disposal. Your opponent will."

"That's what I wanted to hear. Because if I play, I aim to win."

A few days later, Trev had everything packed.

There was no need for him to invite her over to return the favor, pretending in front of his parents. From now on, Tanner could bask in the spotlight with his perfect family, freeing Trev to breathe for the first time in ten years. He still couldn't believe it, but Leanne had texted him the pass code to her condo and said a gate pass would be waiting for him this afternoon with the security guard. His life certainly had taken a wild turn since meeting her at Danica's party. Sometimes he considered sending Titus's girlfriend a thank-you card. Part of him had feared he'd *never* move out of his parents' basement, and yet here he was, carrying boxes up the stairs.

His car looked like it belonged to a college student moving out of the dorms, because he had no furniture, just clothes, books, bedding, and games. Some of his stuff, he had a hard time picturing in her elegant condo, but he could buy a trunk or hide it in the closet. Everything about this was weird, but normal had screwed him over and left him licking his wounds for years.

"You're really moving out." His mother's voice boomed loud and strident behind him, nearly making him drop the carton he was carrying.

Trev turned around. *Damn. I was hoping to be gone before she got back.* "I told you I was the other night at dinner."

The less he had to think about that nightmare of a social occasion, the better. His brother was practically pathological with his need for attention. When Trev mentioned he had a girlfriend, Tanner interjected to talk about an impossible surgery he pulled off. Then Trev tried to tell the family that he was moving out, and Tanner announced that he and Amelia—his wife—had decided to try for another baby. Like, why did that need to be shared over spaghetti and meatballs? He could've lived without knowing they were focused on procreative sex.

"Dad and I thought you were joking. Tanner said—"

"I was entirely serious," he interrupted, wedging the box in the back seat.

Mom followed as he went back down to continue loading the car. *Good times.* Now that he was leaving, she wanted to talk.

"I see that now. But is this a good idea? We haven't met her, and you can't have been dating long. It seems rash."

Irritated, he stopped on the basement stairs. "How do you know?" he asked. "You and I haven't had a real conversation in six months. I do the laundry when you chuck it down the stairs. You ignore me otherwise."

Barb sucked in a sharp breath, pressing a hand to her sternum as if he'd hurt her. "That's not fair. And it's not true either."

"Oh? What have we talked about? Apart from you telling me to get my act together."

When she remained silent, he offered a wry smile and shook his head. "See? Nothing. I'm not attacking you, but facts are facts. Look on the bright side, you can build that party room and focus on Tanner. He's proof you and Dad raised us right. *I'm* the problem, and I'm getting out of your way. Never thought you'd see the day, huh?"

"What's your girlfriend like?" she asked in a small voice.

He took a ridiculous amount of pride in the answer. "Her name is Leanne. She's smart and beautiful, and she works for the mayor."

Barb's eyes widened, visible even in the dim light filtering from the garage. "She sounds lovely. How did you meet?"

"Through mutual friends. We hit it off immediately." Everything sounded so…normal when he explained it this way. He couldn't resist bragging a little, so he got out his phone and pulled up the city website then clicked on Leanne's page. There was a flattering headshot, along with a short bio about her early life, education, and professional experience. "This is her."

He handed the phone to his mother, waiting for her reaction.

Mom skimmed the whole profile and glanced up with genuine amazement rounding her eyes. "She's gorgeous! And so impressive. I take back what I said before. I'm happy for you, and I hope it works out. Do your best!"

He'd forgotten how it felt to have her smile at him proudly;

it probably hadn't happened since he got admitted to college. "Thanks," he said, hoping she wouldn't notice the ironic edge to his tone.

She didn't. "I'll help you pack the car. Many hands make light work!"

That was one of her favorite truisms, trotted out when she wanted him to help with some shit he didn't want to do. "Thanks."

It was faster with her carting and loading alongside him, though. Soon he had everything, and the trunk and back seat were filled to the brim. "Anything I left behind, you can sell or donate. I've sorted through everything fully."

"I love you," she said, ignoring his comments on disposing of his remaining junk. "It might not seem that way, and I'm sure it appears that we favor your brother, but he's...easier. He likes approval, and he works for it. You...you are not motivated in the same way. It's tough to know what to say, and you're—"

Don't say "sensitive."

"—sensitive."

Of course. He couldn't count how often he'd been called that, usually in a derogatory fashion. In this house, it was *never* a compliment.

"Moody," Barb added, as if she hadn't said enough already.

"Yeah, well, I'm someone else's problem now. Take care." He got in the car, grateful he still had some cash and gas in the tank.

This was a huge leap of faith, entrusting himself to someone he'd just met, but Leanne seemed to have a plan, and that was more than Trev had. He backed out of the driveway and drove across St. Claire to the gated community where Leanne lived. As promised, she had a card waiting for him with the guard; he just had to show ID to claim it. Then he scanned the pass card and found a place to park. She'd said she would register his car and get him an assigned spot, but visitor parking would do for now.

He grabbed the first box and took the elevator up. The pass code worked too. *I can't believe this is actually happening.* When he went in, he found Junie still in the condo, and she beamed as he carted the first box into Leanne's bedroom. Junie would think it was weird if he stashed his stuff elsewhere.

"This is so exciting! I was afraid LeLe would never take the leap again. Let me help you unload. I could use the exercise. I'm sick of sitting around all day." She sighed. "I thought I'd get to spend time with her if I dropped by, but all she does is work."

"Yeah, she's driven," he said.

If she wasn't, he wouldn't be here, bound by a verbal agreement to be her First Gentleman. *Mom will be so proud. Hell, Tanner might even be jealous.* It gave him a disconcerting amount of pleasure imagining how much his brother would hate seeing Trev getting positive press coverage.

Junie chatted nonstop the whole time they unpacked his car. Trev understood why Leanne avoided her; she was so desperate for company that she treated Trev like they were best friends already. When they finished up about forty minutes later, he knew an embarrassing and frankly inappropriate level of detail regarding her...colorful past. Bemused, he locked the car, headed back upstairs, and glanced around his new home, fighting a wave of incredulity.

This is so fucking surreal.

"Her taste is boring," Junie said, misreading his expression. "It looks like a fancy hotel, but with even less personality."

Trev turned, folding his arms. Junie seemed to agree with his parents: no qualms about disrespecting her kid. "*You* might not like it, but I do. Leanne has fantastic taste."

"I sure do," Leanne said.

She stood in the open door of the condo, and he hadn't heard her come in, too busy starting an argument with her mom. *Not the best beginning.* Or that was what he thought, until she added, "I picked *you*, after all."

She crossed to him and kissed him passionately, only pulling back to whisper, "Loving that loyalty, Trevor Montgomery. Knew I made the right call with you."

CHAPTER 9

IT DID SOMETHING TO LEANNE, coming home to hear Junie complaining about her "hotel bland" home decor, and then—

Trev, defending her without a flicker of hesitation, like she was really *his* person, the one he'd back all the way to the wall. No questions asked, no explanations needed. *I've never had anyone like that.* She was the woman they wanted to possess—for a night or a week—but they rarely imagined what a future looked like with her. She was a conquest, not a life mate.

Fuck, whatever.

The kiss was awesome. He was red-cheeked and glowing when she pulled back, running her immaculately manicured nails through his shaggy hair. It was impossibly soft, silky, and she wrapped a lock of it around her fingers before giving it a gentle tug. *Mine. I'm keeping you.*

For as long as I need you, she added hastily.

She didn't believe in forever, and they hadn't discussed the duration of this agreement. They'd mentioned keeping it flexible, but no matter what Trev said about sticking around, he'd go eventually. It just couldn't be before she got what she required out of the situation. Once the election was over, then they could reassess.

"I found a place to stay," Junie said. "I'll be out of your hair tonight."

"Oh?" That was the best news Leanne had gotten since she found out the deputy mayor was taking a vacation and wouldn't be around to ogle the admin staff for the next two weeks.

"I answered a roommate ad like you suggested. Blair is so nice, and we have a lot in common. They just got divorced and need someone to help with the bills."

Leanne knew she shouldn't, but she had to ask, "Are you still doing online tarot readings and...other stuff to earn a living?"

Trev's attention seemed to sharpen when Leanne said "other stuff," but he didn't interject.

"Yep," Junie said cheerfully. "Business is booming too."

If it got out that her mom did certain things online for cash, Leanne could absolutely kiss the election goodbye. Maybe it would be better to control that revelation and disclose it immediately. The gig-and-hustle voters might not hold it against them, but the asshole demographic probably would. *Maybe I have to decide between them.*

It wasn't a problem she could solve today, however.

"Is Blair okay with you moving in right away?"

Junie nodded. "I hope you don't mind—I gave several of your... book club friends as references. Blair already talked to Ethel."

"You're in a book club?" Trev asked.

"Yeah, we're pretty close. You met everyone at Danica's party."

"Can anyone join? I'm into reading, and I could use a wider friend circle."

Oh wow. Usually, people heard "book club" and changed the

subject because they either didn't like to read or didn't want to be told *what* to read. She hedged, "Sure, but I need to talk to them first. We vote on it. Majority rules."

"That's fair."

"I'm glad you see it that way," she said.

Good thing Trev was so chill. Otherwise, he might get annoyed at the prospect of being vetoed. Junie cut her a look, and Leanne raised both eyebrows. *What was I supposed to say? You're the one who brought it up!*

"What do you read? Is it heavy lit fic?" Trevor asked.

"Hell no. We pick sexy books or deeply touching ones. I think all our favorites to date have been romance or fantasy with a romantic thread."

"No science fiction?" he asked, mimicking a space cowboy drawing a laser pistol, then he made the *pew-pew* noise.

Damn, why is he so cute?

"Not so far, though we'd be open to it if there's hot banging."

"In space no one can hear you scream," Junie said.

Trev blinked. "I'm guessing you mean the good kind of scream."

In answer, her mom made an *O* face, and Leanne face-palmed. When some of the secondhand embarrassment faded, she said, "You were just about to get your stuff and head over to Blair's, right?"

"I was hoping you'd let me cook dinner for everyone first," Trev cut in.

Startled, Leanne took a step toward him, gesturing at the kitchen. "Are you sure? I don't even know what I have on hand."

"I bought some groceries," Junie said cheerfully.

"Let me take inventory." He headed for the fridge like a

professional, and eventually, he added, "I can do honey Dijon chicken with vegetables. Sound good?" Trev tied on an apron and washed his hands before setting out ingredients and locating kitchenware like he'd done this countless times before.

He's really selling us as a couple. She read Junie's silent approval and mentally patted herself on the back.

"Sounds incredible," Leanne said.

Without even changing out of her work clothes, she settled on a stool across the island to watch him work. He chopped up peppers, zucchini, and onions then quickly whisked together a sauce. Trev prepped a sheet pan with aluminum foil, laid out the veggies and put chicken breasts on top, basting them in the deep yellow honey Dijon. Once it was all done, he sealed the packet and slid the pan into the oven.

"Half an hour, maybe forty minutes. It'll be awesome, trust me. Sheet pan foil packets are impossible to ruin, and you can do all kinds of flavor profiles. Teriyaki, lemon pepper, spicy ginger, barbecue..."

"You're so talented," Leanne said, propping her chin on her hand to admire him.

Honestly, he looked fucking hot in an apron, his cheeks flushed either from working by the oven or from her praise. *I didn't even know I had an apron.* In gradient pastel hues—with ruffles, no less—it was so adorable on him that she wished she could grab him with both hands.

"I agree," Junie put in. "I've never heard of this foil packet thing, but it sounds versatile."

"Definitely! You can use whatever meat you want or no meat at all. I'm not sure I'd try tofu, but chickpeas might work."

He rounded the counter, coming up behind Leanne to set his hands on her shoulders. When he started kneading, it felt so good that she let out a moan. She hadn't realized she was tense until he found the knots, applying the perfect amount of pressure to smooth away the aches in her neck as well. Sighing blissfully, she closed her eyes.

"How are you this wonderful?" Junie asked, obviously talking to Trev.

"I'm committed to looking after Leanne," he replied. "That means home-cooked meals, back rubs, and cuddles...if she wants them." He finished up with one last, gentle squeeze. "Take a hot shower and get changed, babe. You have time."

Babe? They'd used it jokingly before, but she hated that endearment...but after him cooking dinner and giving her a back rub? *I'll let it go.*

With Trev as a buffer, she didn't even mind that Junie was still here. She practically floated to the bathroom, lost herself in a warm shower, and by the time she came out in yoga pants, he was checking their meal. He cut into a breast to make sure it was cooked properly then served up three plates with a proud flourish and added a little more sauce to the chicken.

"Dinner's done." He did a double take when he saw her, knuckling his eyes with exaggerated shock. "Okay, how do you look glamorous, even in that? It's sorcery, I tell you. Every angle, every time of the day, you're a knockout."

Swapping a look with her mother, Leanne offered him a sly and teasing half smile. "Just one of my many charms."

———

If Trev's arms bent that way, he'd pat himself on the back.

Such a basic recipe, and it was a huge hit. There was no food left, and Junie hugged him once she cleared her plate. Now she had all her bags by the front door; Leanne wasn't offering to see her off, but it felt wrong to do nothing. Especially when he was the reason she was leaving in the first place and his relationship with Leanne wasn't the way they portrayed at all.

"I'll help carry your stuff," he said to Junie, hefting a shoulder bag and taking hold of her wheeled suitcase.

"That's so sweet!" Junie beamed as she crossed to hug her daughter. "Come here, you."

Trev went ahead to call the elevator, and Junie caught up with him as the doors dinged open. He kept them apart long enough for her to hurry past, then he joined her. Surprisingly, she didn't chatter his ear off on the way down. Instead, she maintained a meditative silence, as if she had something heavy on her mind. As they stepped into the foyer, she tried for a smile, but it came out crooked.

"Everything all right?" he asked.

"Not exactly. I'm sure she's told you we're not close. And it's my fault. I put my needs—and my social life—ahead of LeLe when she was growing up. It left scars on her heart, and I want us to be closer now. But...I don't know how to make her forgive me."

At least you know what you did wrong.

"You can't," he said bluntly.

"What?"

"You can't *make* her forgive you. Have you apologized for your actions?"

Junie nodded. "Lots of times, for all the good it does."

"See, that's the thing. If you're apologizing because you're lonely and you want her to fill the void in your life, then your sorry won't come across as sincere. Because it *isn't*. You're still thinking about yourself, not how she feels. It's a different flavor of self-absorption, but if you only care about your desires, even now, then you haven't learned anything."

She pressed a hand to her mouth, eyes wide and teary, but Trev didn't feel even a flicker of sympathy. He folded his arms and waited.

"That is really harsh," Junie sniffed.

"It's accurate. Take some time and put yourself in Leanne's position. Do you have any idea about what she wants from life? Have you ever asked? What I'm hearing from you is that you want a relationship with her, but you'd rather not put in the work. If you care, you'll stick around and get to know her."

"Wow." Her eyes overflowed, and she stared at her feet for a long moment.

He suspected she'd relied on this "pitiful little girl" routine for most of her life, but it was strange seeing it in a woman old enough to be his mother. And his loyalty was to Leanne anyway, so he waited to see how she'd respond.

The silence built, and finally, Junie whispered, "She's lucky to have you. I'll...take my bags from here."

This time, he didn't argue. Maybe he should've pulled his punches a little, but he could see how Leanne tensed when Junie was around. That meant this woman had hurt her a lot over the years, and if he could stand as the wall that kept it from happening again, he'd damn well do so. He watched as she crossed the parking lot and got into a beat-up, blue Dodge Daytona. The thing was so old that it qualified for the "classic" car label, but it looked like it had been driven hard all those years. It must've been sporty and fun in the nineties, but like Junie, it showed all the miles of hard road.

When she put the car in gear, she didn't wave as she drove by, and he turned back toward the elevator. He felt weird heading back up. Leanne wasn't his girlfriend, but "roommate" didn't seem quite right either. Their relationship frankly defied definition, and he hesitated outside the door, staring at the keypad. Finally, he input the code and stepped in. When he came in, she was still on the couch, curled up with her feet tucked to the side.

"Do you like this show?" she asked, nodding toward the TV.

"I've never watched it. Just let me clean the kitchen, and I'll check out an episode."

"Need any help?"

Trev shook his head then realized she couldn't see him. "No, it's fine. This is part of my job description."

Leanne angled her body enough to flash him a grin. "That's good because I was just asking to be nice. I had no intention of getting up."

He laughed. "You shouldn't offer to do things you don't want to do. When people take you up on it, then you're stuck and feeling resentful. That's no way to live."

She paused the show and popped up on her knees, her pretty face bright with surprise and enthusiasm. "See, that's exactly how I feel. Normally, I *don't* offer. Politeness is for chumps. Who wants to live like a martyr, constantly helping others but wishing they didn't feel obligated? Bad enough I have to put up with that shit at work. It's so not for me. I'd rather save my energy for stuff I truly want to do. That way people know I mean it when I suggest pitching in."

"I'll remember that," he said, getting into a rhythm rinsing cups and plates.

It didn't take long to put everything that fit in the dishwasher and scrub the sheet pan by hand. He went the extra mile and wiped down all the counters and appliances then joined her in the living room. Since he wasn't sure about the rules, he chose the other end of the sofa.

Leanne cut him a sideways look. "Are you drawing lines, warning me not to cross?"

"No, I just—"

"Good, because I'm *really* bad at following the rules. I mean, if you tell me no, obviously, I'll back off, but I'd prefer to keep it fluid between us."

He had no idea what to say and finally settled on, "I'm fine with that. We don't need labels. It's enough that we enjoy…hanging out together."

That seemed like the wrong thing to say, but she didn't take offense. Instead, she said, "Awesome," and slid toward him, pulling his arm around her shoulder. "We're watching TV tonight, and later, there will be ice cream."

"Will there?"

"Absolutely. You got rid of Junie in less than a week. That's a new record."

"She's still in town, you know."

Leanne waved a hand. "But she's not my immediate problem. I'm choosing to live in the moment and...bask."

"In what?"

"You," she said, surprising him. "I hope you're a high-quality cuddler."

"I'll do my best." To that end, he snuggled her against his side and tried not to think about how good she smelled, fresh from the shower. But he couldn't resist one long, deep inhalation, drinking in the sweetness of her skin.

"Are you sniffing me?" Leanne asked.

Trev froze. *Busted.* It seemed better to admit it than make it worse by lying. "Yeah. Your shower gel smells amazing. I was wondering what it is."

"Orange blossom and juniper. It's pricey, but worth it."

"No kidding," he mumbled.

"You're cute when you're shy." She kissed his cheek and settled in, choosing a different show without him asking, presumably so they could watch together from the beginning.

That was quietly considerate in a way he wouldn't have expected. And while the program was interesting enough, he paid more attention to how she felt tucked into the crook of his arm, her weight on him gradually increasing as she relaxed. Her hair occasionally brushed against his arm when she laughed, and she was so warm and soft that it drove him wild.

How the hell did I get this lucky?

CHAPTER 10

IF ANYONE HAD TOLD LEANNE that she'd have a live-in "boyfriend" by the end of the summer or that Junie would stick around St. Claire after having her plans wrecked, she would've laughed.

But two weeks later, that was *exactly* the situation. So far, Trev had been a quality housemate. The only issue was she didn't want him smoking in the condo, and he agreed to stick to edibles while they were cohabiting. She didn't have any sense of how often he went that direction, but the place was always clean, and he usually had dinner ready when she got home. Already she'd gotten into the habit of texting him when she was on the way, and he'd greet her with a hug and a kiss on the cheek.

Mostly, he'd stuck to the guest room, claiming he didn't want to encroach on her space. In the past fourteen days, there had been two occasions when they had some wine after dinner and fooled around, but he seemed to prefer taking it slow. Which made her nervous, like he believed they had a shot at a real relationship, but she didn't let it mess with her head too much.

Today's the day.

She tugged at the hem of her jacket and strode boldly into

Mayor Anderson's office without knocking. His brow furrowed over that, but he didn't have a chance to say a word before she set her resignation on his desk. The frown deepened as he read the letter, then he flattened his palm with an audible thud.

"Is this a joke, Vanderpol?"

"Not remotely, sir."

"Cut to the chase. What do I need to offer to make you stick around?" Leaning back in his ergonomic leather office chair, he seemed confident this was a power play.

And it *was*, in a way, but not in a manner he could predict or obviate.

"There's no 'closer' here," Leanne said. "I'll save you some time in offering random bennies to sweeten the pot. I'm done working for you because I'm planning to run for city council, and I need the time for my campaign."

"You have family money to fall back on? That doesn't pay a living wage," Anderson said, like he was telling her anything she didn't already know.

"I'm aware. I'll work freelance in the interim and look for a suitable position once the election is over."

Mayor Anderson smirked when she said "suitable position." *Damn I hate this asshole. Just one hex. He would never know it's not a natural infection.*

"You're going after Dan Rutherford," the mayor said then.

In all honesty, it surprised Leanne that he recalled where she lived well enough to place her in the correct district. She froze. "Yes, that's why I'm resigning."

Meaning she didn't want Mayor Anderson poking around in

her business, calling it "good" because she worked for him, and then passing on his insights to Rutherford. It would be an uphill battle as it was, without fighting the mayor and all his cronies at the same time. No, the way she had the battle planned, it would happen in stages, and it wasn't time to take on Tom Anderson.

She had a list, she'd checked it twice, and Dan Rutherford was the first name on it.

No question whether he's naughty or nice.

Suddenly, Anderson's manner became jovial, and he sat forward in his seat. "Fair enough. If I can't talk you out of this, then I'll congratulate you on deciding to take such a momentous step. You're a smart, capable woman. Dan will have his work cut out for him."

Leanne could tell from his half smile that Anderson didn't think she had a chance in hell of pulling this off. Her mouth compressed before she blurted something she'd regret. "Do you want to choose my successor? If you decide before my notice is up, I'll do my best to prepare them and hand all the work over in the most efficient manner possible."

"I'll leave that up to you," the mayor said.

Leanne blinked. "You want me to hire my own replacement?"

"That would be ideal. You know the job, as well as my expectations. Hopefully, it won't prove too much of a challenge."

In addition to my actual work. She couldn't believe he was handing off this responsibility as well. Then again, it was par for the course, and maybe it was the final obstacle he could chuck in her path, all in solidarity with his deep-pocketed pal, Dan. *But sure, whatever. This is the last time you get to screw me over, Mayor Asshat.*

"I'll get right on it."

"Excellent. And don't forget about..." The mayor listed a bunch of stuff that technically didn't fall within her purview. Hopefully, Leanne's successor would do better at enforcing boundaries. She tuned him out for a while and only started paying attention when he added, "You know...Dan's wife, Molly, is just invaluable. You're divorced, aren't you?"

You son of a bitch.

"Good luck with the interview later today," she said.

They'd recently sent her a list of amended questions, but right then and there, she decided not to share them. Passive-aggressive? Absolutely. Listening to Mayor Anderson flounder should prove an excellent distraction. She whirled and stepped smartly out, returning to her own office with a spike of rage so profound that she could *feel* the magic gathering, just itching for her to turn it on him.

I shouldn't. Dammit, I don't care.

After locking her office door, Leanne checked her schedule, and yeah, she had time for this. This hex didn't require too much preparation, and she could cast it in her sleep. She pulled a few herb pouches from her briefcase and arranged them on the desk. Candles would help strengthen the spell, but she didn't have any, so her resentment had to do the job.

She swirled the herbs around and fed the working with the certainty of her intent. "When a man can't tell truth from lies, there should be an awful prize. Whenever he attempts to deceive, a terrible itch he shall receive." The spell itself sounded like a nursery rhyme, but it popped off with the force of a cork launched from a champagne bottle, and she sensed it arrowing directly to Mayor Anderson.

Perfect. Now when he tries to bullshit the interviewer over those new questions, he's going to look like a lice-infested chimpanzee. She waited a few beats for the guilt to kick in, and when it didn't, she shrugged and got to work. *It's good to be a witch.*

Some assholes had it coming.

––––––––––––––

Am I...happy?

Trev asked himself that as he set out the ingredients to make dinner. In the past two weeks, there had been no passive-aggressive comments, nobody asking what the hell he was doing with his life. He'd even gotten a few friendly texts from Mom. There was only radio silence from the old man, and he'd never been close with Tanner, so lack of contact from his father and brother didn't surprise him. He suspected they had a family chat that excluded him, but he'd never asked because his brother would take satisfaction in confirming it.

Happy. Yeah, I think I am.

It had been a long-ass time since the word applied, and while he still had days when he woke wondering why he was still breathing air and taking up space, they were a little less now, and he didn't need to be baked constantly to withstand the endless march of days. A whisper in the back of his mind suggested he needed more than a change of scene, but he closed his eyes and shook his head.

I'm okay.

If he repeated that enough, it might even be true. Cooking was like meditation; the repetitive motions of chopping vegetables for soup soothed his mind. He was making classic chicken noodle soup with chunks of carrot, celery, and onion. The chicken was already simmering in broth, and he added the vegetables, scraping the knife across the cutting board. This wasn't what he wanted to do with his life, however, and he'd gotten no further than entertaining the question.

Forty minutes later, Leanne let herself in, and he heard the click of her heels on the tiles in the foyer. He popped out of the kitchen and smiled at seeing her face. Even after a long day of work, she was a marvel, brilliant red hair flowing smoothly past her shoulders. Her lipstick matched, and her skin was flawless, highlighting the brightness of her eyes.

"Welcome home," he said. "It seems like you have news."

"I do. Let me get changed, and I'll tell you."

Trev paused her with a light touch on the shoulder and kissed her cheek. "I'll be waiting."

Leanne grinned. "Why are you so cute?"

Shortly thereafter, she came to the kitchen with her hair up in a ponytail, wearing lemon-yellow yoga pants and a green T-shirt that read BIG WITCH ENERGY. Even barefoot and dressed down, she was the most gorgeous person he'd ever seen. She leaned against the counter, watching as he blew on a spoonful of soup then tasted it.

"Dinner's ready. Talk while we eat?"

"Sounds good," she said.

He settled at the counter. "Junie came by earlier today."

Leanne sat beside him with her bowl of soup, stirring it idly with her spoon. "Oh God. I'm sorry. What did she want?"

"Not sure. I think she's lonely and..." He hesitated.

"And?" she prompted.

"Maybe she was also checking our story. I made up something about working from home, and she seemed to buy it. I fixed her a tuna sandwich for lunch."

"You're really going above and beyond," Leanne said, smiling. "This soup is delicious, by the way."

He basked in the pleasure of that simple compliment, and let the warmth sink in, feeling like someone experiencing the sun for the first time after a long winter. "You had news?"

"Don't freak out, but...I may have quit my job today."

It would make sense if he did panic since he'd just moved in—with the tacit understanding that she'd be footing the bill while he did household chores, played the role of her live-in boyfriend, and figured his shit out. Instead, he asked, "Are you okay?"

She tilted her head. "That's not what I expected you to say."

"You're deflecting. Did something happen?"

She smiled. "I mean, the mayor *is* an asshole who talks to my tits, but that's nothing new. I gave my notice to focus on my campaign for city council. I have enough in the bank to pay the bills until after the election."

"Wow, that's incredible." He couldn't find the words to tell her how inspiring it was to see her set a goal then go after it, like she couldn't imagine the prospect of failure.

"You're not worried at all?" she asked, seeming incredulous.

"Nah. But I am wondering if there's something I can do to help out. I've never volunteered on a political campaign, but it doesn't look too hard on TV." He grinned. "I can pass out flyers, and my paper collation is excellent. I can stand around at rallies and yell your name. What else is there? Oh, canvassing. Is that a thing? I'll totally knock on doors for you."

She reached over then, cupping his chin and turning his face toward her so suddenly that he dropped his spoon. Then she kissed him softly, tracing a fingertip down his cheek to his jaw. When she pulled back, her eyes were bright.

"Thank you for believing in me."

"Was that even a question? You're smarter than half the people currently on the council. I'm proud to be in your camp."

"If you're serious, I could definitely use the help. There's so much to organize, and I don't have a huge PR budget. I'll need to rely on volunteers."

"Start at the coffee klatch," he suggested.

"I will. I'll be at the office for two more weeks, then everything will ramp up. I'll be able to do more with social media than Dan Rutherford. He probably says 'on the Facebook.'"

Trev laughed and went back to eating his soup. "Nothing is guaranteed, but I'm betting you'll do great. Just let me know how to help."

"I will."

After dinner, he tidied up the kitchen and joined Leanne in the living room. She had a documentary queued up, and he wasn't all that interested, but when she leaned against him, nudging him with her shoulder, he circled an arm around her. *I missed this.* It might not seem like a big deal to anyone else, but Sarah had been his first and only serious relationship. Before that, he'd been Party Trevor and paid way more attention to doing keg stands than his GPA. When he'd met Sarah, he'd tried his best to recover, but she'd graduated and he… Well, the less said about that the better. And once she'd left, it was years before he could even imagine himself with anyone else. Cliché but true: he'd fallen hard when it finally happened, and he'd landed in a deep, dark hole when it all went wrong.

But he'd missed being cozy with someone, feeling the slow, steady shift of their breath, their body nestled into his. Others might judge him for lacking drive, but this was basically what he wanted in life. To be needed by someone, to be the reason they were glad to get home at the end of the day. It wasn't ambitious, and according to his dad, it wasn't manly either. Probably, he should desire to make a lot of money, but he didn't care about that and never had.

When the documentary about bees ended an hour and a half later, he said, "Damn. Now I know way more about this than I ever expected."

"I find insects soothing," she said in the tone of one making a confession.

Trev made a show of shuddering. "*Really?* I find them so creepy. I was going to bite the bullet, but if you're not afraid, then you're in charge of getting spiders out of the bathtub."

"Not a problem." She angled her body, propping a knee up as she leaned on her elbow resting on the back of the couch.

"You're looking thoughtful," Trev said, hoping the other shoe wasn't about to drop.

Leanne smiled. "I suppose I am. The first time I asked you to be my third husband, I admit it was a line. We discussed the possibility briefly over lunch, and you moved in. We've been really solid as domestic partners, so I'm asking again, this time for real. How about it, hon? You and me. We can catch the next plane to Vegas."

Is she seriously proposing?

He stared, unable to figure out how he should answer. "Are you sure about this?"

"Totally. We get along great, and I need to be in a stable relationship to do well in the polls against Dan Rutherford."

Oh right. It's all for show—a piece of paper that makes her more appealing to constituents.

Even so, he didn't hesitate because being Leanne's housekeeper and fake husband was still better than living in his parents' basement. He wouldn't let himself hope for more; taking one day at a time had gotten him this far, and all his instincts insisted this was the right move.

Taking a deep breath, Trev nodded. "Pack a bag. I'm down."

CHAPTER 11

SINCE LEANNE BELIEVED IN STRIKING while the iron was hot, she booked plane tickets for the next day.

The mayor might be pissed about her calling out on a Friday, but she didn't want to see his lying ass. *He's probably all blotchy from the hex and scratching his way through the interview.* That made her laugh as she clicked through a few more purchases: hotel room and a wedding package that included everything. Trevor should enjoy the trip at least—and frankly, she would too. If nothing else, this would be a fun, whirlwind vacation.

Quickly, she texted Danica: You owe me. I need a ride to the airport, no questions asked. I'll explain everything when I'm back. Deal?

The reply came immediately. Absolutely. What time should I pick you up?

Leanne: Nine should be early enough. Ride or die.
Danica: Don't you mean fly or die?

Leanne tried not to, but she laughed. If only you were as funny as you think you are.

Danica: See you tomorrow.

She only glanced up from the text exchange when Trev kissed the side of her head. "I'm going to bed now. What time are we leaving tomorrow?"

"Be ready by quarter to nine. Danica is driving us to O'Hare."

"Does she know where we're going…and why?" he asked.

Leanne shook her head. "I'm not telling anyone until it's done. My friends mean well, but I don't want to hear that I'm being reckless. I have a plan, and you're an important part of it." That wouldn't win her any awards for Most Romantic Proposal, but it had the chief virtue of being completely true.

Trev pretended to wipe a tear. "That's the nicest thing anyone's ever said to me."

He turned toward the guest room, but she stopped him with a hand on his forearm. "Hey. Do you plan to insist on separate beds even after we're official?"

Laughing softly, he covered her hand with his. "Does it seem like I'm playing hard to get? Guess it worked. I was hoping you'd put a ring on it."

"Wait for it," she teased.

Though she expected to be too full of nervous energy to sleep, she fell into dreamland right away and didn't wake until her alarm went off at eight. She took a long shower and did her hair up in a casual but elegant chignon. No need for makeup—magic took care of that. She packed her favorite royal-blue duffel with care, checking her closet for wedding dress options. Wearing virginal white was out of the question, but maybe…

She pulled a cream swing dress out and held it up. The fabric packed well and would look gorgeous after being hung up overnight, pure vintage charm with a sweetheart neckline, a fitted bodice, and a skirt that begged for a swishy petticoat. *This will do.* Leanne added the perfect pair of shoes and accessories and, as an afterthought, put in some sexy lingerie along with the rest of her clothes. Then she ordered the swing underskirt to be sent to their Vegas hotel.

If I'm getting married, I'll dress for it.

She checked everything in the condo one last time then led the way to the elevator. "Are you nervous?" she asked.

"I should be."

"But?" After stepping into the elevator, she moved to the back, a courtesy in case they stopped at other floors on the way down.

"I dunno. I can't explain it, but I feel the most chill I ever have. Like if I'm holding your hand, you won't let anything bad happen."

Oh. Oh wow.

She hadn't been holding his hand until that moment, but she reached for him instinctively, lacing their fingers together. Neither of them said a word until the elevator doors opened, and she tugged him forward. Though it was only five till nine, Danica was already parked out front with the engine idling. She waved with both hands, presumably one for Leanne and the other for Trev. While Leanne didn't possess that kind of joie de vivre, it amused her. Danica was the bouncy puppy of the coven, always quick with a smile or a hug, while Clem was more of a hedgehog. She could've gone further with the animal comparisons, but she stowed their bags in the back then swung into the back seat instead, beckoning Trev to do the same.

"You're making me your chauffeur?" the other witch joked.

"I should've told you to dress in black and white and to wear a jaunty hat."

"Welcome aboard, Trev. I hope you're going somewhere fun," Danica said.

She felt Trev's gaze lingering on her face, and when she glanced over at him, he smiled. "It should be."

Leanne connected her phone to the car audio and selected a road trip playlist. Trev surprised her by singing along to all their in-group favorites, tapping out the beat on his knees. He was pretty good at harmonizing, and Leanne didn't miss how Danica smiled at him in appreciation in the rearview mirror. The rest of the coven hadn't liked either of her first two husbands, but it seemed like things might be different this time.

They made good time, and Danica dropped them off at departures. Trev grabbed their stuff while Leanne leaned into the passenger window. "Thanks for always being in my corner."

"I can't wait to hear the whole story." Danica waved as she pulled away.

Leanne found Trev waiting by the automatic doors as people surged around him, but he kept his gaze locked on her. He had one hand on the raised handle of her small rolling duffel, and it struck her as sweet that he took it for granted that he'd manage her things. She wasn't used to that sort of care, but...she liked it.

Five minutes at the kiosk, and she had boarding passes. With Trev keeping pace in long, easy strides, she led the way though security. His bag got searched while hers didn't, and she waited for him on the other side. She'd booked business class seats, so they headed to the lounge. Trev seemed to be trying to play it cool, but she noted how his eyes widened as they got scanned in and found chairs in the corner, tucked away from everyone else.

"Wow, this is amazing. Do you usually travel this way?"

She shot him a wink. "First class all the way, sweetheart. Well, business anyway. But don't be too impressed, I upgraded using points."

He ducked his head with a rueful smile, another expression she found ridiculously adorable. "I'm pretending I have any idea what that means. Is that a credit card thing?"

"It is. Want something to drink? I can't cook, but I can use coffee machines like a boss."

"A latte or cappuccino?" he asked, seeming unsure.

"Coming right up. I'll get some snacks too."

He arranged their bags behind his chair, keeping them safe. Leanne smiled over that as she strode toward the drink bar. First she fetched their coffee, then she served two plates with a variety of fruits and pastries. They hadn't taken time to eat breakfast; she'd figured they would eat at the airport, and Trev never questioned her plans. While some might disparage his easygoing attitude, she favored the faith it demonstrated.

"I never thought it would happen to me," he said, obviously parodying one of *those* stories. "But here I am, being swept off my feet."

Business class was way better than coach.

Trev hadn't traveled much in the past ten years, but before

that, family vacations had him wedged in with Tanner and Mom while Dad enjoyed an upgrade alone. This time, though, he sat beside Leanne on the aisle, and she smiled at him before taking his hand. The flight attendant asked if they wanted juice or water before takeoff, and afterward, they pulled the curtain separating the front of the plane from the back.

They had lunch in the air, and he watched a movie while Leanne took a nap. The flight took four hours, and soon, they were on the ground in Vegas. He grabbed their bags from the overhead and stepped back so Leanne could precede him, blocking those trying to press forward behind him. She shot him a soft smile and glided forward. Her walk was a force of nature, drawing multiple eyes as her hips swiveled.

And she's with me.

That was the wildest part of all this. She took his hand again as they walked up the jet bridge to the airport proper. Harry Reid International Airport was clean and modern, and Leanne led the way as if she could navigate this place in her sleep. Soon, they joined the taxi line and got a ride to their hotel, a posh place that looked like a cathedral in Europe. Trev tried not to stare in awe at the frescoes on the ceiling and the gilt everywhere.

Leanne took care of check-in while he stood back, silently marveling that any of this was happening at all. Mom and Dad would be so surprised. Probably, he should feel bad about doing this in secret, but they'd written him off years ago. He did feel a bit guilty about leaving Titus in the dark, but since Leanne wasn't telling her book club besties either, he'd roll with her desire to keep everything on the down low until it was too late for anyone to argue.

"All set?" she asked, tapping the counter with her nails to get his attention.

"Totally."

Even the elevators were fancy, requiring the key cards to access them. Their room was on the thirty-eighth floor, with an incredible view of the skyline. At night, the city probably glittered like a heap of jewels. He tucked his backpack out of sight in the closet and laid her suitcase on the folding rack meant for that purpose. She nudged into the space with him and started hanging up her clothes, perfuming the air with sweetness that went right to his head.

What did she say about her body wash? Orange blossom and juniper.

Her lotion carried a matching scent, and she didn't seem to use perfume, relying instead on the layering from her other toiletries. She looked like a woman who would favor a stronger signature blend, but instead, she smelled unexpectedly innocent, like the last blooms of summer, that moment just before they ripened from flowers to fruit.

"Did you bring a suit?" she asked.

He flinched, glancing at his ratty backpack. "I don't even own one."

"It's fine. We need to shop for rings anyway. Adding your suit to our to-do list isn't a big deal." She ran a hand through his hair, gently stroking a strand between her fingers. "I'm glad I'll get to pick it out with you."

"You're not suggesting I get a haircut too?"

She lifted a shoulder in a graceful half shrug. "That's up to you. The suit is to make our pictures pop."

Surprised but pleased, he stepped away before he indulged the urge to hug her. "We're even taking wedding photos?"

"Seven, to be precise. I got a ninety-nine-dollar package. It includes use of the chapel, ceremony, traditional music, filing of paperwork afterward, and they even provide witnesses if you need them. And it's close to the office where we'll get the license tomorrow."

"You've thought of everything. Can I make a couple of requests?" He tried not to sound too tentative, but with her footing the bill, he felt like he had no right to be picky.

"Of course."

"I've heard there are places here that you can get a deal on jewelry, and vintage suits are more interesting anyway."

Leanne raised a brow, seeming amused. "You want to get our rings at a pawn shop and your suit from a thrift store?"

"Does that bother you? It's because...I want to pay for both since you're covering everything else, but I don't have a lot to work with." The admission shamed him, and he dropped his gaze, unable to face her derision.

Manicured fingers traced down his cheek, tilting his face upward. "There's nothing wrong with living within your means. I didn't choose you expecting a big, glittery rock, hon. In fact, I'm touched that you want to do what you can. Just let me find a few prospects, and we'll head out. We can get dinner afterward."

"That sounds awesome." This time, he couldn't contain himself, and he wrapped his arms around her, kissing her with the tenderness and longing he'd been repressing for weeks.

Her lips were so soft, pillowy against his, and she knotted her fingers in his hair, pressing closer even as their tongues tangled. His emotions swelled, baffling and complicated; this wasn't supposed to be real-real, but the further they went with this, the more he *felt*.

"Mmm. You're a good kisser. Can we do that more once we're married?"

He laughed softly. "You want more of me?"

"Definitely. Let's get moving, unless you need a nap?"

"This *has* been a lot more exciting than I'm used to, but I'm enjoying the journey. Let's get a rideshare and paint the town pink."

Leanne cast him a smiling glance over one shoulder. She probably didn't mean for it be so seductive, but his heart still skipped over it. Impossible not to react when a woman like this focused all her attention on him.

"Not red?" she teased.

He shook his head. "That's such an aggressive color. Not the vibe we want for a whirlwind wedding weekend."

"Are you commenting on my hair?"

Trev froze. He loved her hair, actually, and he hadn't meant to make her feel bad with his random joke. It took confidence and commitment to look after and—

"Relax, I'm joking. I agree with you. It's sort of a violent phrase. When I think of painting the town red, slasher movies come to mind." She slung her bag over her shoulder and beckoned. "How do you feel about random facts?"

"Generally? I enjoy them," he said, as they left the hotel room.

"There's a fun story that people tell about how the phrase got started, likely inaccurate. They say 'paint the town red' comes from this British nobleman who loved a good prank. Apparently, he led his crew to paint a tollgate and several front doors...bright red."

"Huh. So it's not blood after all."

"Probably not."

They took the elevator down with a couple who couldn't stop kissing. Trev spared a wish that Leanne felt that way about him then sternly warned himself to be happy with what he had.

There was a special rideshare pickup area away from the taxi line, and they waited for five minutes before a young driver in a gorgeous black BMW collected them. Trev mouthed "wow" at Leanne, who shrugged. Apparently, she was used to this. They got dropped off at the freestanding silver and gold resale shop, a dated-looking white-and-blue building not far from the Strip. He had his doubts going in, but the prices were reasonable.

He found a set of simple silver rings that Leanne liked and he could afford; the shop said they could have them sized to fit in two hours. Next, they ordered a ride to an upscale consignment shop, trendier than he expected, and he found an elegant gray pinstriped suit in his size right away, almost like it was predestined. Normally, Trev didn't believe in fate, but Leanne stared at him with naked admiration when he stepped out, dressed to the nines in clothes he would've said didn't suit him—until he saw his reflection in her eyes.

Trev picked up a trilby hat and twirled it then set it on his head. "What do you think? Does it work?"

"Love it. We're not leaving until we find you the matching wing tips."

The salesclerk overheard. "Actually, we have a good selection in the back. Not many can pull off vintage gangster style, but your boyfriend is rocking it."

"Fiancé," Leanne corrected.

The most incredible pride rushed through him—that she felt strongly enough to claim him. He just had enough cash left from working for Titus to get everything he needed. Before, he hadn't let himself imagine how his wedding might go, but now, apparently, he'd be dressed like a mafioso from the '20s, and he was all in, if Leanne liked it.

I'd do anything she asked. Anything at all.

CHAPTER 12

"WOW," LEANNE SAID.

Trev stood just outside the fitting room, decked out from head to toe in clothing she'd chosen, and his willingness to put himself in her hands did something to her. Not only did he look fantastic—he was also gazing at her like all he cared about in the world was her approval. He touched the trilby hat and flashed her a smile.

"I take it that's a good wow?"

She grinned back. "Generally speaking, 'wow' is positive. I guess I might say 'wow' if a giant golem punched through the floor, but my tone would definitely be different."

"I'll bring a few pairs of the shoes. What size?" the clerk asked.

Trev answered, and the second pair he tried on was perfect. Leanne was prepared to pay for everything, but he gently nudged her card away and paid cash for the lot, accepting the bags with a friendly smile for the woman who'd helped them shop. His credit card was nearly maxed, and he didn't earn much, yet he'd spent almost everything he had on wedding attire and simple silver rings. She recalled arguing with her second husband about—*no, hell no.*

Not today.

"We have a little time to kill before we can pick up the rings," she said.

"I'd like to get my hair cut, if you don't mind."

His adorably tentative expression prompted her to kiss his cheek. "Absolutely. Let me find a place that can fit you in."

She made a couple of calls and got him a spot if they could be there in fifteen minutes. Thanks to the rideshare driver, they made the window, and she sat at the front of the salon, feeling a strange sort of pride as Trev transformed from shaggy to elegant. She hadn't weighed in on his choice, but she approved of the low fade with the wavy, side-part swoosh. It would look fantastic with the trilby and should photograph well.

Discreetly, Leanne signaled the stylist at the front desk. "I'd like to pay before my fiancé realizes I have. It's a wedding present."

The woman beamed. "Is today the big day?"

"Tomorrow."

"Congratulations! I'll give you the special newlywed discount." She ran Leanne's card and took care of everything before Trev even noticed Leanne had gotten up. She was in her seat when he joined her ten minutes later.

Trev glanced at the stylist. "How much is it?"

The woman smiled. "You're all set."

He bit his lip, eyeing Leanne for a moment. "You didn't have to—"

"Never mind that. You look fantastic. Let's swing by and get the rings then have dinner?" she suggested, ordering a ride as they left the salon.

Leanne input the first stop as Trev said, "Sounds amazing. Do you have someplace in mind?"

"Not really. I've done a few girls' trips to Vegas, but we usually eat whatever while we drink and gamble. Come to think of it, I don't remember ever seeing a show while I was here."

"We should check this out." Trev flipped his phone to show her a listing for *The Rat Pack Is Back*, a dinner show that offered a full-course Italian meal while performers paid tribute to Frank Sinatra, Dean Martin, and Sammy Davis Jr.

On impulse, she opened the link on her own device and checked while waiting for their driver. "Looks like I can get tickets, if you're serious. There are seats available."

"Whoa, really? I would love that. It's so Vegas, you know? I mean, it's a little embarrassing to admit, but I've always been weirdly out of sync with modern music. My favorite song of all time is 'Beyond the Sea' by Bobby Darin."

She tilted her head as a shiny red VW pulled up. "Hold that thought. I added a second destination," Leanne said to the driver. "I'll update the addresses in the app."

The driver nodded. "No problem. Yep, got the change."

"Excellent," she said.

She slid across the back seat, busily booking tickets for the show. Her husband-to-be gazed at her with open admiration. She'd had people stare at her tits like that a *lot*, but this might be the first time anyone had been so impressed by her competence.

She turned to Trev as he settled in beside her, still holding the bags. "Do you mind running in to get our rings?"

"Not at all."

"To make the show after, we don't have time to drop those off at the hotel, but we should be able to tuck them out of the way. I'm excited at how everything came together, like—"

"It was meant to be?" Trev suggested. "And...me too."

Leanne couldn't bring herself to agree, but she didn't argue either. Sometimes everything aligned just right; that much was true. "Anyway, back to your favorite song. How did you even hear it in the first place?"

"Promise you won't laugh?"

"Cross my heart," Leanne said solemnly.

"Okay. I heard the Robbie Williams version on the *Finding Nemo* soundtrack first. It's also in *BioShock*. I played that a lot, and then I kinda went down a rabbit hole listening to different covers. I even checked out the original French version. It's a freaking *great* song," Trev added in a defensive tone, like she might mock him.

"That's cute. You must've been..." Doing the math quickly in her head, Leanne said, "Around fourteen when you saw *Finding Nemo*?"

"That sounds about right. I liked cartoons even as a teenager. Hell, I might as well be honest. I *still* like them...love *Clone Wars* to this day. I'm all about Ahsoka." He ducked his head, evidently afraid to make eye contact after this confession.

People probably told him to grow up all the time. Combined with his lack of a steady job, the interest in animation and video games likely earned him all kinds of censure, particularly from his parents. But Leanne couldn't get on board with such criticism; people ought to live however the hell they wanted, chase happiness in their own style. Being an adult didn't mean all the things you loved as a kid had to be chucked along the way.

"You and me both," the driver mumbled.

"We should watch it together," she suggested. "I've been known to star a war from time to time."

Trev brightened, his pretty eyes sparkling with surprise and delight. "Oh my God, that would be awesome."

When the car stopped at a traffic light, the driver fiddled with his phone, and suddenly, the car filled with mellow violin strings and a velvety-voiced woman singing "La Mer" in French. "Romantic, am I right? I'm totally getting five stars from this ride."

Trev gave him a thumbs-up in the rearview mirror. "Definitely, dude."

Soon, they arrived at the pawn shop and Trev retrieved their rings in record time, then they continued to the show venue. The driver dropped them off, and Leanne hurried ahead, showing confirmation emails and QR codes when necessary. Staff seated them straightaway, and Trev hid their bags under the table, to her amusement. Everything was a bit posher than she'd expected, though the dress wasn't black tie.

As for the menu, she picked salad instead of soup, chicken marsala, and cannoli for dessert while Trev went for minestrone soup, eggplant lasagna, and gelato. Though they hadn't planned this even slightly, she allowed satisfaction to wash over her. The arrangements really had been incredibly smooth, everything unfolding as if by some greater design.

"Thanks for suggesting this," she said, as the server expertly opened the bottle of Chardonnay she'd ordered.

"I didn't think you'd go for it. When I go out with the guys, I basically never suggest anything because…" He hesitated.

"Because?"

"Only Titus knows anything about what I'm really like," he admitted in a quiet voice.

"You're afraid to show them?"

"That's part of it, I guess. But it's just easier to let people fill in the blanks, make assumptions based on how I look. Correcting those ideas looks an awful lot like effort."

"Which you haven't cared enough to make? They're *your* friends, Trev."

He shook his head, taking a sip of the wine. "No, they're Titus's friends. I'm his platonic plus-one. I'm his drinking buddy, largely because I never turn him down. I'm reliable as a Toyota, right? Knew a dude in college who put two hundred thousand miles on his Camry."

With an odd tightness in her throat, she touched the back of his hand, and that moment felt more significant than fucking in Danica's downstairs bathroom, somehow. "But you're not worried about putting me off? Letting me see the real you."

"I should be," he whispered. "But…I'm not. It feels like…"

"What, sweetheart?"

"That you're *my* person. That no matter what I say, you won't judge me. I…trust you."

———

Before Leanne pulled away, Trev caught her hand where it rested on his and lifted it to brush his lips over her knuckles.

Hopefully, she wouldn't crack a joke because he might never

work up the nerve to say something like that again. But her gaze stayed on his, quiet and steady as a rainy night. "I'll do my best not to disappoint you," she said.

"That's not possible. Everything we've done together has turned out, like, a thousand percent better than I expected...or frankly, than it should have, all things considered."

"I was thinking that too," she admitted.

"Like, about what?"

"Grabbing business class seats on such short notice for instance. Getting a discount on our gorgeous hotel room. Finding a vacancy at such a pretty chapel and then lucking into same-day tickets for this show. Just...all of it, really." She cocked her head, a flirty little gesture that never failed to make his heart flutter, and added, "It *is* pretty magical."

Trev didn't quite get why she was smiling so much, and he couldn't stop staring at her mouth. "Could not agree more."

If he leaned over the table to kiss her, he'd likely spill the wine. So he contained the urge and just admired how gorgeous she was as the restaurant served their meal in courses. *Freaking courses*. He thought about how he used to subsist on whatever he could microwave or make on a hot plate. The show started as their dessert arrived, and he loved that too.

Trev had never told anyone that he preferred old music or that he'd gotten into it in a big way after hearing a variety of songs in games like *BioShock* and *Fallout*. It was easy to talk to her, a level of comfort he'd never achieved with another partner. He'd never put too much thought into what he wanted from a relationship, but now, one unshakable certainty coalesced:

It shouldn't feel like work.

Sure, it would require effort and nurturing down the line. But each moment shouldn't feel like being a salmon swimming upstream to spawn. He watched her every bit as much as he did the singers, sneaking glances at the performers now and then, because it was more fun to see her smile, to watch her eyes light up at something happening onstage.

When the show ended, he collected their bags as Leanne linked her arm through his with a content-sounding sigh. "This was fantastic. We'll have such a great story to tell when we get back."

He missed a step, nearly stumbling, and she helped him stay on his feet. *That's not what this is all about, right? It's not only a ruse, keeping up a front for her political aspirations.* But maybe it was? Grimly, he reminded himself that he'd agreed to help her craft a certain image, one more marketable to voters, and to keep Junie from moving in.

Don't push past what's been asked. You're already getting a lot out of this.

Mumbling a noncommittal response, he ordered a ride for them. Awesome thing about Vegas, there were drivers nearby, usually four or five minutes away, pretty much all the time. Not like St. Claire. Their driver this time was an older man who reminded Trev a bit of Howard Carruthers, who drove to keep busy. Their driver was also a talker, preventing them from making any private conversation on the way back to the hotel.

When they got to the room, he hung up his wedding clothes with reverent hands. While it was Leanne's third run, this was his first time, and truthfully, it probably wouldn't happen again for Trev. He stood for a moment, admiring the gray pinstriped suit and the charcoal-and-white wing tips. To his surprise, Leanne came up and hugged him from behind, resting her head between his shoulder blades.

"What a long, awesome day it's been."

Trev savored her warmth for a moment then loosed her hold on him and turned so he could cuddle her in return. "I hope you don't think this is weird, but...I'd like to hold off on sex stuff until tomorrow."

She smiled and kissed his jaw lightly. "So we can have an actual wedding night. You're secretly a romantic."

He felt heat bloom in his cheeks. "It's not really a secret. More that there was nobody interested in finding out."

"I am," she said. "Interested, that is. And it's no problem, I'll keep my thirst in check. Tonight we spoon, but it would be knife if we fork tomorrow." Leanne caught his gaze and winked at him, utterly shameless about that pun.

"Why are you so cute, even when your jokes are this bad?" he demanded.

"Generations of anthropological scholars will ask themselves that very question." After pressing another little kiss to his throat, she pulled back. "Gonna brush my teeth. You?"

Trev smirked. "I endorse oral hygiene as well."

Probably better if he didn't admit how long it had been since he'd been to the dentist or how there had been days when he couldn't bring himself to shower or brush his teeth because everything seemed so fucking pointless. Hell, he didn't even know how to bridge a subject like that or tell her that LBL (Life Before

Leanne) had been one endless dark night with no promise of light, each day the same as the last. And he knew simply meeting someone new couldn't fix everything that was wrong in his head, but fear made it difficult to consider confiding in her, and he couldn't have afforded therapy before either.

Maybe I can soon.

His old man didn't believe in it, and he'd have mocked Trev for even considering it. Real men didn't admit to having emotions, let alone get dragged around by them. Tanner seemed to be the exact same way. It was only Trev who didn't fit the mold, weak and sensitive and—

"Your turn," Leanne said, saving him from that dreadful loop without even realizing it.

"Thanks. I'll be there in a sec."

He spent some time in the bathroom, just breathing as he brushed his teeth, trying to understand what she saw in him. In Trev's mind, he might as well have the loser *L* tattooed on his forehead. *Cut it out. You've got potential.* Damn, but he loathed that word. Eventually, the breathing exercises calmed his brain enough for him to act like he was okay when he wandered out of the bathroom five minutes later.

Leanne was already under the covers, and the lights were off. "Come to bed," she mumbled. "I'll only grope you a little, I swear."

"Don't threaten me with a good time."

He slipped under the covers, and she immediately rolled over, curving her soft body against his side. She seemed to be wearing shorts and a T-shirt. *Aw, she's trying to honor my request for us to have an actual wedding night.* It moved him that she cared to that extent. How long had it been since anyone heeded his requests or cared about how he felt?

Hell if I know. What an unsatisfying answer.

"We're getting married tomorrow," she whispered into his shoulder. "You nervous?"

It took him a while to answer, trying to decide if the truth would upset her. He swallowed hard and finally answered, "So much."

But she was already asleep and didn't hear his honest response. Hopefully, he could keep his shit together long enough to roll around in this delightful fantasy.

Because when they got back to St. Claire, Trev suspected the magic wouldn't last long.

CHAPTER 13

LEANNE WOKE UP WHEN ROOM service arrived.

Since she didn't order it, Trev must have. He'd chosen an assortment of options: pastries, yogurt, and fruit, along with a heartier breakfast that they shared. Before he moved in, she usually grabbed a protein bar and coffee. This qualified as luxury. There was something subtly charming about a partner who tended to the details, taking care of her without being overt about it.

She genuinely liked Trev, and she enjoyed sleeping next to him, which wasn't the norm. Generally, she preferred for people to get out of her bed when she was done fooling around with them. In a rom-com, Leanne would be the character who rolled over right after sex and offered to call a rideshare without a flicker of hesitation. While she loved the idea of marriage, she'd never been able to get comfortable with relying on someone else, and she knew herself well enough to accept that her marital failures were mostly her own fault. The fact that someone could choose to go always hovered in the back of her head, so she pulled the plug before anybody bailed on their own.

Better to leave than be left, right? But here I go again.

Yet this time, her heart ached when she imagined the inevitable ending of this agreement. Nothing lasted, no matter how much she wished otherwise. The important thing was to get what she needed before Trev decided to go his own way. It wasn't that she *planned* to discard him once he served his purpose, but the minute he showed signs of restlessness, she knew herself. When the time came, she'd pull the trigger preemptively on reflex, to preserve her dignity.

With effort, she put aside those negative thoughts and set up their food on the two-person table in front of the window. They ate a lazy brunch, then her phone beeped. She glared at it. *If that's Junie…*

"It might be important," Trev said.

If it was about work, they could go to hell. Despite her better judgment, she read the text, and sure enough, it was from her mom. You're really not home? Are you avoiding me?

As her mother had done to her *many* times, Leanne left the text on read. "Should we go for a swim? We have time before we need to get our license."

"I packed my trunks," he admitted with an endearingly sheepish grin. "Better to be prepared, I thought."

"I'm into it. I'll put on my bikini." She wrapped up in the hotel robe and slipped on some flip-flops.

The pool was outside, and there was a massive stretch of people sunning themselves on rows of lounge chairs. A few families were in the water, but there was still plenty of space to swim. Leanne dove in without hesitation, a clean slice through the water. Magic tickled over her skin as she broke the surface, and she skimmed the pool area, trying to pinpoint her fellow witch. Impossible without doing a little spell work of her own, and she didn't care that much either. Pretending she hadn't noticed, she cut toward Trev in a brisk breaststroke.

"You're an incredible swimmer," he said. "I thought you'd be a toe-dipper."

"What's that? Sounds vaguely offensive."

"You know, someone who perches at the edge of the pool, slathers up in sunscreen, maybe puts a foot in, and eventually decides to work on their tan instead."

"Are you judging me for how I look?" Leanne asked in a neutral tone.

"A little, I guess. Should've known better." Instead of apologizing, he splashed her, and she went back at him hard. "Okay, but seriously, how is your face still perfect? What brand of cosmetics do you use? The world needs to know your secret."

She tossed her head, slinging water everywhere. "I'll never tell. Maybe she's born with it, maybe it's..."

"Witchcraft," Trev said.

Leanne froze, then she forced herself to laugh. "That's not how the ad slogan goes."

She ducked under the water and swam through his legs like a seal, lifting him up as she passed. He tried to grab her, and they spent a glorious hour horsing around, until well past the point when her skin was shriveled up like a prune. Eventually, she stretched an arm out, staring at her wrinkled fingers in disapproval.

"Time to go?" he asked.

"I think so. I need time to get myself together for the wedding."

The hotel robe was delightfully absorbent, so she didn't drip water all through the halls. Back in the room, it was odd and quiet after the silly, playful pool outing, and she kept stealing looks at Trev as she gathered her toiletries for a long shower.

Finally, he said, "Something on your mind?"

"You're not saying much… If you're having second thoughts—"

"Not even slightly," he cut in.

"I'd understand if you were. It's a big step, and maybe you'd rather hold out for the perfect person or the perfect moment."

With a faint, melancholy smile, Trev shook his head. "Perfection is a lie. It's just hitting me, that's all. We're really doing this. No matter the reasons, I'll legally be your husband in like two hours. That's wild."

"I was thinking about that," she said. "Do you mind if I take a hyphen?"

His eyes widened. "Why would I? I haven't even thought about the name-change stuff. Leanne Vanderpol-Montgomery is quite a mouthful, though. Have you imagined the signs?"

She grinned, loving that he was already picturing her political ambitions. "It sounds fancy, doesn't it?"

"Sure does. Do whatever you want. I wasn't expecting you to take my name at all."

Impulsively, she hugged him, wrapping her arms tightly around his shoulders. "It's a good-faith gesture. I'll take the first shower."

"No problem. I'll watch some TV in this badass bathrobe."

She washed up properly but didn't linger, aware that he was waiting for a turn in damp trunks in an air-conditioned room. *He's probably freezing.* Trev seemed like the kind of person who would always go second, never putting himself first. *Maybe I need to nudge him in that direction. Wait, no. I'm thinking like this is a normal relationship instead of a mutually convenient arrangement.* Even Leanne occasionally lost track of why they were together, so maybe it was confusing for him too.

She stepped out of the shower and wrapped up in a towel. "All yours," she called.

He ambled into the bathroom and pulled her close, brushing a kiss against the wet hair at her temple. "Thanks, Butterfly."

"What?"

"Just an endearment I'm trying out. I noticed the face you made when I called you babe. How's it working for you?"

After a moment of proper consideration, she said, "I think I like it."

"When will you know for sure?" he asked.

"When you share the reasoning behind it."

"Butterflies are beautiful, obviously. And so are you. But they're also super helpful—they pollinate flowers and nosh on weeds. Yet go ask anybody, 'What's a butterfly's deal?' They'll be like, 'Well, it's pretty. It flutters around being colorful, right?'" Trev shook his head. "Nah, if you pay attention, they're about *way* more than looking good. Just like you."

She closed her eyes, more touched than she wanted to be by his artless explanation. With effort, she kept from tearing up. If any droplets slipped out, hopefully she could blame the recent shower. "Yeah, I *love* that. Carry on."

In appreciation, she gave him a long, deep kiss, and he responded by pressing close, leaving no doubt about how ready he was for their wedding night. Finally, Trev pulled away, breathing hard. "Out, temptress, or my pants won't fit."

She smirked, but she sauntered out anyway, quickly touching up the glamour spell on her face, and she extended it to her hair while he was busy. The magic lent luster to the bright-red strands and added dexterity and skill to her hands, so she coiled it into a style she'd seen in a beauty tutorial.

Her phone rang, actually rang. And what the hell was that about? Leanne answered, although she didn't recognize the number. If it was a coven sister calling from a different phone due to an emergency, she'd never forgive herself if she didn't pick up.

Hell, I hope the witch hunter isn't—

"Hope I'm not disturbing you, Ms. Vanderpol." Dan Rutherford's oily voice oozed over the line, making her feel like she needed another shower.

Obviously, you are.

"I'm out of town, and it's the weekend," she said, letting him draw his own conclusions.

"Well, I won't keep you long. Just wanted to let you know that a little bird told me you're planning to go up against me. You sure that's the right move, darling? I absolutely hate making a pretty girl look bad."

"I guess we'll see."

"Indeed we shall. You'll soon learn you've bitten off more than you can chew. At every turn, I've tried to—"

Leanne hung up without letting Rutherford finish the rest of his bullshit sentence, then she blocked the number for good measure. This wasn't his cell phone—that would've popped up in her contacts—so it might be his landline at home. Irritation popped in her head like firecrackers, but she refused to let that asshole ruin her mood.

Not today. Not with this witch. Get it together, and remember why you're here.

With effort, she calmed herself. This was *exactly* why she'd given notice, however. The mayor hadn't wasted any time spilling everything he knew her to opponent, and she hadn't even officially announced her candidacy. Rutherford must already be contemplating strategies to use against her. *It'll be fine. I expected this.* By the time Trev emerged from the bathroom, she was putting on her dress and checking herself from all angles in the mirror.

He dropped the towel he was using to dry off his hair, his face glowing with awe. "You are a goddess. How is this real life? Seriously. *How?*"

"Good question! Put your fancy suit on and let's get married."

Vegas had quick weddings down to an art form.

There were five other couples in their wedding clothes getting marriage licenses as well, and thanks to Leanne having filled out the forms ahead of time, they breezed through the process, made the payment, and moved on. The wedding chapel was nicer than Trev had pictured. He'd imagined "Vegas style" and that there would be sequins, rhinestones, and Elvis impersonators in white spandex jumpsuits everywhere. But he was pleasantly surprised at how elegant everything was. A young woman greeted them and explained the process. Their officiant was included in the package, and two witnesses would be provided from the chapel staff. It all happened so freaking fast that it felt like he was sleepwalking through his own wedding.

He must've said all the right things, because the next thing he knew, he was slipping the ring on Leanne's finger, and she did the same to him. They'd been sized perfectly, and he stared for a moment at the silver band marking him as Leanne's husband. *Holy fuck, I'm her husband.*

"You may kiss the bride," the officiant said.

Silently, he tried to convey his wild emotions with a deep, sweet kiss. Hard to know if he succeeded, but when he pulled back, she was smiling up at him, perfect as a pinup model. It still absolutely blew his mind that this woman had carved through a crowd straight to his side. Hell, he'd never been picked first for anything in his life, not even dodgeball in elementary school.

Just her. Only her.

"We'll file the necessary paperwork," the woman said, smiling. "If you'll both sign here, and witnesses, if you please..."

Soon, it was all done, and they moved along to the brief photo shoot included in their package, seven poses that would be provided in digital form: classic side by side, one with Trev behind her, another with them kissing, a fourth back-to-back and laughing wildly. Number five showed them facing each other while holding hands, six had them making silly faces, and in the last one, the photographer said, "Gaze at her like she's the person you love most in the world."

Trev had no idea how that expression was supposed to appear so he just...looked. At Leanne, envisioning a real future with her. That moment left him breathless, aching with want edging toward need. *If you were mine, Butterfly—truly mine—I would never ask the universe for anything else.*

"I'll send you the digital pictures via a link in your email," the photographer said. "You can order prints from us or print them yourselves. These photos are yours."

Leanne smiled brightly, and Trev swore he saw stars in the dude's eyes as she said, "Thanks. I can't wait to see them."

"You two look great together," the man added.

Do we? Briefly, Trev imagined a big, framed photo hanging on the wall of the condo. Maybe she'd get a smaller one for her desk—

Breathe. You did it without giving her any clue how much of a mess you are. Maybe that was unfair? Like selling a car without disclosing it's been in a wreck. Making a face, he tried to shut his brain up. *Can't you leave me alone for even one day?* Thankfully, the awful voice that whispered how he was doomed to misery and failure quieted.

The chapel owners came to greet them afterward and thank them for their patronage. "Congratulations again. We hope you'll be happy together."

"Thanks." Trev offered his hand to Leanne and experienced a gentle frisson when she interlinked their fingers.

"We did it, hon." She squeezed lightly as he followed her out into the fading heat of a late-summer day in Vegas. "Our flight back leaves at eleven tomorrow, but we still have tonight. Anything you want to do?"

"Besides you?"

Her smile gained teasing layers, and she canted her head to gaze at him through absurdly thick lashes. "That's a given. So, yeah, before that."

"Nah, I got to pick last night. It's your turn."

She lifted his hand to her lips and brushed a kiss across his knuckles—such a romantic gesture that his breath caught. "Is that the secret to our lasting love story? Taking turns."

"Hope so," he said, more seriously than he intended.

"Then...I've always wanted to try the High Roller, but the friends I vacation with would rather go clubbing or try their luck at the casino. Are you afraid of heights?"

"Might be the only thing I'm *not* afraid of," he joked. "When I was doing more in the lawn care and maintenance line, I went up trees to trim them and on roofs to clean gutters."

"According to the reviews, it's not scary even if you're acrophobic because the pods are slow-moving and very stable. Should I book the tickets?"

Trev nodded. "Go ahead, I'm looking forward to it."

She bounced a bit, endearingly enthusiastic at the prospect of riding an upscale, touristy Ferris wheel. If he'd judged by her looks, he never would've imagined Leanne would want to do something like this. Then again, he'd skirted perilously close to pissing her off this afternoon by assuming she was a cover girl who preferred not to get her hair wet.

Note to self: don't presume anything *about my wife.*

"If we time it right, we'll be able to take some gorgeous selfies at sunset. Afterward, we'll find something delicious for dinner, and then—"

"I'll make you mine." He couldn't stop the words, even if they made her mad.

Thankfully, she slanted a sizzling look in his direction. "Sounds perfect. The paperwork's already in order and everything."

"Do you come with a warranty?" he joked.

She shook her head. "Sorry, some wear and tear is inevitable. What's the phrase in Latin? Caveat emptor. Yeah, that's the one."

"I have no idea what that means," he admitted.

"Let the buyer beware."

"But I *didn't* buy you. There's no way to put a price on perfection."

"True enough. The first thing, not my perfection," she added quickly. "It's my choice, and I'm giving myself to you."

Giving myself to you.

It took all Trev's self-control not to push her against the chapel wall and kiss her like the world was ending. They were probably used to PDA here, but if he started, he might not be able to stop, and it would not be ideal to do it for the first time as a married couple in a public bathroom. Doing that at Danica's party had been wild enough.

"Can't wait. All night long, I hope."

Their eyes locked, and Trev swore his body temperature spiked to the point that he felt the heat everywhere. He inhaled slowly. Exhaled.

She smiled. "The stamina ball is in your court, sweetheart. Okay, we're all set, tickets purchased. Let's head over and get ready to admire the city from above."

The wedding chapel was about half an hour from the High Roller attraction in south Las Vegas, so they called for another rideshare. This driver was quiet, respecting the mood, and he played a medley of soft, romantic songs. The car was clean and smelled of cinnamon, details Trev noted and stored away, because he wanted to recall every last trace of this perfect trip. He might never experience anything so wonderful again.

On impulse, he leaned over and kissed Leanne on the cheek. "Thanks for making this so incredible and memorable."

"I'm having fun," she said, waving off his gratitude, but she did lean over to return the kiss, her soft mouth lingering on his jaw.

The resultant thrill did things to him, feelings he probably shouldn't focus on. Not yet anyway. There would be time for that tonight. *Our wedding night.*

Oh my God.

A short while later, he stepped into the pod behind Leanne. It was huge, much larger than it looked from the ground, and the view was breathtaking. They shared it with a few others, but they were quiet, admiring the slow, golden slide of the sun sinking in the sky. Since he'd grown up in the Midwest, he hadn't realized sunset could be so glorious elsewhere. Out here in the desert, the colors were electrifying, making him feel like he'd never seen the sky before in his life. Or maybe it was the woman holding his hand, the last rays of sunlight gilding her hair like she was a flaming angel come to bless mere mortals with her grace.

"Take a picture," she said, catching him gazing at her face instead of the skyline. "It'll last longer."

To her evident amusement, he did, clicking away with his phone like he could freeze this moment for all time.

CHAPTER 14

ELECTRIC CANDLES, A BOTTLE OF champagne, and rose petals scattered around the suite did an amazing job of setting the mood.

There were also strawberries dipped in chocolate, arranged like a bouquet of flowers. No doubt about it, the hotel had gone above and beyond in creating the perfect ambiance for their wedding night. Leanne surprised herself by feeling a tad nervous as she changed out of her wedding dress and into the sexy number she'd packed specially for tonight. Not that she planned on wearing it long.

Trev stood in the middle of the room in his boxers, seeming confused as to what he should be doing, like he'd paused to think about it and not reached any conclusions. She sauntered toward him, grabbed his hand, and led him over to the table for two placed before the inspirational view of the Vegas Strip. The champagne was open already, so she poured two glasses and settled into the nearest chair, crossing her legs slowly to draw his attention.

"To happily ever after," she said in a faintly ironic tone.

"Sounds like you don't believe in that." He clinked his flute against hers and took a sip then set the drink aside.

To avoid answering the question, she slid out of her chair and perched on his lap. He immediately shifted to accommodate her, snuggling her against him with gently encircling arms. With a soft sigh, Trev rested his chin on her shoulder, grazing her loose curls with his cheek. One nuzzle, another, then he swept the hair aside entirely to press kisses up and down the side of her throat. That felt exquisite, tender and sexy at the same time. She looped an arm about his shoulders and let the pleasurable sensations wash over her.

"We didn't talk about it, but I got tested in case you want to—"

"So did I," Trev cut in with a soft laugh. "Looks like great minds think alike."

"I'm clear. All good on your end?"

He nodded. "Want to see the email?"

"I trust you. We can forego the condom if you like. Contraception is covered."

It occurred to her then that she often went hard at sex—more interested in getting off and getting out than enjoying the experience. For some reason, she didn't feel that way with him, as if she didn't need to keep both hands on the wheel. So, when he shifted his arms and lifted her, carrying her toward the bed with bold strides, she merely curled closer.

Trev took his time, toying with the straps on her slip of a nightgown and laying delicate kisses on her shoulders. She slipped her arm out, silently amazed at his patience. He lavished her chest and throat with attention, never once straying lower, until she twisted beneath him, her fingers curling into the nape of his neck. Normally, she'd be on top by now, driving the action with innate dominance. Probably, she preferred it overall, but it also felt good to find out how he liked to touch her, left to his own devices.

And he caressed her body like he had all the time in the world. No limits, no tomorrow. He licked and nuzzled her breasts and then lower still, tracing his name on her stomach with his tongue. She only knew that because he whispered each letter into her damp skin, creating pleasurable goose bumps and a sweet little chill with each breath. When he murmured the V, he veered lower and kissed the tops of her thighs, his palms gentle when he parted her legs.

"Just making sure this is still good," he asked on a soft pause, eyes locked on hers.

She propped up on an elbow, drinking in the ridiculously appealing picture he made. "I'm aching to see how this all ends up. Don't keep me in suspense."

"Wouldn't dream of it, Butterfly."

With delicate fingers, he parted her sex and went in with his lips first, more heated kisses exactly where she wanted them. Leanne sank her fingers into his hair and tugged, trying to get his mouth on her clit, but he teased her with slow, languid licks everywhere else. He liked to draw everything out, like she was a Popsicle that would melt for him. The heat blazing through her backed up that theory, and she lifted her hips, rolling her pussy against his face.

"You're getting so wet and squirming so much. It's incredibly hot."

"So is your mouth. *Please* stop talking." The truth was, even the rumble of his voice felt good, but she needed more.

He pulled back long enough to strip off his boxers, then he

returned to her, and stroking her just so, his body hanging over hers. Leanne pulled him down on top of her, twining their legs together. Then he rocked against her, seeming in no hurry to push inside. More tantalizing thrusts, and he shuddered, so hard that it must have been torture. She couldn't remember ever wanting to fuck more in her life. *That's it.* Leanne shoved him back and straddled him, taking charge the way nature had designed her.

Trev's lips parted, but no sound came out as she sank on his throbbing cock. He clutched her hips and then shifted the touch to a slow and gentle massage, rubbing her butt as she rode him. It felt so good that she wanted to scream, but she bit him instead, marking his shoulder with hungry teeth. That snapped the last of his control, evidently, and he pushed up as she dropped on him. Their bodies made slippery, liquid sounds with each movement, and he couldn't hold in the groans, nonsense promises of the filthy things he'd do to her next. Everything about this man drove her wild.

His cock was fucking glorious.

Maybe it was shallow, but she loved riding it, rolling her hips just right until her clit rubbed against him perfectly. And he knew exactly when to thrust, exactly when to hold still—that was when she ground down in a tight circle. Then there were the kisses, drugging and soulful, each time he could reach her mouth. He breathed hard and fast, the sounds gone urgent and uncontrolled. Partners who fucked in silence didn't do it for her; she needed to hear their pleasure to get there herself. The sounds played into her own satisfaction, filthy, delicious stimuli driving her out of control.

"I can't get enough of you," she gasped, brushing her hair over one shoulder.

The orgasm built up as he shaped her back, dragging his fingers down her spine. She watched his face, drinking in his dazed pleasure, the way he spilled for her without even trying to stop it. Trev got there a little ahead, his body going rigid, and she felt the pulsing heat of his come deep inside her. She rubbed her clit frantically, peaking with a moan right after he did. Her heart thundered in her ears, and she would've fallen over if he hadn't caught her, cradling her in his arms with absolute reverence.

"That was one hell of a wedding present," he said, breathless.

Leanne smiled, closing her eyes. "Guess I can return the ceramic knife set, then."

Tickling fingers scraped over her ribs. "Don't you dare."

"Mmm. I'm too tired and blissed out to mess with you more tonight. Probably it's the sex haze talking, but your dick is flawless, seriously."

Trev burst out laughing. "I'm so putting that on my business card, whenever I figure out what job suits me."

"Being my husband suits you."

"That's not a job."

"Isn't it? Because you totally aced the interview and accepted the position."

———————

A week later, Trev was back in his own life.

Oddly enough, it didn't *feel* the same. At Leanne's invitation, he'd moved into the main bedroom, and they'd set up his game console in the guest room, configuring it as a place where he could hang out if he wanted to game while she watched something in the living room. It was incredibly sweet, an accommodation she didn't need to make when he contributed so little.

Or at least that was how he felt when she went off to work. He started getting up when she did to make her breakfast and pack her a lunch. Hell, if his dad got wind of this, he'd be calling Trev a pretty little wife. Gender roles were bullshit, but both Dad and Tanner went all in on them, and his mom never contradicted them. Now that he had some distance from his family, he entertained the idea that maybe *he* wasn't the problem.

They're toxic.

The condo was so quiet. He studied his phone, scrolling through the gallery of wedding photos. Seven pictures, proving he'd really flown off to Vegas and gotten married without saying a word to anyone. *That's one way to get out of a rut.* Gathering his courage, he chose the best photo and sent it to Titus with the caption: *Guess what I did last weekend?*

It didn't take long before his phone rang. At this hour, Titus was normally up to his elbows in baked goods, and the fact that he was actually *calling?* Yeah, the dude must be intervention-level worried.

"What did you do?" Titus demanded, as soon as Trev picked up.

"It's not a costume party, if that's what you're asking."

"Did you seriously get married without me? What the hell, I thought we were friends."

He blinked a bit over that. In all honesty, he expected to hear how foolish and impulsive he was, but it sounded like...Titus was hurt? "We are."

"But you didn't tell me, didn't ask me to be your best man, or even invite me to watch a livestream of the occasion. You always know what's going on with me. I told you everything about me and Danica, about my dad, and...*fuck*. You're my first call whenever I need a friend, but I guess you don't feel the same way."

Oh shit.

"I'm sorry," Trev got out. "Truly. I guess I thought I was more...convenient than anything else. I didn't know that I..."

"Really matter to me? Of course you do. I mean, I won't lie, it is convenient that you're always willing to help, but you're a hell of a lot more than my odd-jobs guy. You're my best friend. I thought you *knew* that."

He didn't know how he was supposed to feel, but simultaneously pleased and chastened about covered it. "Apparently not?"

In the background, Trev heard a relentless beeping. Titus swore. "I have to take these trays out of the oven, but we're absolutely talking more about this later. Oh, and Trev?"

"Yeah?" he asked warily.

"Congratulations, you reckless, secretive son of a bitch."

"I have some serious amends to make, huh?"

"You think? I'll let you decide how to go about it." With that, Titus hung up.

A few days passed with Trev feeling guilty about how he'd treated Titus, and he struggled with the realization that maybe the way he viewed himself didn't match up to the way others did. *I matter after all.* He buried his remorse by looking after Leanne, and that night, she showed her gratitude in the hottest possible way.

As she rose and fell on him, her phone buzzed. *Leave it*, he almost shouted, but she grabbed it and swore. "Sorry, sweetheart. This is a book club emergency."

"Are you serious?" he groaned.

Leanne leaned down, kissing him on the nose. "Keep it warm for me. I'll be back as soon as I can."

It was fucking impossible to wait, so he cranked one out on his own, mildly alarmed by the secrets she seemed to be keeping. *What kind of book club requires its members to rush out in the middle of sex?* Maybe he didn't want to join after all. More worrying, those secrets might hurt her chances in the election.

Is that why she needed to distract voters by getting married? What the hell is up?

When she returned, she didn't offer to explain, and he feared pissing her off, so he pretended not to be curious about the parts of her life that didn't include him. *I need to find my own thing.*

The silence and the secrecy bothered him, though. How could it not? Some days Trev did feel more like an employee who occasionally fucked his boss, and that...didn't feel awesome.

But he pushed down those misgivings as they fell into a comfortable routine—maybe not the passion and excitement one would expect from newlyweds, but their relationship was atypical. And, as promised, she got him on her insurance with a pledge to keep paying it even after she switched over to COBRA.

Junie dropped by on Leanne's last day of work, and Trev gave her a framed wedding photo, feeling like he was supplying a consolation prize. *Sorry your relationship with Leanne is terrible. Have this fine framed memento instead of personal interaction.*

With tearful eyes, Junie touched the glass. "She looks so beautiful. I wish I could've been there. You know I haven't been to even one of her weddings? The first one, I was traveling in Peru, and I didn't get the message until it was far too late. The next time, she got married on a cruise. This time—"

"We eloped to Vegas."

"How was it? Tell me everything."

Feeling like an absolute tool, Trev did because his mother-in-law looked so pitiful that he couldn't bring himself to be harsh with her again. He spent over an hour sharing the experience and showing her the photos he'd snapped at the various places. Buying rings, picking out the suit, the hotel lobby, the city skyline, and the wedding chapel.

"I can't really think of anything else," he said eventually.

"This is perfect. I feel like I was there." Impulsively, Junie hugged him. "I'm glad you're my son-in-law."

That made him feel shitty when their marriage was primarily for show. With Leanne's city council election campaign kicking off, he lacked the time to dwell on it, though. Trev stayed busy ordering stuff for her; communicating with online vendors; and getting hats, signs, stickers, banners, and posters printed up. As suggested, Leanne rounded up volunteers from the coffee klatch, and Howard Carruthers agreed to let her use the space over the hardware store. It was supposed to be a suite of offices, but he'd had a hard time keeping it rented since the lawyer who used to occupy it left St. Claire. Trev felt incredibly out of place among the retirees and housewives who mostly made up the volunteers willing to devote their precious time to getting Leanne elected to city council.

But nobody commented on his joblessness, and he ended up partnered with Mrs. Carmenian for the canvassing. She went right in for the gossip. "What's this I hear about you two getting married on the sly? Do you have baby news to share, hmm?"

He stopped walking and almost dropped the bag of election paraphernalia he was holding. "Uh, yeah, we did get married. And no, nothing like that."

It always suffused him with pride when he saw Leanne's whole name on the promotional materials—Leanne Vanderpol-Montgomery. Though it made no sense, he felt like a piece of him went with her because she'd chosen his name. He hadn't told her yet, but he'd quietly decided to take her name too. God, the old man would hate it. That was reason enough to make the change, but he suspected it would also make Leanne happy.

"Well, that's disappointing. Why did you sneak off, then?"

"I'm not sure what you're hoping to hear," he said, as they walked toward the next house in their zone. "There's no scandal. Why spend twenty grand when you can do it for a few hundred and enjoy a honeymoon in Vegas after?"

Mrs. Carmenian put a hand on her well-padded hip. "When you put it that way, it sounds entirely reasonable. And you don't have to listen to your families fighting over who sits where and how many vegan entrées are needed."

He imagined listening to his mother and Junie bicker over font choices on the invitations and shuddered slightly. "That sounds awful."

The old woman leveled a shockingly astute expression on him then. "They do say the wedding is a test for the relationship, though. How do you know yours will stand up to life if it hasn't been stress-tested?"

Good question.

Trev knocked on the front door of the well-kept ranch house without responding, saving him from the need to reply. Soon, a middle-aged woman with light-brown hair answered. "How can I help you?"

He recited the script about Leanne's bid for city council, a short and tasty sound bite, and then asked, "Can we put this sign in your front yard to show your support? The council has had far more men than women on it for years now."

The homeowner studied the election sign before breaking into a broad smile. "That's true. Go ahead. She looks so capable! I can't wait to see Dan Rutherford's face. He hasn't had a real challenger in ages."

For four hours, he drove around with Mrs. Carmenian, and they managed to put up all their signs and gave away a fair number of bumper stickers as well. Eventually, the old woman said, "My dogs sure are barking. You're a good worker, Trev. Leanne's lucky to have you."

"Thanks," was all he managed to say.

The old woman added, "Drop me off in front of Sugar Daddy's. I deserve a treat after all that free labor."

"No problem." He found a parking spot on the square, not directly in front of Titus's bakery—just as well because he wasn't ready to face his best friend after finding out he'd hurt the guy.

Instead of going home, Trev returned to the office above the hardware store and found the place bustling. A table of volunteers was calling while others seemed to be assembling some sort of mass list for texting. There would probably be email campaigns as well. Leanne stood with a stern-faced old man with a big nose, Leon...no, Leonard Something. The whole coffee klatch basically followed Gladys's orders, and she'd told them all to help Leanne, it seemed. If you wanted to win, you got the seniors on board first. His wife glanced over—

Oh God. My wife. For the first time, it truly sunk in. This incredible woman was his wife.

"What else can I do?" he asked Leanne.

CHAPTER 15

LEANNE WENT TO DANICA AND Clem's house once the volunteers left for the day.

It was difficult to believe how many people were willing to set
their noses to the grindstone to put her in office. Trev had made a
few reels for the campaign; he was surprisingly adept at it, and the
timing was spot-on since they had the coven meeting today. When
they asked if anyone had spell work, she'd ask for assistance in
getting her promotional reels to go viral.

After the way Clem had outed the witch hunters, it should be
a piece of cake. Leanne had mostly been on the outside for that,
but she did appreciate how Clem risked everything for her sisters.
She wouldn't forget it in a hurry. For now, she had no clue how it
would all shake out in the long run in terms of hunters becoming
witches and how it all related to council matters. But that was for
Gavin, Clem, and the council elders to figure out.

On the way over, she grabbed a box of wine at the market and
carried it in, mostly because that was what the others expected.
She could try harder, but why? They had her pegged a certain way
and it was easier to meet those expectations than to deviate from

them. Teeth clenched, she endured the ribbing that was still ongoing because of her runaway nuptials. And she still hadn't clued in the rest of the coven regarding her plan.

Not sure if I will.

Though she trusted these witches with her life, she didn't enjoy the prospect of them thinking less of Trev for agreeing to this plan. And she didn't come off great either since she was using him for personal gain. *Is that so bad when it's mutually beneficial? We both get something we need from this arrangement.* In all honesty, she was happier than she'd ever been in a relationship with none of the usual panic about him packing up suddenly after deciding she wasn't worth the work. He needed what she could provide and vice versa.

That's the definition of codependency.

Exhaling in an annoyed huff at her own thoughts, she hugged Vanessa first. "Let me get a load of the new hair."

Today, Vanessa had complex, beautiful braids gathered on top of her head. It must have taken twelve hours. "Definite witch queen vibes, am I right?"

"All the way. You're gorgeous."

"Always am," Vanessa said.

Leanne smiled, handing off the box wine to Danica, who ferried it to the kitchen. Everyone filled their plates with finger foods and raw vegetables, settling in for a good chat. They'd taken to parking their cars all around the neighborhood instead of right in front of the house. If they didn't go in covertly, Hazel Jeffords would be at the door in twenty minutes. Not that Leanne disliked the old cat fancier, but she made it difficult to conduct coven business.

"It feels like ages since we were all together." Margie crunched into a carrot stick after dipping it in ranch dressing.

Tilting her head, Leanne noticed that Margie was wearing a new shade of lipstick and she'd chosen a new hair color, just a skosh lighter and brighter than usual. Everyone knew she and Dante had struck up some FWB agreement, but nobody was talking about it. As long as the man didn't hurt Margie, it was all good in Leanne's book. But if he messed Margie around, she'd hex him into next week, even if he *was* Titus and Trev's friend.

"You look like you're scheming," Ethel whispered. "Can I get in on this?"

Quickly, Leanne shook her head. "Nothing serious."

Clem grabbed a sandwich with the crusts cut off—Margie's handiwork, as her kid refused to eat them for some reason. "So you're running for city council. How's that going?"

"I'll talk about that when it's my turn. First off, how's everyone else doing?"

Danica frowned at her. "Like you can get off the hook for—"

"We didn't talk about my wedding when you dragged me off Trev's dick for a witch hunter emergency, and we're not getting into it now."

"Can we talk about how Trevor moved in before the wedding and you lied about it to get out of pitching in?" Clem nudged her.

Leanne tried to control the blush. "I didn't want to deal with everything, okay? I'm sorry. Back to the main point—it's my third time. Making a huge thing of it doesn't even make sense. Even *I* think it's bizarre to keep trying." Not that she *was* trying to make the marriage work in a traditional sense.

Not this time.

Vanessa eyed her sharply, but she kept her mouth closed. And that was why Vanessa was her best friend in the coven. Witch knew when to keep certain details quiet. Margie was equally discreet, but that was more of a personal brand because she genuinely disliked gossip. If "nice" needed an illustration the dictionary, they could use Margie's photo, and that was part of how she ended up getting so screwed over by her ex.

"You'll end up like that one actress," Clem predicted.

"The one with seven exes?" Leanne asked.

"That's her."

She shook her head, trying not to get salty over what felt like Clem pronouncing a curse. "This is my last go-round. You wouldn't understand them, but I had my reasons."

"Why are you just assuming we won't?" Clem demanded.

Kerry and Priya had been lost in each other's eyes for the whole exchange, but Priya, like Danica, tended to live in the rose-wreathed "please don't fight" cottage. So she spoke up. "Let's take a breath and give Leanne some space on this topic."

"Agreed," said Kerry.

But Leanne had noticed Kerry would concur if Priya said clouds in the sky had purple polka dots. These two were adorable, still delightfully deep in the honeymoon period. But unbiased toward each other? Definitely not.

"That's good advice," Danica put in, right on cue.

There was no benefit to being shy. "Moving on. I didn't want to start by putting my request first, but if nobody else has anything, I'll make my case. I'd like for Clem to use the same spell she dropped on the hunter's guild. This time for my benefit." Quickly, she showed them the reels Trev had made.

They were short and cute, with catchy slogans like, "If you want someone great for city council, you want my wife," and then Trev would make an "oh no" face, like he'd just realized the implication of the endorsement, then the cheesy wink. People would most likely eat it up, if Leanne could gauge such things.

And I can.

There were a few more, none of them long, but memorable and clever, full of quirky humor and unexpectedly adroit filters and transitions. His grasp of the necessary touch must be instinctual because she didn't think he had formal training. When the witches watched all the reels, Danica stared at her in amazement.

"I had no idea he could do this," she said. "Titus never mentioned it."

Leanne nodded briskly. "Then you see it too. Right now I can't pay him, but down the line, I'm thinking of asking him to be my social media manager."

"Wow," Ethel said. "Do you think he'd evaluate my TikTok channel? Based on the market appeal of a cussing parrot, I should have more followers by now, but I can't get a handle on the algorithm."

"I can ask him," Leanne offered.

"Chris is trying to do an Instagram for the robots he builds," Margie said then.

Leanne grinned. "Let me guess. You want me to see if Trev will look at it."

This was so unexpected, but also such a good feeling. Others could discern what she saw in him, that raw promise and artless appeal. Kerry even asked if Trev would assess the company website, and a few more asks came up.

Then Clem said, "It's no problem at all. Send me the reels, and I'll make sure you—and Trev—are an internet phenom by morning."

Ethel gave an endearingly evil grin. "Dan Rutherford won't know what hit him."

———————

Trev woke to hundreds of notifications.

Silently, he slipped out of bed, unable to believe what he was seeing. He padded barefoot into the living room so he could look at his phone with full brightness. His reels had gone viral in a huge way, and people were posting duets and response videos, using the catchphrase "you want my wife," and all of it had attracted a ton of attention to Leanne's political social media accounts. As director of communications for the mayor's office, she hadn't paid her own socials much attention at all, so Trev had started fresh, creating new accounts dedicated to her city council campaign.

That meant he had all the passwords and a ton of traffic to be managed. While he made breakfast, he responded to all the @s, posts, reels, and comments while keeping in mind the tone he wanted to convey, relative to his wife's political career. To his surprise, he found he enjoyed the work, playing Oz behind the curtain for Leanne, making the magic happen.

By the time she came up to the kitchen island, he had a veggie omelet ready for her and a cup of coffee, just the way she liked it.

She pecked him on the cheek then sat down at the island, eyeing him with an inscrutable smile. "Any news you'd care to share?"

He narrowed his eyes. "It seems like you already know."

"A suspicion, not a certainty." She picked up her fork and dug in. "Wow, this is fantastic. I love the gooey cheese pocket."

He shrugged. "It's not hard. I keep diced veg in the fridge. In the morning I just whip the eggs and put it all together in the pan."

"Look at you, refusing to take a compliment and minimizing your achievements. You're a great cook. Say thanks and tell me what's up."

He swallowed, gaze locked on her ridiculously glamorous face. Seriously, who looked like this at breakfast? "Thanks, glad you like the food I make. Anyway, it seems people are massively digging yesterday's reels. I've posted responses, don't know if you want to—"

"I trust you," she cut in, eating placidly.

"Are you sure? This is your public image we're talking about, and you're the pro here. Compared to you, I'm just—"

"Doing an awesome job. It's rude to cut you off, but I won't let anyone put my man down, even if you're doing it to yourself. Real talk, hon, I went to school for years to train on shit you grasp intuitively. If you took a couple of online courses in social media management to hone your instincts, you'd be the real pro, an unstoppable force."

He stared at her, stunned but aware of a cautiously rising excitement at the prospect. "Do you really think so?"

"It doesn't matter what *I* think. Only if you can imagine doing this as a job."

Quickly, she finished her food and kissed him again, then he heard the water running while she brushed her teeth. His breakfast got cold while he fretted the idea like guitar strings, scrutinizing it from all angles. Suddenly, he realized he *could* imagine it. Making those reels had been fun. And while he wouldn't want his face on every account he managed, he'd still like doing this for other people, making their socials funny and relatable, creating content to brighten other people's days without making himself the focus.

Shit. Yeah. This…is what I want to do.

Right now, he was a househusband, though, so before he headed to the campaign office to pitch in, Trev fulfilled that requirement by cleaning the kitchen and the bathrooms, then he dusted and let the Roomba run wild while he put in a load of laundry. Anyone who said this wasn't a real job had never done it, that was for damn sure. He had to hang certain clothes up to dry and load the dryer before he went out, so while he waited for the washer to finish, he searched for the classes she'd mentioned.

Soon, he had a bunch of potential courses to assess, along with one online school that offered a certificate in social media marketing and management. Trev bookmarked the sites and then hung up the delicates and tossed the rest of the clothes into the dryer with a sheet. *Wonder if I should sell my car. An electric bike would be cheaper, and I could pay for classes with the rest.*

There was no need to decide now, but for the first time in ages, he felt hopeful about the future. Of course, none of this was a cure for the dark cloud he didn't want to term *depression* that'd gripped him tight for years. That would require talking to someone and maybe getting on the right meds. He just had to work up the nerve to do it and try not to let his old man's brainwashing succeed in making him feel like this was mental weakness of some kind. In fact, when he considered therapy an act of rebellion, it got easier.

That's the next thing I'll do for myself. If I sell my car, I can afford it.

He had no doubt Leanne would pay for sessions, but he didn't want her to. It might be vanity, but since he couldn't do a lot for her financially, he wanted to cover his own repair work, so to speak. Making up his mind, he went out to the parking lot and took some pictures. The title was in his name, and he earned enough annually to pay for the plates and insurance, doing whatever work came his way. His father would probably blow his top since he'd bought this car, but it was Trev's now, right? His solitary asset. People shouldn't bitch about what you did with presents after receiving them.

Before he could second-guess himself, he posted the listing on several free local sites. Maybe this was another mistake, but he didn't think so. It felt more like selling his past to pay for his future, one he was finally fucking on board with. Belatedly, it occurred to him that he hadn't thought about Sarah in quite a while or wondered about her wedding.

Hell, I'm married too.

At some point in the future, he might even be brave enough to tell her she'd been right to leave, though she could've been kinder about it. He still had dreams in which she told him he'd never amount to shit and that he'd die in that basement. Taking a breath, he hopped into the car and drove over to the campaign office.

Leanne was conferring with her team, going over the latest poll numbers. They were better than expected already, considering how long Dan Rutherford had held that city council seat. His camp was already hitting back; he'd apparently done an interview at a local radio station that painted Leanne as a ditzy party girl who would bankrupt St. Claire with her addiction to designer shoes.

"That son of a bitch," said Mrs. Carmenian.

"Took the words right out of my mouth," an older woman added.

Trev couldn't come up with a name, though she looked vaguely familiar. She trundled toward him and shook his hand vigorously, an absolute vision in puce velour covered oddly in ginger cat fur. "Hazel Jeffords. I'm in Leanne's book club! We need some new blood on the city council, and that's a fact. At this rate, she could go to the White House one day. Are you ready to change the world, young man?"

"You know what?" he said, not even needing to think about it. "I'm with her all the way."

CHAPTER 16

IT AMUSED LEANNE KNOWING HOW much Dan Rutherford would scream if he knew she was literally using magic against him.

He was the kind of man who said "females" when he was alone with his buddies and slapped women on the ass then pretended he hadn't known it was offensive. And she couldn't manipulate the votes; that qualified as mind control, and even the most powerful neuromancer couldn't manage it. At best, she could nudge someone in a direction they were already inclined toward. It would probably surprise Trev to realize the reason he saw her as the most beautiful and glamorous woman in the world was because he was already disposed to think so. Her glamour spells didn't work half as well on someone who disliked her profoundly.

Talk about the ultimate "beauty is in the eye of the beholder" test.

It was also why it had been impossible to force Margie's ex to pay child support, no matter what spells they worked. So ironic— technology was *way* easier to influence than people.

As expected, Clem's spell had worked like a charm. Trev had been so surprised and delighted when she mentioned that multiple "book club" friends wanted his help with their accounts as well. Frankly, he was doing a magnificent job with Leanne's professional socials. She'd peeked a few times in the past week, and she couldn't do better herself. He had an eye for nuance, and he was relentlessly charming when responding to constituents. People might believe it was impossible to turn patience and an inherently kind nature into a career, but look at him go.

Her favorite part of this whole viral deal was the tribute videos. A whole slew of people praising their partners had cropped up online, and it wasn't limited to wives and husbands either. There were videos of people saying, "If you want your house rewired, you want my partner," and "If you need someone to build the best treehouse ever, you want my spouse," and she was so here for it. Because it made her campaign truly part of the community, and people were finding each other, and...

Okay, I'm definitely not crying. I wanted wholesome, and he's giving 120 percent.

Tonight, she had a speaking engagement, and she wanted Trev there, but he'd left the campaign office early. He didn't say where he was headed, and she didn't want to be one of *those* partners, the kind who had to know everything about every minute. In fact, she wasn't even sure if she had any rights at all. Since their wedding night, they slept in the same bed, but he seldom made any moves on her. Despite his amicable exterior, her husband was hard to read. He smiled a lot, but it didn't reach his eyes, and he rarely volunteered his thoughts.

With effort, she squared her shoulders and offered her loyal volunteers a reassuring smile. The most shocking development?

Hazel Jeffords was among her staunchest supporters. Leanne had heard through the grapevine that the old woman had thrown a handful of chip and dip samples at Dan Rutherford, after she heard him shit-talking Leanne in the local supermarket. Though she'd once been opposed to the woman's intrusion on coven meetings, she now stood firmly in favor of Hazel dropping by anytime she wished.

What would that be like? If we could really invite mundanes to join our coven, let them see how our magic works, and treat them as true siblings? Wistfully, she decided the world wasn't quite ready for that step. *But one day, maybe. Hopefully in my lifetime...*

"Thank you," she said warmly. "I appreciate all of you so much."

"It's my pleasure," Gladys replied with a wink. "Break a leg, dear child."

It took a woman of a certain age to call someone who was nudging forty a "child," but Leanne didn't argue. She merely left the others to lock up and headed downstairs. When she stepped out the back and passed through the alley toward the street, she spotted Dan Rutherford standing with his chief aide some distance away. They were speaking in low voices, and she glanced around, making sure she had cover from the buildings on either side, then she whispered a spell that would turn the wind in her favor, allowing her to listen in. Next, she pulled out her phone, which gave her a plausible excuse to linger, too far for most people to eavesdrop.

"...find something," Rutherford was saying.

"She's been unfortunately candid about her private life.

Everyone in town knows that she's been married twice, but nobody seems to care."

"I refuse to believe that woman has no skeletons in her closet. I want all her dirty laundry, all of it! Have you seen the numbers? This is the last time I can run, and I refuse to have my term cut short by that little bitch."

"*What* did you just say?" Suddenly, Hazel Jeffords was on the scene, upending the entire contents of her travel mug on Rutherford's head.

Guess the chips-and-dip incident offered a clue that Hazel's not having it.

"Today is not the day," Hazel was saying, both hands on her round hips. "How dare you talk about Leanne that way?"

What would it be like if I had a mom like Hazel? Junie wasn't the scrappy type; she would never react like Hazel. And while fighting might not solve anything—

Just then, her phone pinged with a message from Mrs. Carmenian. Normally I wouldn't want you to see this because it might hurt you, but I suspect you can make use of this clip. Do as you see fit.

When she played the video, it was the incident she'd just witnessed—Dan Rutherford, running his mouth then getting schooled by Hazel. Right now, Leanne couldn't make a decision regarding the dispersal of the footage. She had somewhere to be. So she wheeled and cut through the alley, avoiding the main street, and took the long way to her car.

If it looks like I need a boost later, I might circulate it. We'll see.

She drove slowly, reflecting on the clash between her people and Dan Rutherford. *Get your head in the game. Don't let him rattle you.*

This particular talk was small, a gathering of local women at the public library, but there were no unimportant moments of connection. She truly believed that. Twenty people or forty or a hundred, she'd speak sincerely every time. On the way, she rehearsed her speech until the words blurred, probably not the desired result.

When she hopped out of the car, she spotted Trev propped against the faded brick of the St. Claire Public Library, legs crossed at the ankles like he had all the time in the world. He had on faded jeans, a T-shirt that had been washed so often that the logo was faded beyond recognition, and a gray zip hoodie. Somehow, just seeing his face calmed her rioting nerves, and she rushed toward him. Before she even got there, he opened his arms and drew her in, reassuring and warm and—

Home. He smells like home. Trev was laundry detergent and lemony dish soap with just a whisper of grapefruit bodywash. Nothing glamorous, but so familiar and precious.

Have I ever been with anyone long enough before to be comforted by their smell? The answer terrified her.

He misread the tremor that ran through her. "Breathe, Butterfly. The people who signed up are interested in what you have to say."

"You came," she whispered.

Gentle hands smoothed down her back, stroking her until she closed her eyes at the pleasure of his touch. "Of course I did. I'll be rooting for you."

She'd never been the cuddly sort, preferring the quick satisfaction of sex to anything more intimate. But if she wasn't careful, she could get used to this. "But I didn't ask you to. I never told you I wanted you to be here."

"Yeah, you might want to work on that. I'm not a mind reader. But I *want* to be here, so our interests coincide." With his usual serene smile, he pretended to scoff. "Some First Gentleman I'd make if I didn't attend my wife's events."

"What?"

"Ask Hazel Jeffords. Let's get you inside."

Everything melded into a congenial montage of her shaking hands and presumably saying the right things, then suddenly, she was at the podium, trying to remember her speech. Leanne took a breath, focused on Trev, and smiled. "For years, I've helped public figures put their best foot forward. Written their speeches and moderated social media accounts. But it occurred to me that I don't want to do that anymore.

"I don't want to help others polish their images. Rather, I want to make a difference. Other candidates will allege that I don't have the political experience necessary to help the city of St. Claire, but after observing from behind the scenes, I'm certain I can address problems that have been swept under the rug for far too long."

She went on to outline her ideas, trying to be precise and succinct. And, when she finished, Trev beamed at her and gave two thumbs-ups. Judging by the applause from those gathered, she must have come across well. Some of the tension left her shoulders. *Damn.* Her hands even hurt from gripping the sides of the podium. Public speaking was a *lot* different than simply typing out the words.

With as much dignity as she could muster, she added, "I hope

I can count on your support. I'm Leanne Vanderpol-Montgomery, and I want to work for *you*."

If Trev hadn't already been on his feet since he didn't want to take up valuable chair space, he still would've given Leanne a standing ovation.

He clapped enthusiastically, stirring the rest of her listeners to greater fervor. After the speech, interested parties became enthusiastic supporters, and they spent a good half an hour bending his wife's ear with helpful suggestions—both about her campaign and changes she should propose if she got elected to the city council. The proposal about improving the recycling program was a good one, and it would even create some jobs, but he understood such innovations had to pass through a daunting number of approvals to become reality.

Twenty more minutes passed, and Trev settled in a back row seat with his phone, now that the crowd was thinning out. Indefatigable, Leanne kept chatting and shaking hands until the last two guests excused themselves. Only then did she make her way to the back of the room, balancing graceful as a swan in heels so high, they could stake a vampire dead.

"How was I?" she asked.

"Perfection. You slayed the hell out of that speech, and you were so charming that I feel like marrying you all over again, just because."

She smiled, her lipstick perfect, teeth bright and white, but it was the faint crinkles at the corners of her eyes that he noticed today, along with the deeper blue specks in her smoky eyes. Odd, he'd never realized she had a dark limbal ring before, contrasting beautifully to the brighter hue. The longer he knew her, the more he observed the small details. Not that these observations detracted from her beauty—quite the contrary. He found everything about her beautiful, even the tiny mole behind her left ear.

"My cheering section is open for business, I see." She reached for his hand, her expression different than he'd seen before.

Trev curled his fingers around hers, finding her hand chilled to the point that it probably hurt. *Was she that nervous?* Gently, he rubbed her hand between both of his to warm her up. Leanne didn't ever show weakness, so this felt...significant, somehow. That she was reaching for him when she needed someone.

"Always. Are you hungry?" he asked.

Now that her hand was warmer, she produced a smile, but he still detected shadows in her gaze. "If I say yes, what will you do about it?"

"I'll take you to Titus's house. He's cooking for us, apparently." Later, he would ask if something had happened. Right now, she seemed to want to lose herself in prosaic conversation. Maybe it grounded her after public speaking? That didn't seem to come naturally to her, even if she'd nailed it.

"Just us?" Leanne asked.

Trev shook his head. "Danica will be there too. Maya is spending a lot of time at her girlfriend's place, and he wants to hang out. Suspect he also wants to talk to me about our quickie wedding. But it *is* short notice. If you're not up for it—"

"No, sounds fun. I'm always happy to see Danica. She's a

good friend, and I want to get to know Titus as well. He's your bestie, right?"

Laughing, he said, "I've never used that word, but yeah. We're BFFs. In fact, he chewed me out for keeping quiet about our Vegas plans."

"You could have told him," Leanne said.

When she upgraded their connection by looping her arm through his, it seemed like a proud declaration of their relationship. She tugged him toward the front doors, and a little thrill went through him. He tried not to look at her as a status symbol, but the woman was incredible. Beautiful, fun, smart, successful, and ambitious—the total package. Sometimes it was difficult not to wonder what she saw in him.

"Who did you tell?" he wondered aloud.

And how much do they know?

"To be honest, I told Vanessa and Margie that we've come to a mutually beneficial arrangement," she said.

He let his arm straighten so her hand slid out of the crook of his elbow. "Then they know I'm not your real husband?"

She shot him a reproachful look and grabbed hold of him again. Trev didn't resist as she towed him outside toward her car. "Watch what you say," she cautioned, glancing around. "And how are you not real? We eat together, sleep together. We have sex. We spend leisure time together. Doesn't that tick all the boxes?"

Somehow he swallowed some of his unhappiness. Trev couldn't even say why it bothered him, imagining the convo with her book club friends. What would she have said? *I found some loser and*— suddenly, her fingers were on his chin, and she was kissing him, not gently either. She shoved him back against the car and curved her hand around the nape of his neck. Leanne leaned into him as she bit his lower lip and swept her tongue against his. Her body felt fierce and urgent against his, and he got hard immediately.

"It might not be *traditional*," she said against his mouth. "We didn't do things like everyone else, but don't ever say it's not real. Hear me?"

"Yeah, but..." With her gaze locked on his, he couldn't bring himself to voice his doubts. That this likely had an expiration date and when she reached her goals, she'd discard him like a pair of shoes she'd worn out. Yet, even if that was true, he still chose to stick around because at least he'd have these precious memories when it was done.

And the knowledge that someone like Leanne had wanted to be with him, even briefly.

"But nothing. Let's work on your self-esteem. How about some affirmations?" she said, rounding the car to open the door for him.

Little details like that were so freaking charming that he didn't know what to do with himself. He probably wasn't supposed to like it when she took the lead, but he did. Just as he enjoyed cooking for her, making sure the house was clean, and supporting her quietly from the sidelines. His old man wouldn't approve of any of it, but that wasn't news. Trev hadn't made him happy since he quit baseball in fourth grade.

Trev got in the car. "What kind of affirmations?"

"Repeat after me." Leanne flashed him a teasing smile. "'I am a valuable human being.'"

"I am a valuable human being," Trev said.

She started the car and put it in gear, then drove toward the other side of town. "You don't sound like you believe it. How about this one…? 'I deserve to be happy.'"

Stealing a glance at her profile as she drove, he wished he could believe that. While he didn't know if he deserved it, per se, he did feel incredibly content. Jubilant, even. "I deserve to be happy."

"Maybe this one will work better for you… 'This cock is a gift to humanity.'"

Trev almost repeated that on automatic, and then he burst out laughing upon realizing what the hell she'd actually said. "I'm not saying that."

"I suppose me declaring it will have to be enough." She glanced at him sideways, her smile growing into a ridiculous grin completely at odds with her political persona.

He adored seeing her like this, loved putting that glint of mischief in her gaze. "You're ridiculous. What am I supposed to do with you?"

"I'd help you figure it out, but we're expected for a double date. I hope we play games. Do you think Titus has *Mario Kart*? No, I bet he's a board game guy, am I right?"

He snorted. "Spot on. Sorry in advance. At least the food will be delicious. He's a better cook than my mom. I learned from watching him."

Leanne touched his knee. "Nothing to apologize for. All jokes aside, I want to get to know Titus. He's your BFF *and* Danica loves him, so he's someone I value on principle. People who are important to you matter to me, hon. End of."

How am I supposed to react when she's so freaking sweet? Three words came to mind, but he feared she wouldn't want to hear them.

Instead of those, Trev settled for saying, "Thank you, Butterfly."

CHAPTER 17

ON THE WAY OUT OF St. Claire, Leanne stopped at the garden center.

Trev got out of the car with her, glancing around in apparent bafflement. "What are we doing here?"

She'd never visited Titus's house before, and it seemed impolite to show up empty-handed. Since she didn't know if he was a drinker and she had to drive home afterward, it didn't make sense to bring her usual gift of box wine. Judging by the way he appeared to enjoy nurturing others—he lived with his grown sister, and he'd taken in his stepsister as well—Titus would probably like looking after a plant.

For ten minutes, they wandered, looking at various shrubs while Leanne checked the type against whether they were toxic to dogs.

"This one?" Trev asked, about a green plant with pointy leaves and purple blooms.

"Nope," she said.

Finally, they found one that would work, and she paid for it. Trev ported it to the car. "He'll love it," Trev predicted. "You're positive this won't hurt Doris?"

"It's fine," she assured him. "Plus, it's literally called a friendship plant. What could be better as a gift?"

"You make a good point."

From the garden center, it was fifteen minutes out to Titus's place, and she settled as she drove. The tension eased out of her shoulders. Between constant preparation and the mess with Dan Rutherford earlier, Leanne hadn't realized how nervous she had been, worried about how people would react to her candidacy. Today's speech had been the first step down a long road.

"You're really quiet," Trev said. "Did something happen?"

Without even thinking about it, she passed him her phone. "Play the video Mrs. Carmenian sent me. Volume on."

He did, and she snuck peeks at the way his expression darkened. "That dirty bastard. No wonder you needed a hug."

"What do you think? Should we put this on the internet?"

Trev paused as she turned onto the county road that led to Titus's place. "I don't know. You might get sympathy votes, but I think it could blow back on you as well. Certain voters might say you set him up, or they might feel sorry for him for getting jumped during a private moment. My gut says you should try to win without unleashing this."

"That's what I thought too. Don't delete it, though. You never know."

"Whatever happens, I'm here for you, Butterfly."

When she pulled into the driveway, she spotted Danica's car already parked. *She probably won't be sharing it with Clem for too much longer.* It must be a little sad for the cousins to think about going their separate ways. Though they weren't divorcing—Danica had simply started a serious relationship—it did still feel like the end of an era, at least to Leanne, who had been through two splits of that nature. At some point, goods got divvied up, and she'd find herself arguing about a box of crap she didn't care about, mostly because she couldn't say what was truly on her mind. It would make sense if Clem kept the house, gave Danica the car, then paid her the monetary difference. There was no reason they couldn't keep working together, but there were still household goods to divide.

I hope they'll be okay and not fall out over who gets Gram's good tea set.

"Ready?" she asked, determined to put on her board game face.

Trev touched her arm before she could get out of the car. "You seemed so sad for a minute."

Wow. I can't believe how well he reads me.

Most people couldn't. They rarely looked past the surface, past her bright, insouciant facade. He had a knack for making her feel defenseless. Normally, she'd be pulling back by now, building walls and shoring up defenses to keep him from seeing all the emotional scars and unhealed wounds. For some reason, she didn't fear Trev, though, like his touch might be gentle enough to tend the hurts she'd never allowed anyone else close enough to touch.

"I was just thinking about Danica and Clem going their separate ways. Though I'm not sure what's up with Clem lately, I'm positive Danica's serious about Titus. They'll end up moving in together, likely get married at some point, and—"

"Your friends have a house together, plus the business. Are you worried it could get messy?" As usual, it was like he could read her mind.

"Somewhat. But it's their issue. I'm not the type to meddle. I'm there for my friends the minute I'm asked, but..." She lifted a shoulder. "I guess I don't see any point in sticking my oar in *before* I'm asked to row."

Trev leaned over and kissed her on the forehead. "That makes total sense. I love the way you put things."

Before he could withdraw, she cupped his face in her palm and nuzzled her nose against his. "That goes for you too, by the way. If you need me, I'll be there. I'm giving you space to figure things out, but I don't want you to think I don't care."

"I know," he said. "And I appreciate it."

Judging by the softness of his tone and the gleam of his hazel eyes, he meant it. Smiling, Leanne slid out of the car, letting him deal with the houseplant. As she carefully made her way to the front door, it opened before she could knock. It was already getting dark, long summer days well behind them. Danica stood in the bright-yellow backlight, bouncing with excitement.

She pulled Leanne into an impulsive hug. "I can't believe we're doing this. I'm so excited. It's like we're sisters-in-law or something, dating best friends who are like brothers."

Leanne restrained a chuckle at the other witch's excitement. She had to admit it was pretty unlikely, but she let herself be drawn into Titus's house and accepted another hug, this one from Titus. The place smelled incredible, fresh bread and lemons, and her mouth watered over the richness of an aroma she couldn't even place.

"That's chicken marsala," Trev predicted. "His go-to when he wants to impress someone. *You*, by the way. These days, he barely bothers making me a sandwich."

Titus protested immediately, "That's not true. But you've been here so much, you even rearranged my spice cupboard last time you stayed with Doris."

Trev narrowed his eyes, folding his arms with a distinct lack of discernable remorse. "Is it my fault you had a jumbled mess up in there?"

"That's enough," Danica said. "Leanne will think you're arguing for real."

To her surprise, Trev slung an arm around her shoulders and kissed her cheek. "Nah, she knows me better than that. Sustained bickering takes too much energy."

"It's true." She added to Titus, "Your house is so inviting. Thanks for having us over."

"My pleasure. And Trev's right, I made chicken marsala. There's also roasted potatoes, a green salad, and some fresh-baked bread. I thought we could have it with balsamic vinegar and olive oil. But if that's too many carbs—"

"It sounds delicious," she cut in with quiet amusement.

She could practically smell how nervous Titus was. The poor man was nearly wringing his hands, and now she got why Danica liked him. For her part, he wasn't her type physically, as she wasn't a fan of burly or bearded, but that wide-eyed earnestness and eagerness to please, yeah, she saw it. At least his beard was well-groomed. She'd seen a few where the owners appeared to be storing food for winter or something.

As predicted, she enjoyed the meal down to the last bite. In fact, she ate until the band of her skirt pinched at the waist, and she didn't even finish a whole slice of cheesecake on her own. She nibbled a few bites then gave the rest to Trev, while Doris looked on with huge, sad eyes. At first, Leanne wasn't sure what to make of such a huge dog. Truthfully, she was a little scared of them, but Doris seemed docile enough. Leanne gave her a wide berth anyway, just in case.

And, of course, Trev noticed. "Does she freak you out?" he whispered, once the other pair headed to the kitchen with their plates.

She eyed the dog who was currently lying on the rug in the kitchen, watching while Titus and Danica tidied up after the meal. "A little," she confessed.

"Did something happen?" he asked.

How does he always know?

Normally, she wouldn't share a story like this. What was the point? But she found herself saying, "When I was eight, I was walking home from school. It took forever if I stuck to the sidewalk, but if I cut through people's yards, it was much faster. Hardly anybody had fences in that neighborhood, and…" Her heart lurched with remembered fear. "The dog was huge, and it came out of nowhere. Baring its teeth, chased me all the way home. I didn't get bitten, but…"

I did wet my pants.

That was how scared she'd been. As usual, Junie wasn't home. She'd spent the night with a guy who was *definitely* the one. Left a note on the fridge that had no food in it. Leanne had dug in the couch for quarters, bundled up her clothes, and dragged them all the way to the laundry building, about a block away inside the crummy apartment complex they'd lived in at the time. She'd learned a long time ago that it was a bad idea to rely on other people, even if they were supposed to be there for you. In theory anyway.

Her husband rounded the table and wrapped his arms around her, giving her a gentle hug from behind. "You were terrified, and you're still nervous. I get it. I won't push you to pet Doris or anything, but she's a sweet dog. She'll be there when you're ready."

Before she could reply, Titus came out of the kitchen with a big smile. "Who's up for some Spirit Island?"

Trev had never seen this game before or heard anything about it from Titus.

That meant his friend had bought it special for this occasion. And it was *fun*, not just a board game. It also had cards and lots of backstory. While he still preferred video games, it was hard to find one that made sense for four players, and the physical logistics would be tough too. This allowed everyone to participate, gathered around the table to learn all the rules, and Leanne seemed to enjoy it as well.

Before things kicked off, Trev got up, ostensibly to help Titus make coffee, but as soon as they reached the kitchen, he said, "Look at you. How long did you hunt for the perfect game?"

"Not long," Titus said defensively. "Just a simple online search. And the reviews were glowing, it's supposed to be—"

"Thanks for making the effort," Trev cut in.

"I just wanted us to have fun. I can't believe you're married!" Titus hugged him around the shoulder, his smile so wide, it looked like it might crack his face. "You owe me since I've decided to be the bigger man and get over being left out of the loop."

"Leanne only told Vanessa and Margie," he pointed out. "So

does this mean we don't need to have the serious heart-to-heart you mentioned before?"

Titus sighed softly. "I just want to be sure you know that I don't call you only because it's convenient. We've been friends since high school. You were the first person who spoke to me after I transferred, and you were popular, dude. *Everyone* liked you— have you forgotten that?"

In all honesty, most of high school and some of college was a blur. To quiet his anxiety, he'd gotten good at substituting booze and weed for confidence. Titus and Trev had gone to the same university briefly, but then Titus left because his mom got sick, and Trev partied nonstop until he met Sarah. Two paths diverged, and—he couldn't remember the rest of the quote. Something about the woods, which didn't apply to their situation anyway.

"It's not comforting to hear my best days might be behind me, you know?"

"Bullshit," Titus said. "You lost your way for a bit, but you're finding the path now. In the beginning, I had my doubts about the two of you as a couple, but you and Leanne look great together. I'm *so* happy for you, seriously."

This was the moment when he should confess his relationship with Leanne wasn't what it seemed. But, as he warmed the milk, he couldn't bring himself to do that. Trev kept quiet while Titus filled the tray with coffee supplies and carried it out. *He wouldn't understand. And I don't want him thinking badly of Leanne.*

Whatever. Let's live in the moment.

He surprised himself by letting go of all the worry and just enjoying the evening. Spirit Island was genuinely entertaining as well as incredibly challenging, and he lost himself in the game for several hours. In fact, it was later than he expected when Leanne yawned. Trev didn't think it was a "wow, I'm tired of being here" cue, but she must be sleepy after the stress of dealing with Dan Rutherford, her first speech, and then all those carbs.

"Thanks for a fun night," Leanne said.

Danica and Titus walked them out, and everyone swapped hugs. Trev offered to drive, and his wife smiled as she slid into the passenger seat. The other couple stood in the farmhouse doorway as he backed out onto the quiet country road. This far from St. Claire, the sky was ablaze with stars since it was a clear night. If he thought it would do any good, he would wish on one of them.

Don't let this end. Don't let me fuck it up.

"Did you have fun?" he asked.

"I did. Obviously, I'm close to Danica already, and I can imagine us being annoying couples who go on vacation together." The light from the dashboard illustrated the most beautiful smile he'd ever seen.

He cut her a look, surprise warring with warmth in his chest. "Wow, really? You like Titus that well already?"

"How could I not? He's your best friend, and he cares *so* much. Tonight, he did everything but a backflip to make sure I had a good time."

There was no arguing that. In fact, in high school, people made fun of Titus for that tendency, while Trev had been one who never put effort into anything. Not because he wanted to be cool, but he just couldn't see the point since no matter what he did, it was never enough. His grades would never be as good as Tanner's even if he studied every waking hour.

"Where would you like to go?" he asked.

"For what?"

"Our first vacation. Not necessarily with Titus and Danica, though you can include them if you want."

"Oh. I hadn't even thought about it, but...off the top of my head? Fiji. I've always wanted to go. I hear it's gorgeous. Or maybe Macao. Ethel went a few years ago..."

Her quick answer took his breath away. Trev lost the thread as she repeated a story about the older woman who was in her book club, an amusing adventure Ethel had in Macao. Before, he hadn't gone *anywhere*. Or done much of anything. After he'd dropped out of college, the years blurred together, partly for lack of funds, but the problem went deeper, and it wouldn't get better until he faced up to it.

"Or maybe you'd prefer somewhere closer to home to start," she said eventually.

"Maybe Aruba or the Bahamas?" Geography wasn't his strong point, but he thought he remembered one of Wade's friends saying he'd taken the boat from Miami. "I've always wanted to do a boat trip."

"A cruise?"

"Oh, hell no. I wouldn't want to be trapped on it long term. But it would be cool sailing somewhere, you know?"

She touched his arm with a gentle hand. "That might be doable. We could travel by boat to Freeport. Would you settle for a day trip by boat and a beach vacation to start?"

"Absolutely. It's fun to think about," he said, deflecting from the fact that it seemed unlikely they'd ever go anywhere else together. And he shouldn't be sad about that. He'd already gotten more than he could reasonably expect from Leanne.

"Something wrong?" she asked.

"Not at all." Quickly, he changed the subject and told her about the courses he'd found online, asking her opinion about the ones she thought were most important or worthwhile. "I was thinking about learning some web design as well. That way I could eventually offer a full-suite of freelance services."

They chatted about that for the rest of the drive, and once they got home, she insisted on checking the descriptions herself, then she bookmarked the ones she assessed as the most useful. Since she'd done this sort of work professionally for years, her opinion carried weight, and he appreciated her honest appraisal.

"You're better at this than I am," she said matter-of-factly. "With me, it's training and experience, but you're ahead in terms of instincts and the way you relate to people."

He ducked his head, embarrassed but pleased. "I can't get used to you randomly saying nice things about me."

"You deserve only the best. Do you mind if I shower?" She kissed him lightly on the lips after he shook his head.

As Leanne headed to the bathroom, her phone vibrated on the kitchen counter. He picked it up to see if it was urgent, possibly related to the campaign, and a message from Junie popped on the lock screen. He didn't set out to read it, but the message practically leaped out at him:

We need to talk. It's about your father. Lunch tomorrow?

While he didn't know all his wife's secrets, he understood she had a complicated relationship with her mother and that she'd had a rough time growing up, complete with a bunch of stepfathers. *Wonder which one this is about, or if it's about her biological dad?* Whatever bomb Junie was about to drop, it would likely put Leanne on her ass when she could least afford to be distracted.

He had Junie's number in his own cell, and he knew the code to unlock Leanne's phone from watching her. Maybe he shouldn't do this—*No, fuck it. I'll protect her even from her own parents if I have to.* Quickly, he keyed Leanne's pin and deleted the message from Junie, then he texted his mother-in-law from his own cell.

> Leanne is busy with the election. Will you talk to me first?
> I'll help you break the news, whatever it is, but let's time
> it for when it won't mess with her head.

Within five minutes, he had a reply from Junie. Sorry. This is why I get on LeLe's nerves. I have something to get off my chest, but I didn't consider her feelings. She's lucky to have you.

At least she's capable of realizing that. His own parents seemed to have no sense that they ever did anything wrong. To the best of Trev's recollection, Wade had never once apologized, not even when he laid into Trev for something he didn't do.

> **Junie:** Lunch tomorrow then?
> **Trev:** Sounds good.

She sent the time and place, leaving him to wonder what terrible revelation Junie was about to dump on Leanne this time.

Whatever it is, I'll be there to pick up the pieces.

CHAPTER 18

THE NEXT DAY WAS JAM-PACKED.

Leanne campaigned nonstop, starting with a chat at the coffee klatch. More than half of the gathered seniors were already on her team, but she reinforced the message by stopping in personally with a huge assortment of goodies from Sugar Daddy's.

"Good morning," she called, as she trekked through the fire station into the conference room, where a number of retirees awaited.

Gladys winked at her. "Can't get enough of us, huh?"

"I'm hoping to get the most powerful voting bloc firmly in my camp," she said seriously.

"We're yours, honey." Hazel hurried over to take the bakery box from her and carried it to the table where the coffee was set up.

"Not me," said Leonard. "I belong to Gladys."

"Stop being so literal," Howard grumbled.

"I hope to see everyone at headquarters later. But mainly, I wanted to talk about outreach. Even if you're not actively volunteering…" She made eye contact with a few seniors and smiled. "I hope you'll mention that I'm running to your friends. At church and bunco, bingo and the singalong, or at your weekly breakfast catch-up."

"You're trying to get on our gossip circuit," Mrs. Carmenian said with a chuckle. "I'm already canvassing for you, darling. And yet you want *more*?"

She bit her lip, trying to look rueful. "Is that wrong? I probably shouldn't—"

"I'll take care of it," Hazel promised.

Impulsively, Leanne crossed to the doughnut table and gave the old woman a hug. She whispered, "I appreciate you so much. Read the book for this month's club meeting yet?"

Hazel grinned. "I'm halfway through! It's pure filth and I love it."

Leanne let her go with a final pat on the back. "I saw how you went after Dan Rutherford. Don't get in trouble, okay?"

"Please, that rodent can't mess with me. My grandson is a lawyer."

While Hazel filled a plate with pastries, a few other retirees offered to spread the word to folks who didn't get online. Leanne said, "I truly appreciate it. I don't have the same resources as Dan Rutherford."

Howard patted her arm in a comforting gesture. "Of course you don't. He's sixty-eight and owns a car dealership."

Leanne headed toward the door, content with what she'd accomplished. "Thanks so much. I won't take up more of your time—"

"Oh, please," Mrs. Carmenian cut in. "We don't have that much of it left at our age, but ironically, there are so many hours to fill with our families busy and no actual job."

That cut close to the bone. She went back to Hazel, who'd

unexpectedly become her fiercest defender. "Can I hug you again before I go?"

She'd never met any of her grandparents. Junie had been disowned before Leanne was born, so she'd never known the witch side of her family, and Junie had said her biological father was some random mundane, a man she couldn't track down if she tried. Since that was just classic Junie, she'd never questioned it. But over the past few months, she'd come to view Hazel as a surrogate grandma, and the altercation with Rutherford underscored how precious this woman was. While she seemed grumpy as hell on the surface, she was lonely deep down and longing to feel necessary and be included.

"Bring it in," said Hazel, her round face creasing in a bright smile.

Smiling, Leanne hugged her and patted her back. "I'm completely out of corn muffins, you know."

"You ate the lot already?" Beaming, Hazel gave Leanne another squeeze. "I'll make a double batch this time, and you can put some in the freezer. They microwave real nice."

"Thanks, you're the best."

"You never make me corn muffins," Howard complained.

"That's because you're not in my book club." Hazel tossed her dandelion perm and then patted the curls with a superior sniff.

Before, she'd wondered why Clem bothered attending these meetings, and while she'd started with an ulterior motive, Leanne genuinely liked these seniors now, all of them, not just Ethel and Gladys, who had always been cool witches in her book. With another wave, she rushed out, as she'd spent more time chatting than she planned.

The rest of the morning, she visited businesses downtown and did her nutshell pitch without taking up too much time. By lunchtime, she was exhausted, but she kept working at headquarters even as she ate, reaching out to community groups like the Kiwanis and the VFW via email, along with youth organizations, agricultural foundations, and a variety of other special interest groups that might make good allies.

Volunteers trickled in, and to her surprise, some of the retirees had high school–age grandchildren with them today. Leanne immediately put the Zoomers in charge of social media outreach, after showing them some of Trev's efforts. *Speaking of which…*

Normally, he'd arrived before now. She checked her phone, but she didn't have any messages from him. *Well, maybe he's researching classes?* Mentally, she shrugged and dove back into work, scheduling six more meetings or speaking engagements for the following week. Ideally, she'd have a professional manager to do this, but she was running this thing on a shoestring, having given up her stable and reliable future for one in which she theoretically could make a difference.

"How're you doing?" Ethel asked, squeezing the back of her neck gently.

The sudden touch made her jump and belatedly realize how tense she was. "I feel like I ran at this too suddenly. I should've been making plans to do this for years, but…"

I couldn't let Dan Rutherford win, and I couldn't stand working for his cronies. Watching incompetent assholes take credit for my hard work? It sucks.

But she couldn't say any of that in front of the volunteers.

Even people who were on her side gossiped, and it often came across as bitter when a woman told the truth about workplace dynamics after leaving a job. So she bit back the torrent of words and basked in Ethel's kind smile. Stretching her neck from side to side, Leanne got up from her laptop, aware of the aches from sitting too long.

"Pace yourself," Ethel advised. "Yes, you're running behind the curve right now, and you don't have as much time as would be ideal, but you have two months. You can do this."

Most of the tension drained out of her body. "That's exactly what I needed to hear."

"Then how about this? No matter what happens, I'm incredibly proud of you." The older witch delivered the short speech in a serious tone, quite unlike her usual breezy jokes.

"I don't know what to say. What's with you and Hazel today? You're both trying to make me cry or what?"

"Not even slightly. I'm having lunch with Angelica. Gonna try and talk some sense into her. She needs to leave Danica and Clem alone."

Leanne chuckled. "Good luck with that."

"I'll need it. But before I go, I wanted to give you this."

Leanne accepted the sweet-smelling herbal sachet. To a mundane, it would look prosaic as hell, potpourri to keep clothes smelling fragrant. A text popped up on her phone as Ethel sauntered toward the door. I spent hours on this. Put it with your campaigning clothes, and it should attract success. When we get closer to election day, I'll do a divination to check your chances. We're with you, every step of the way.

This was the kind of message she deleted immediately. It contained too much information for her to risk leaving it be, but Leanne did stare at Ethel for a long moment, letting the support soak in. Junie had raised her like a nomad, and her mother had never really connected to a coven. Leanne had been lucky to find her heart's home in St. Claire.

I appreciate it, she sent back. You're my hero.

Back atcha.

With a whisper of regret, she purged the whole chat then, as she had countless times before. Witches tended to speak in code even online because of past persecutions. But...what would it be like to live a world where she didn't need to worry about this or perpetually hide her identity?

My existence isn't a crime.

Sighing slightly, she decided to focus on what she could change—for now.

At 1:00 p.m., Trev sat at a table at the Coffee House.

He didn't want to do this with Junie, but the alternative was letting Leanne get ambushed, and that didn't seem right either. He tapped his fingers briefly on the table while scanning for Leanne's mother, then he decided to check the campaign socials. At least he could respond to comments and like some posts to amplify engagement while he waited.

As expected, Junie was twenty minutes late, and she ran into the café wearing what appeared to be a man's overcoat and two different socks. Her hair looked like she had slept in the braid, and

Trev pretended not to notice her disarray, standing up to greet her because he did have manners when he bothered to trot them out. Normally, he didn't waste his energy, but however scattered Junie might be, she'd produced a treasure like Leanne. Looking at her mom, he seriously couldn't imagine how Leanne had become so organized and ambitious.

Maybe it's a form of rebellion?

Breathless, Junie plopped down at the table in a swirl of patchouli. "Sorry, I overslept."

That made him smile because he'd done the same. People with a regular schedule didn't stay up all night and go to sleep when the horizon got bright and the birds started singing, but before moving in with Leanne, he'd been quite a night owl. Not because of his circadian rhythm, but because it didn't matter when or even *if* he went to bed.

"It's fine. I feel awkward about doing this, but—"

"No, you're right. It's better if I do a test run with you. And if you think I should wait until after the election to tell her, I will. But…this is time sensitive, so…" She trailed off. "Well, let's grab some food, then I'll fill you in."

"I'll get it. What would you like to eat?"

"Oh, anything's fine. A sandwich and a drink—why don't you surprise me?"

With a nod, he got in line and waited his turn then ordered two turkey and Swiss, one green tea lime twist, and an iced latte for himself. To deal with this crisis, he felt like a fair amount of caffeine would be required. Soon, their food was ready, and he went back to the table.

"Hope this is okay," he said, passing Junie's meal to her.

"It looks great, thank you." The older woman took a breath and flipped her unraveling braid over her shoulder. "So let's get down to it. How much do you know about LeLe?"

"Uh." That wasn't how he imagined this would go.

Fortunately, Junie misunderstood his hesitation. "I guess she's told you a lot if you're worried about hurting my feelings. Whatever she said, I deserve it. But how surprising...she doesn't ordinarily enjoy shining any light on the dark places."

"She did marry me," he said, hoping a blanket statement would cover all the gaps.

"Fair point. Then, do you know anything about her father?" she asked.

"She hasn't said much." Not a lie.

"That's because I told her I didn't know who he was," Junie announced.

"Like, *Mamma Mia* style?"

"No, there won't be four ashen ferrets showing up to vie for the privilege of being LeLe's dad at this stage in her life."

Trev burst out laughing. "Do you mean silver foxes?" Come to think of it, there might only be three potential dads in *Mamma Mia*, but he wasn't an expert and he didn't care enough to correct her.

Junie shook her head. "No, I heard my friend's son say 'ashen ferret,' and it made me laugh, so I use it now myself."

"It's funny," he admitted. "Have you considered 'titanium tanuki' for strong candidates?"

"I will now. Tanukis are Japanese raccoon dogs, right?"

"Yep."

Deliberately, Junie unwrapped her sandwich and took a bite. "I appreciate you giving me time to put my thoughts in order, but it really won't help. I'm always like this."

"I'm listening, whenever you're ready." He tried to keep his expression neutral.

"The situation is this. When I was young, I had an affair with a married man. He... I was a toy to him, a flavor of the month, I guess. I told him about LeLe, and he said to get rid of her. He had no use for either of us. I wanted her, though. And I tried my best to raise her on my own, but...I wasn't great at it."

"I see why you lied," Trev said tightly.

Imagine being that much of a bag of dicks.

"Yeah. It was the right decision then, but the situation has changed."

"How so?" he asked, as a bad feeling trickled in like slow-drip coffee.

"Her father is from a...prominent family." Based on her hesitation, he suspected Junie had almost used a different word. "His wife has since passed away, and he's become nostalgic in his old age after receiving an unfavorable diagnosis. He wants to meet LeLe before it's too late. She also has three half siblings she could get to know, and..."

"And?" he prompted.

This was a hell of a lot to take in. If he felt overwhelmed, God only knew how Leanne would react. But like Junie said, this was a now-or-never decision, most likely. Depending on how dire the old dickbag's situation was, the meeting might not keep until after the election.

"There could be multiple benefits," she finally said.

"Like, inheritance? If I'm reading between the lines right."

Junie didn't meet his look, busy tracing patterns on the table. "Pretty much."

"If you expect Leanne to fall in line with some asshole's plan for money, you don't know her at all. And if you don't tell her why you kept her dad's identity a secret in the first place because you're hoping for a payout..." He couldn't bring himself to finish that sentence.

Junie's gaze snapped up, as she choked on a swig of lime tea. "What are you saying? *I* don't want anything from that rat bastard. But she *is* his child, which means she's entitled to anything he wants to give her. It might come in handy later. They say it takes money to get anywhere in politics."

He clenched a fist, trying to keep hold of the fraying reins of his temper. "I doubt Leanne will want anything from this man. But...you should tell her. Not because she might get something, but because she has a right to decide."

"Do you have any advice as to how I should put it?" Vulnerable eyes stared across the table, begging for guidance.

Somehow this woman still isn't a grown-up. It was like time stopped when she met the wrong person as a kid, and she never ceased looking for someone to take care of her. An unsettling realization to have about his mother-in-law.

"I wouldn't tell her that he asked you to have an abortion. That's too hurtful even if it's true. I guess I'd just say you were ashamed because he was married."

Her shoulders rounded slightly. "Maybe it doesn't matter, but in the beginning, I didn't know. I call it an affair now because that's what it was, but at the time, I thought I was so cool, dating an older guy. I got pregnant thinking it would make him stay. But there were too many restrictions, times I couldn't get in touch with him, and then…"

"You found out."

"Yeah." Junie sighed and lowered her head, the perfect picture of injured innocence. "I think you're right. I'll lay it out, bare bones, and she can take it from there."

Yeah, I definitely did the right thing, even if Leanne gets mad. She didn't need to hear the unfiltered version. It's bullshit for Junie to expect Leanne to comfort her in a situation like this.

"Can I give you one more piece of advice?" Trev asked.

Leanne's mom nodded. "Please do."

"I know you want a better relationship with her, but you can't just…insist on it. You weren't around when she needed you most, and now that she's grown, she gets to choose how often she sees *you*."

"Whew. No punches pulled." Junie stood abruptly. "I appreciate your time. I'll give you a heads-up before I talk to LeLe. I'm really, truly glad she has someone like you watching her back. I wish I'd been that lucky."

Funny, once, he'd have said he hated confrontation, but before anyone—even her mom—upset his wife, they had to deal with him first.

CHAPTER 19

FOUR DAYS LATER, LEANNE SAT in her car numbly staring at the steering wheel.

The day had started so well, then Junie messaged unexpectedly, asking her to meet up. That never boded well. Then Trev gave her a heads-up that Junie had news about her bio-dad, and she wasn't sure how she felt about him screening Junie's content. On one hand, she'd liked it because it meant he cared enough to try and protect her, but it also felt like maybe he'd crossed a line. Yet she wasn't *sure* if she thought so, as she wasn't the most experienced in such matters. Maybe it was normal for partners to get involved under those circumstances?

In the end, it had helped that she'd known what to expect heading to the meeting, as Trev had outlined his discussion with Junie already. It didn't take long for her mom to sum it all up. She'd been young, and she'd had a torrid affair with a married witch from a prominent witch family. Apparently, Leanne had two half brothers and a half sister somewhere out there, not that she was in any hurry to meet these new relations. If her so-called father had cared about her genuinely, he wouldn't have waited until he was dying to look for Junie and Leanne.

"What, does he need a kidney or half my liver?" she'd asked. "None of his other kids are a match, is that it?"

"LeLe, please. It's fine if you don't want to meet him, but it's not like that. He just wants to see your face before it's too late."

"It was too late when he let you walk thirty-eight years ago."

And despite letting the news sink in, her fundamental opinion hadn't changed. She'd never had a father before, and she didn't need one now. It felt like the height of selfishness to ask her to invest her time, energy, and emotions into someone who was likely dying and was looking to expiate some sin at the end of his time on earth, if one subscribed to that view of the afterlife. Which she didn't.

Muttering a curse, she finally bounded out of the car and stormed toward the condo. She felt like throwing a fit, but she was too old to shout and throw things. Leanne took the elevator up, and when the doors swished open, she smelled the warm, comforting scent of dinner cooking. Something meaty, maybe with root vegetables. The fact that Trev was home, waiting for her, sliced the edge off her agitation.

She keyed the pin to the front door and stepped in to find him right there. He hugged her without saying a word, letting her choose what to say and how much. Exhaling slowly, she wrapped her arms around his waist and closed her eyes. Funny, her condo had never felt as much like home as it did since Trev moved in.

"Do you feel like talking, or would you rather eat?" he asked.

"I'll change, then we'll catch up." She was still trying to decide how to feel.

He gave her space while she put on a pair of sweats and a cozy old sweater. The weather wasn't chilly enough to turn on the heat, but she needed fuzzy socks and some snuggly clothes to feel comfortable after dark. Trev was plating pot roast with potatoes, carrots, and onions when she got back.

"Here you go."

Briefly, she ate a few bites before addressing the elephant in the room. "So you met with Junie to find out what she wanted to tell me. Without talking to me about it. Which means you either answered my phone or deleted a message. I don't particularly enjoy either option."

He flattened his palms on the counter, head lowered. "I wasn't sure it was the right move. But letting her careen toward you while you're running for city council didn't seem like the best idea either. I'm sorry for deleting the text and meeting her without informing you."

Leanne sighed. "I didn't need to know all the details, but you should've told me about the text. And you should've looped me in about your lunch plans." She laid down her fork and stared at him, where he stood like a penitent across the kitchen island. "Trev."

"Yeah?"

"I'm not mad. And I appreciate that you were trying to run interference. If you'd given me a heads-up, we wouldn't even be having this conversation, because frankly, I've wished someone would save me from my mom more than once in my life."

Finally, he lifted his face and made eye contact. Wow, she'd seldom seen anyone so miserable about a minor misstep. Leanne reached for his hand, and Trev hesitated before taking it. He scanned her face, seeming to search for...what? Maybe confirmation that she truly wasn't pissed? Then he appeared to conclude things were fine and wrapped his fingers around hers.

"Why don't we eat? Then I'll rub your feet while we talk everything through."

Her fake smile edged a little closer to being real, and some of the tightness left her chest. "Are you trying to earn points?"

"Maybe," he mumbled.

"It's not necessary, but I'm not silly enough to turn down a foot rub."

"I don't know how you walk around in those heels all day. I'm awed by your skills," Trev said, clearing away the dinner dishes.

She couldn't exactly admit that her shoes were enchanted to prevent pain and posture problems. Probably, she should offer to help with the cleaning, but the day had been exhausting, so she settled on the couch and let the news really sink in. *I have a dad. He's dying, and he wants to meet me. I have brothers and a sister.* It was all hard to digest, but especially that part. She'd made peace with the idea that she was alone in the world, apart from the coven and occasionally Junie, when she was feeling maternal. Now she had Trev too.

Well, sort of.

Suddenly, Leanne realized she hadn't texted the coven group chat at all today. Actually, it had been more than one day. Messages from the other witches had been pinging, but not only had she not read them, she hadn't shared her news either. *I refuse to drift away just because I've got a lot going on. I'll talk to everyone later.*

A few minutes later, Trev joined her on the sofa and pulled her feet into his lap, delivering on his promise. "More pressure or less?"

"A little more. That's perfect." She sighed as he dug into her arches.

"So what's your first reaction?"

"Honestly? To hell with all of them. When I was a kid, I wanted a normal family, but I grew out of it." She smiled slightly, tipping her head back as a wave of pleasure washed over her. "Not that anything about this mess qualifies as normal."

"Sounds like you don't plan on meeting your dad," Trev said.

"You think that's a mistake?"

He shook his head. "It's totally up to you. Hell, sometimes I wish I'd never met mine."

She laughed softly, as she was meant to, but she could tell talking about his father hurt Trev. "Part of me wishes I wasn't so obstinate because if I went, put up with some bullshit, and pretended to be moved by this nonsense, I might get something out of it. I can't muster any motivation, though. Even if he's an asshole, it's immoral to run a game on a dying man."

"Words to live by," Trev said with a mock-somber air.

Before bed, Leanne caught up on everyone's news and made a mental note to check on Vanessa, who was quieter than usual. She responded to everyone then apologized: Sorry I've been unavailable, I'll do better.

Margie: It's understandable. Win the election.

She sent a private text to Vanessa: Everything okay? Do you want to talk?

Vanessa: There's some stuff going on, but I'd rather not get into it right now.

Leanne: Okay, but I'm here if you need me. Day or night.

Vanessa: I know. And thanks.

———————

A few days later, Trev got a message from Dante, a little unusual.

Among their poker pals, Trev was closest to Titus. Everyone else, he joked around with in the group chat, but he'd never hung out with Dante, Calvin, or Miguel one-on-one. Poker night was the height of him being social, and he never hosted because why the hell would the guys want to get depressed in his basement? It occurred to him that Leanne might be okay with him inviting the guys over, though, maybe on her book club night?

Trev read the text twice. I need some advice. Want to get a beer?

Does he actually think I can help?

Leanne had said she'd be late at the campaign office tonight. She had some local media interviews lined up, so he mentally shrugged. Sounds good. When and where?

Dante: Seven Grand at 7.

Trev had sold his car a couple days ago, and now he actually had money in the bank. He hadn't bought the electric bike yet, as he couldn't decide between a cheap, low-speed model and a Vespa-type ride. It would make sense to go with the former, though, to pay for classes and pay down the balance on his card and bank the rest until he started earning.

Thus making up his mind, he registered for the two courses Leanne had endorsed and noted the start dates on his digital calendar. How...wild. Since moving in with her, he hadn't spent more than a few hours here and there playing games. While he'd expected to miss it, he enjoyed having stuff to do and places to be. He spent the rest of the day tidying the condo and updating Leanne's campaign socials. Pics from her past few talks went up, then he made some more reels, as the first ones were still spinning out there, gathering interest and responses. Before heading out, he left a note for Leanne on the fridge *and* texted her his plans.

She replied right away: Have fun, sweetheart. See you later.

There was no need to dress up, but if he recalled correctly from the single time he'd been to Seven Grand, the place had a business-casual vibe. So he put on a gray-and-white striped button-up and his good jeans. After checking the time, Trev got a rideshare from Howard Carruthers and arrived before Dante.

Seven Grand was a freestanding brick building toward the highway, decorated with ornate shrubberies and fairy lights. The place probably hoped to grab traffic from the freeway and from town; he wasn't sure how successful it was. Inside, it was all burnished wood and well-dressed people with mellow music purring from the speakers. He suspected the fixtures and sconces weren't real antiques, but they were excellent reproductions.

He grabbed a table and ordered a beer while scrolling through memes. Soon, his phone started pinging nonstop with new notifications, as his newest post went viral. It turned out if you suggested your wife hire a goofy ginger cat to run the city—why not put the fat cats in charge for real?—netizens loved it. He was laughing at a list someone had made of Goliath's qualifications when a shadow fell across the wood.

Glancing up and expecting Dante, he felt like the room went still around him, and his heart practically froze in his chest. *Sarah. Sarah Croft. Wait, that was her maiden name.* The room seemed to get smaller and hotter as she smiled at him as if she hadn't once ripped his heart out and stepped on it.

"You look amazing," she said, scanning him in a manner that felt intrusive.

Sarah didn't have the right to look at him that way. Nobody but Leanne did. As if from a great distance, he noticed she'd lost weight, the last ten pounds he'd always thought looked good on her, and her light-brown hair was streaked blond. She'd always preferred natural makeup, and that hadn't changed, though her brown eyes were darker than he recalled. After the way things ended between them, he couldn't bring himself to return the compliment.

His face might as well be covered in cement, like the muscles wouldn't even move, and his throat felt tight. Trev prayed that his voice didn't reflect the strain. "Thanks."

She cocked her head with a friendly smile, setting a hand on his table as if she meant to linger. "You must be wondering why I'm in St. Claire."

He just stared at her because, in fact, he wasn't. Words wouldn't come for this awkward, awful situation. What even *were* words? Instead, he got a live-action replay in his brain of how hard he'd cried when she'd left, the way he'd pleaded for one last chance to get his shit together. *You'll die in this basement.* In all likelihood, the only shock from their breakup was that she hadn't left when he was forced to move back home—that she'd given him a little time.

Somehow she was still talking. "I'm here for my cousin's wedding. Sent you the invitation for mine, but you didn't respond."

Are you surprised?

If only teleportation was a thing, he'd vanish, or hell, maybe he'd poof her somewhere else, so she wouldn't be standing there staring at him, waiting for...what? Did she need closure or something? Until the request for RSVP arrived, he'd have said Sarah would answer any questions about him with a head toss and, "Trevor who?"

"I've been busy," he said. "Did you need something else?"

"I just wanted to say I'm sorry."

He blinked. That was the last thing he'd expected to hear from her. "About what?"

"For cheating on you."

I had no fucking clue. It shouldn't matter now. It *didn't.*

Though he tried not to give anything away, he must've failed because she said, "Shit. You didn't know. But Titus saw us together. I thought—"

"Trev! Sorry I'm late," Dante called to him from across the bar. The guy strolled through the crowd with an awe-inspiring confidence that drew second and third looks.

No surprise because he *was* a handsome man, dark-skinned, brown eyes, clean-shaven with black hair worn in short twists. He dressed like he came out of a catalog too. In fact, Dante made Trev secretly feel like a hairball that a stray cat horked up in the yard.

When he got to the table, he eyed Sarah with obvious perplexity. "Who's this?"

Trev finally found his voice. "No one," he said coolly.

She flinched. *Good.*

Dante turned to Sarah with a practiced, lady-killer smile. "Tell you straight up, you're wasting your time. My man Trev is married, and his wife is a four-alarm fire."

He could've kissed Dante on the lips, seriously. Suddenly, the situation felt wholly different—not disastrous, just...annoying. Managing a smile, he said to Dante, "All true. And no worries, I kept busy." To Sarah, he added, "Want to see my wedding photos? We kept it intimate because Leanne thinks it's better to save the money for our life together than to waste it on a single party." He let that sink in because he knew damn well Sarah had spent forty grand on her glorious, perfect gala. "But the pictures turned out fantastic."

"No thanks," she said tightly.

Yeah, this isn't working out how you thought, huh? Figured you could rub my nose in it and make me even sorrier I lost you? Nah. I'm not that guy anymore. Possibly, he was being unfair to her, and maybe she truly did want to make amends, but from his perspective, she'd just injured him further by revealing past infidelity, piled on top of a brutal breakup.

And Titus knew...

"I heard you're changing your name," Dante said, as Sarah turned.

That froze her in her tracks. He could tell she was still listening. *Okay, this is sort of fun.*

"Just submitted the paperwork. We're both hyphenated now. Trevor Vanderpol-Montgomery has quite the ring, doesn't it?"

"Sounds like yacht money," Dante agreed with a laugh. "How's her campaign going for city council, by the way?"

Bless Dante, all his ancestors, and his descendants. He must be doing this on purpose.

"Extraordinarily well," he said in a voice that carried. "The numbers on her socials are excellent, and she's gaining ground on Dan Rutherford."

"Nice work. You want to take over my accounts too?" Dante gave him a nudge and a broad smile that plainly said he did know something was up.

"We'll talk." As Sarah walked away, he leaned over and gave Dante a hug, whispering, "Thanks, man."

His friend stared after Sarah, brows furrowed. "Yeah, I got a definite vibe, none of it good. Did I back you up okay?"

"Couldn't have been better," Trev assured him.

"That's your ex, I'm guessing."

He nodded. "*The* ex."

"The one who broke you?"

Once, Trev might've argued about that or denied it. In fairness to Sarah, he had been a mess, and there was no need to re-tread old ground. He sipped his beer and said, "Enough about me. We got together because you needed advice, am I right? I'm your guy. Tell me everything."

"Long story. You sure?"

Trev nodded.

"Okay, so it's like this…" Dante began. "I've been…seeing Margie lately."

"Right." He didn't argue the verbiage, though he'd heard about their hookups.

"And I actually like her, but whenever I suggest we get together for…other reasons, she shuts it down and tells me I can do better. What the hell is that about?" Dante demanded. "Is she trying to reverse psych me or something? Because it makes me feel like Margie really means *she* can do better."

Trev muffled a laugh. "I don't think that's it. From what I've heard, she had a rough time with her ex, and it's kind of a big step for her to be…seeing you at all."

"Then what should I do? I *like* her. I thought you had no game, but you're already married. So tell me, what am I supposed to do?"

That had nothing to do with game, only with being in the right place at the right time. In another universe, Leanne might have arrowed right to Dante and dragged him off to the bathroom. Since he had a kid, he probably wouldn't have been down for the Vegas elopement, though. Not for the reasons Leanne had laid out. Hell, she might have gone after Calvin. He was the player of the group—not likely he'd have agreed to help her out either.

"The best you can," Trev said. "And be patient."

CHAPTER 20

OVER THE NEXT FEW WEEKS, Leanne tried to keep all the moving pieces in order.

The campaign work was exhausting, and she wasn't even getting paid. It was hard not to worry since she wasn't independently wealthy like Dan Rutherford. His car dealership made him money without too much input from him, as he had staff handling the day-to-day management. Which freed him up to make Leanne's life worse.

His team hit back on social media with footage they'd dug up from an old Christmas staff party, likely recorded by one of the mayoral aides. She stared numbly at herself, dressed like a sexy elf, at fucking Mayor Anderson's behest. *Show some holiday spirit, Vanderpol! And I don't mean an ugly sweater.* In the clip, she was booty dancing with some guy from the maintenance department, and yeah, she'd had a bit to drink because what woman could cope with that costume sober? It hadn't seemed like a big deal at the time, but now—

The video ended in an ominous black screen. *IS THIS THE NEXT CITY COUNCILWOMAN? Vote smart. Vote Dan Rutherford, the candidate you can trust.*

Her phone went wild, vibrating and beeping with social media reactions and texts from volunteers worried about how this would impact her at the polls. She didn't even know where to start with damage control, but there was no question she had to do something.

To her relief, Trev was the first person to call. "Don't worry, Butterfly. I'm on this. Now that he's gone after you personally, it's time to use that footage Mrs. Carmenian sent us."

Oh wow.

"Are you sure? You said it could ricochet."

"He threw mud first, now it's time to wrestle. Wait, does that analogy work? I'm not sure it does."

"Okay. I trust you."

Within two hours, Trev had the reel online, and it was *glorious.* He didn't show the whole scene, just Rutherford's spiteful expression, the sound bite "this little bitch," and then Hazel's furious reaction with the coffee mug, followed by the SpongeBob "Do you kiss your mother with that mouth?" meme. The clip looped it a few times with a soundtrack reminiscent of Benny Hill, and then ended with a confused-looking cat gazing up at a thought bubble:

Is this the candidate you trust?

She got in the coven chat once the content was uploaded.

Leanne: Clem, I will owe you so big...

Clem: You need me to cast the viral spell again.

Leanne: Sorry, I hope it's the last time.

Ethel: You probably don't want to hear this, but all my divinations suggest it'll be too close to call. I wish I could promise you a blowout, but it's not in the stars.

Priya: Let's stay positive.

Danica: I'll help Clem, give it double oomph. I know how to cast this spell too. Just sayin'.

Kerry: Leanne probably figured you're too busy appreciating CinnaMan stick right now.

Margie: I don't know if I should punish or praise you.

Ethel: ...was that a pun too?

Leanne: I love you all.

The next day, Trev's response was everywhere, courtesy of Clem and Danica's spell. In addition, two Zoomers—maybe the ones who volunteered for her campaign—got inspired in the wee hours and filmed themselves writing DO YOU KISS YOUR MOTHER WITH THAT MOUTH in chalk on the parking lot at Rutherford's Reliable Auto Sales, and now that video had taken off without the benefit of a spell. Dan Rutherford couldn't hope to harness the might of the internet when he was still trying to do uber-serious "she's a threat to your way of life" nonsense. Trev had the right idea, being irreverent and mocking the shit out of him. Rutherford would probably retain the conservative vote, but online seniors with a sense of humor and younger voters? Leanne nodded.

They're mine.

By that afternoon, she also noticed Vanessa wasn't responding to coven chats like she used to, and that growing distance troubled her. While she waited to see how their counterattack would be received, she messaged Vanessa. Everything okay?

Vanessa: I have other friends, you know.

Ouch.

Clearly, things weren't all good, but she couldn't make Vanessa talk to her. On the surface, they looked fine, and they joked around at coven meetings, but her friend didn't reach out like she used to. It was easy to drift, and Leanne didn't want that to happen, but she had so much shit going on that she just couldn't drop it all and force a confrontation, if that was even a good idea. If she'd learned one thing from Junie, it was that she had to give other people space. Life didn't happen on Leanne's timetable.

So she did her best to stay in Vanessa's life over the next few weeks while working on the campaign, sending check-in texts and memes she found funny. Vanessa responded, but she still wasn't opening up. *Dammit.*

In the meantime, Leanne did everything she could to win the election.

Waiting didn't come easy to Leanne.

Somehow, it was worse waiting for the results of the election than anything she'd ever tried before. In the past six weeks, she'd given the campaign her all while shoving the issue of her rich witch father to the back burner. If the old man survived until after the polls closed, then she'd consider meeting him. Though it was self-serving as hell, she'd need funding to run for mayor later on. She'd managed the city council race on a shoestring, but it wouldn't be possible on a larger scale.

The volunteers gossiped and paced by turns, while Leanne resisted the urge to nibble away at her thumbnail. As she raised her hand to her mouth for the fourth time, Trev caught it and squeezed her fingers. She smiled at him, unable to settle because of how tight the margins on the race had become. She'd certainly gotten the word out more effectively, but just because someone saw her stances and platforms online or liked one of Trev's reels, that didn't mean it would translate to actual votes.

"We gave it everything we had," Trev whispered. "Nobody could've done more."

Leanne didn't argue, but while she couldn't compel votes, it *might* be possible for Clem or Danica to meddle with election results if technology was involved. She'd never ask such a thing of them, however. Witches weren't supposed to accrue power through magical means; it would rouse suspicion if presidential candidates came out of nowhere and won in landslide victories that no political analyst could have ever predicted.

She smiled and leaned her head against his shoulder, working to reach a peaceful state of mind. "Thanks, hon. Win or lose, we did the best we could."

Hazel came over and wrapped Leanne into a cuddle. "It's so exciting to witness your rise to power. One day I'll be able to tell everyone I knew you way back when."

Leanne laughed. "You make it sound like I'm taking over the world."

"Aren't you, though?" Hazel winked and sauntered off to check the coffeepot.

She drank two more cups while waiting for the results, and when they were finally posted, everyone in the room started screaming. Leanne stared at the final tally, unable to believe her eyes. *I won by 212 votes. A narrow margin, but Team Underdog came through.* Trev wrapped his arms around her, lifted her, and twirled her around, so the room blurred into a sea of cheering faces. As he slid her down his body, he kissed her forehead, and her heart went a little gooey from happiness overload.

Then he asked, "Do you want to say a few words, Councilor?"

She shook her head. "Maybe later. They aren't listening right now anyway."

To get the room even more fired up, Leonard cranked ABBA with "The Winner Takes It All," and Hazel popped open so many bottles of champagne that they were overflowing everywhere. She hadn't brought wineglasses, so they used plastic cups and coffee mugs. Leanne shook so many hands that she lost track. Her entire coven was here, mingling with the volunteers, and it gave her a strange but heartwarming sensation.

She threaded through the office to reach Clem and Danica, each sipping from red plastic glasses. "How do you like my party?"

"I thought you were an independent," Danica joked.

Clem cracked a smile, though it didn't reach her eyes. She'd been quiet and withdrawn since the witch hunter got rounded up by the council a few months ago. "I'm happy to have played a role in your rise, however small."

"Are you kidding?" Leanne nudged Clem. "You're a VIP, babe."

The older Waterhouse cousin wore a crafty look. "Does that mean you'll fix the parking problem downtown and repair the potholes on our street first?"

Leanne laughed. "I literally just got elected."

Shaking her head, she joined Vanessa, who was chatting with Margie, and hugged each of them in turn. "Thank you both."

"I didn't do much," Margie said in a self-deprecating tone.

Leanne drew Vanessa aside at the first chance she got. Because she refused to be like her mother, Leanne tried to give people time, but it was hard to know if that registered as patience or indifference. It wasn't like they never talked these days, but the quality of the conversation was…different, more superficial.

"I've been waiting," Leanne said, "but it's starting to look like you don't want to talk, period. And if that's true, it's fine. Just know that I'm here if you change your mind."

Vanessa said quietly, "I feel like I'm losing you."

She blinked. "What?"

"You're busy *all* the time. I used to pop over whenever, and I could count on you being down 24/7. But lately, it's not like that."

"I'm sorry," Leanne said.

"I wasn't even gonna bring it up because I get it. And I didn't mean to make you feel bad tonight—on your night—but you *did* ask. So, fact is, I can't even figure out if there's space for me in this new life of yours." She leveled a steady look on Leanne, wearing her usual no-bullshit expression. "You think it didn't hurt my feelings when I found out you're hanging out in couples with Danica and her man? Have you even *asked* me if I'm seeing anyone lately?"

Fuck.

"No. And you're right, this is my fault. I'm so sorry. I've been shitty to you. Of course there's space for you."

"It's also possible that I'm sensitive because…honestly, I

thought you were the *last* person who'd settle down. I didn't see our 'single ladies' tour ever coming to an end."

"Wait, back up. Are you seeing someone?"

Vanessa made a sound that was a mix between a laugh and a snort. "Don't even try. I deserve your full attention, and we both know you can't focus on me tonight."

"Sorry again. I'll do better. We'll go out soon, talk about everything, then drink until we drop and dance until we can't see straight."

"Deal."

Leanne hugged Vanessa, relieved to have cleared the air even if she'd gotten confirmation that *she* was the crappy friend in this scenario. But it was impossible to do better if you never admitted you were the problem. After circulating a bit more, she took a break and Gladys caught her eye, signaling silently for a word. She followed the older witch out of the suite of offices and down the back stairs. It must be a serious discussion if it required this much privacy; Leanne stepped out into the brisk autumn evening, tasting a hint of early snow in the air. Briefly, she wished she'd grabbed her jacket, but Gladys wore such a severe expression that foreboding shivered through her. Leanne rubbed her hands over her forearms, trying to keep her face from showing how concerned she was.

"It must be major, or you wouldn't have pulled me away at this juncture," she said.

"You've always been sharp," Gladys said. "That wit will take you far."

"What's this about anyway?"

"I'll be blunt. And brief, as much as possible. Each witch council member is tasked with choosing their own successor. Nobody else is apprised of when the transition takes place exactly. This keeps the process private and anonymous."

"Makes sense," Leanne said. She already had a bad feeling, but Gladys had mobilized the coffee klatch, and they *were* both witches, even if they weren't part of the same coven.

"You were already on my short list as a possible replacement. Now that you've successfully embedded yourself in mundane government, you shot to the top. So this is your formal notification. When the council resumes meeting after the first of the year, you will take over my role and all related responsibilities."

Shit. It's even worse than I expected.

"Am I allowed to decline this honor?" she asked cautiously.

Gladys smirked and folded her arms. "You are not. This is the witch equivalent of jury duty. If your name is called, you serve."

"Dammit," Leanne said. "Would you have still picked me to replace you if I'd lost?"

"Likely not."

"This is maybe the first time I've ever been sorry about winning," she muttered.

"I won't keep you from the revelry long, but do you have any questions?"

Her first impulse was to say no and flee, but that would be irresponsible, and it wouldn't save her from this additional expectation. "I'll think about it and text you. But...is there any compensation relative to all the work? I quit my job to run for city council and I've been managing on my savings. I planned to do some freelancing after the election, but if you're saying I have to do witch council work for free—"

"There's a generous stipend," Gladys cut in with an amused look.

Some of her reluctance faded. While it might be mercenary, the mortgage on her condo wouldn't pay itself. "There's the silver lining. Wait, I guess I do have one more question."

"What's that?" the other witch asked.

"How long is the term?"

"Four years."

Leanne blinked. "Longer than expected."

"You'll receive official notification through council channels. I don't think I need to tell you that secrecy is mandatory. You cannot share this nomination with your coven sisters, other witches, or your family."

Though she'd been in Vegas when Gladys intervened regarding the witch hunter issue on behalf of the council, Margie had filled her in quietly. "I understand. And I'm not sure if I should say thanks or—"

Just then, something clattered to the ground, a plastic plate spilling pizza onto the chilly cement. Trev stood there holding Leanne's jacket in his other hand, and from his look of abject shock, he'd heard a lot, way more than he should have. Gladys fixed him with a terrible stare, and Leanne's foreboding ripened into full-blown fear. He wasn't wearing a coat either, but he'd brought hers. He clutched it like a lifeline. Why did he have to be so freaking sweet, choosing to search for her at the worst possible time?

Oh hell.

"No," she said, stepping between them. "You can't. Technically speaking, nobody told him. And he didn't hear anything. *Please*, Gladys. Don't do this."

This…has to be a hallucination, right?

Since it was impossible to throw a rocking party without snacks, Trev had ordered a bunch of pizzas, and they'd just been delivered. He got some food into all the hearty partiers, then he noticed Leanne was MIA. Her coat was still hanging on the rack, so he figured she must've stepped out to catch her breath and process the good news in private.

But he found her discussing shit that didn't make sense—*couldn't* make sense—at least not according to the world he lived in. They'd definitely been talking about some kind of secret council, but judging from Leanne's expression, he'd better act innocent and do it more expertly than any role he'd ever played. He'd weigh what he'd heard later. Right now, this appeared to be about survival. If anyone had asked him before tonight, he never would've imagined that Gladys—sweet little Gladys—could look this terrifying.

Trev pinned on a blurry, harmless smile. "Whoa, I am not a good drinker. I tried to bring you a slice, but I went and turfed it. Sorry, Butterfly. You must be freezing, though. Put this on. I'll let you finish your chat."

"It's fine," Gladys said, scrutinizing him from head to toe.

It took every ounce of determination not to flinch or back away from that inspection and to keep pretending to be cool-and-casual Trev. "Let's all get back in, then? The party needs its guest of honor. Pretty sure it's written in the big book of winning."

Leanne came over to him and slipped her arms into the sleeves of the jacket he was holding. "Thanks, sweetheart. Pity about the pizza, but the birds will be happy."

As Gladys moved past him, he got a chill that wouldn't quit, and Trev was still shivering when Leanne urged him inside. The back hallway was dark and quiet, with only distant noise from the party upstairs. The old woman slowly made her way up the steps, leaving them in the yellow flicker of the fluorescent light. He had no idea what to say as Leanne stepped closer.

"You don't understand," she whispered. "And I can't explain. Right now, you're doing the one thing you can, the one thing that might save us both. Please, *please* carry on."

The urgency in her low tone genuinely alarmed him. Trev drew in a breath and took a step, only to stumble. Leanne grabbed his arm, regarding him with a worried expression.

"Uh, right. Low blood sugar. I should get some food. Let's rejoin the festivities."

At the party, he did his best to act like he didn't notice Gladys watching him like a hawk that was about to swoop down on a mouse. He argued with Leonard about the music, danced with Hazel Jeffords, and pretended for all he was worth. The celebration ran late, and Howard made a killing by choosing not to drink since he ended up accepting a ton of gigs driving people home through the rideshare app. Finally, the office emptied out, leaving him to tidy up while Leanne walked the stragglers out. Gladys was gone, finally, but he didn't feel safe exactly. The old woman's scrutiny left him feeling like she could still be watching or listening, which was weird as hell and a bit paranoid too.

"Are you ready to go home?" his wife asked, pausing in the doorway.

A hundred words hovered at the tip of his tongue, questions that demanded logical answers. Only he couldn't even come up with a single theory that made sense. Role-play, cosplay, secret society? None of his half-baked ideas added up, and unease gnawed at him. Yet he still took the keys she handed him.

"You noticed that I didn't drink?" he asked.

"I'm always paying attention to you," she said with the smile that normally cut right through him.

Tonight, he wondered what her pretty smile might be concealing. Trev walked to the car silently. Never had he been more aware how little he knew about his wife. Leanne wasn't a St. Claire local, she didn't get along with her mother, and she belonged to a book club. That…was pretty much it. He had no clue where she'd gone to school or even where she'd lived before St. Claire. Their normal conversations didn't extend to asking deeply personal questions; she seemed to prefer it that way.

In the dark, driving back to the condo, he stole glances at her profile. She gazed out into the darkness like it held the answer to a riddle she'd been trying to solve for a while. *Poetic, right?* More likely that she was just avoiding him. When people said they couldn't explain, it usually meant they didn't want to. On the other hand, he truly didn't think Leanne was faking the intensity of her plea to Gladys. Who hadn't seemed like a powerful person until her whole demeanor changed in a blink.

How's that even possible?

The fraught silence lingered between them even after they got into the condo. Without looking at him, Leanne hung up her coat and set her purse on the end table in the living room. Finally, she turned, and her face stopped him mid-stride.

"I don't know what the hell is happening, but you're scared to death," he said softly.

Quietly, she nodded, twisting her fingers together until he stilled her with a touch. "And you honestly can't explain?" he added.

Leanne let out a shaky breath. "Bad things will happen if I try."

Whoa. What the hell.

"Are you in trouble, Butterfly?" The endearment slipped out, even under these circumstances. He couldn't bring himself to picture a reality in which she would seriously do anything to hurt him. Leanne was an honest person, the first to believe in him in forever.

Her smoky eyes were so dark that they looked almost black, and she was pale beneath her tan, fingers anxiously fidgeting with the hem of her blazer once he let go of her. "*I'm* not."

But I will be if I pursue this.

That was the clear message he got from her body language, and then he knew. It didn't matter. Whatever she was into, even if she belonged to some weird-ass secret society or believed she was a witch, it didn't change anything. Not for him. If she needed help, he'd figure out a way to provide it. Earning money wasn't his strong suit, but he'd attracted a few clients in the past few months, and he made more managing socials than he had mowing lawns.

Way less sweaty too. Maybe I can hire someone to look into Gladys quietly? See what Leanne's gotten roped into. But she seems to think that would be dangerous... Maybe it would be safer to stick to learning web design. He was doing simple sites now, nothing too fancy, but he'd get better. "Then it's just as well that I have no questions. I didn't hear anything before I dropped the pizza plate. There was a lot of wind. I'm sure you just had a good gossip with Gladys, or maybe you managed to get her to share her secret streusel recipe? If so, I'm all ears. Even Titus would have a hard time making it so tasty." He smiled then.

Her throat worked as she seemed to struggle to find words, and then she rushed him, slamming him into the wall with a driven kiss. Trev kissed her back desperately, feeling like he'd almost lost something precious even if he didn't understand precisely why. He twined his hands in her hair and fell into the magic of her soft, warm body pressed against him. Her delicious mouth glided over his, and he tasted her again, again, loving the fact that he got to take her home at the end of a long night where everyone wanted a piece of her.

But she's mine. No matter what, this woman chose me. I won't let her down.

When the time comes, I'll prove it, Butterfly.

CHAPTER 21

LEANNE LOST TRACK OF HOW they made it to the bedroom.

It was a storm of kissing and touching, then all their clothes hit the floor around the same time as her back hit the bed. Trev seemed to share her desperation, even if he didn't understand how close she'd come to losing him tonight. She'd saved him from some awful council action by the skin of her teeth, and there were no assurances it wouldn't happen again.

No, I refuse to imagine losing him.

She pushed the bad thoughts out of her brain and focused on the clean smell of his skin, the way he arched and moaned when she kissed a path down his bare chest, pausing on his hip to outline his pelvic bone with her tongue. He twisted and gasped as she teased him, clutching at the sheets with frantic hands.

I'll protect you somehow. I will.

The lights were off, so she only caught a glimpse of his face, Trev biting down on his lower lip as she shifted and curled her fingers around his already-throbbing cock. His hips hitched as he silently pleaded for more with each movement. She stroked him and licked the crease high on his upper thigh. The hot sweep of her tongue drew a full groan, and he gave up on controlling himself.

"You're sending me," he whispered.

"That's the point."

"But I don't want to go without you."

For some reason, those quiet words hit hard, and she crawled back up his body as he rolled onto his side. Leanne slid a thigh across his hip and gloried in the feel of his hands roving down the smooth skin of her back. There was no calculation, just Trev taking a ridiculous amount of pleasure in touching her all over. He kissed her again like their endgame was making out, even as he slid his hard length against her slick pussy. But when she tried to get more friction, he put a steadying hand on her ass and offered the laziest, sexiest smile she'd ever seen. Then he kissed her nose.

"Don't be in such a hurry, Butterfly. Let's enjoy the ride."

Leanne brushed her lips against his chin as longing swelled inside her, contained by sheer determination. "That's what I'm trying to do. But it looks like you enjoy teasing me."

"Seems I do. It's wild how much I want you. Part of me just wants to have you, but I don't want this to be over. I want to feel you and breathe you in, and…"

"What?" she asked.

"Worship you."

From anyone else, a declaration like that might make her laugh and break the mood, but Trev had always treated her like a goddess, someone who would be forever precious, not a good time. And so, the words merged with her simmering desire, infusing it with an unfamiliar ache. There had been plenty of sex, but never quite like this. She wanted to crawl inside him and see if his heart could possibly be as warm as it seemed.

"Trev…" Now she was gasping as his lips traced over her neck and shoulders, his hips still rolling against hers.

Another teasing pass of his tongue on top of her breast. Her nipples tightened, and she ached for his touch with an urgency that was becoming uncomfortable. When Trev finally worked his way down her breast, she knotted her fingers in his hair and tried to swallow her helpless cries. He drew them out of her anyway with each delicious tug of his lips. He knew how much teeth she liked now, how much pressure, and as he sucked and licked and bit, he teased her between her legs with delicate swirls of his fingertip without ever granting the pressure she needed right on her clit.

"Look at you coming undone," he whispered against her throat.

She reached between them and took hold of his cock, working him in her fist until he shivered with pleasure. "Let's go together."

"Yes," he gritted out, rolling on top of her.

She wrapped her legs around his hips and tilted for the first thrust. At first, he held himself up on his arms, gazing down at her with each inward push. But then she dug her hands into his back and urged him down. Trev moaned as she held him tight, feeling each tremor that rolled through him, each puff of breath against her skin.

His cock really was perfect, gorgeous in the way it filled her, and he knew exactly what to do with it. He angled so that he rubbed the right spot, and she screamed his name as an unexpected orgasm banged through her, leaving her breathless and trembling, but he wasn't done. Trev kept up a steady pace as she came down, thighs quivering. He caressed her clit until the tingles came back, and soon, she was lifting to meet each gliding stroke.

The next climax felt like it began in her toes, an all-over glow that brightened every nerve ending, and he intensified it by burying his face in her neck and shoulder. He pumped in jerky little motions, starting to chase his own finish, and she wanted it to be so good for him, so fucking good, that he'd forget about anything else. Leanne urged him on as he shook and rocked into her with impassioned need.

"That's so good. You feel incredible." She heard herself babbling half-intelligible words of praise.

At this rate he'd make her come a third time before letting go, and she didn't know if her body could take it, but she was willing to get wrecked trying. Her vision went starry, but she couldn't close her eyes because she didn't want to miss a moment. The room smelled of salt and sex, and her whole body blazed with heat.

"I need you. I need you so much." His whispered confession sent her again.

Then he pushed deep and held, coming in silence, so deep that the pulses of heat felt almost magical, and she could hear her own heartbeat. Or his? At this point, she couldn't recall where she ended and Trev began. He started to roll away, but she wouldn't let him go. Leanne had never held a man until he went soft, but tonight she did, cuddling him with as much tenderness as she could muster. It was all new, brand-fucking-new.

"You okay?" she finally asked, as his breath steadied and slowed.

"Are you seriously asking me that? I just banged the hell out of Councilwoman Vanderpol-Montgomery. I'm freaking glorious."

Relieved, she laughed and finally let him tumble to the side, though she kept her hands on him. "It's been a hell of a night."

"Why are you so amazing?" he asked.

"It's a good question."

"A better one might be *how*. I've met Junie."

Leanne laughed and shook her head. "Normally, bad-mouthing your mother-in-law gets you in trouble, but these are special circumstances."

"Understood. I'll quit while I'm ahead." He hesitated, seeming to weigh his next words carefully. "Have you considered what you're doing about your dad?"

She sighed. "Not even slightly. Can we not talk about that tonight? I'm trying to ride these endorphins as long as I can."

"Sorry, Butterfly. Whatever you decide, it'll be right."

"See, this is why I married you," she said impulsively. "You always know what to say."

He kissed her on the temple. "Yeah, I'm above average at winging it, and my instincts are pretty good."

As they snuggled up to sleep, Leanne hoped with all her heart that everything would be fine, but past life experience suggested that because happiness was nearly in her grasp, shit would soon go catastrophically wrong.

———

Surprisingly, Trev still didn't know what the hell to make of what he'd overheard, even a week later.

On the surface, nothing much had changed apart from Leanne's win, but the questions in his head wouldn't quit. He couldn't even talk about it with his therapist because the stuff he'd overheard sounded wild even to him when he replayed it. Most of the time, he tried to pretend like he'd misunderstood something or taken it out of context. That allowed him to do what he'd been doing for most of his life: cope with a situation he couldn't change.

He'd been seeing Dr. Grant for about five weeks, once he finally acknowledged he needed to get help officially. At first, talking to a stranger over video seemed weird, but he definitely preferred it to an office visit. And now he looked forward to the biweekly sessions because he was learning to manage his brain and trying to stop treating himself like the enemy.

Damn it, he couldn't even ask Titus because his social circle was too tightly entwined with Leanne's, and he knew his best friend all too well. If Trev hinted at something bizarre, Titus would absolutely ask Danica about it. Plus, he was still chewing on the fact that Titus had evidently known Sarah had been cheating on Trev.

All these years, and not one word. They needed to talk about it, but it made Trev's chest hurt to think about bridging the conversation. Once again, he was alone, struggling with multiple problems, even though he was "married" and supposedly had friends.

Initially, he figured he had no choice but to wrestle this stuff solo, but then it occurred to him: *Dante asked me for advice, right? I can do the same.* Nothing specific, but maybe the guy would have some helpful insight. And if not, Trev could use the company.

As usual, he made breakfast for Leanne, packed her lunch, did a little cleaning, then worked in the afternoon on various socials. His classes didn't require attendance; it was all modular work, augmented with forum support and video lessons he could watch at his convenience. Sometimes he marveled at how much his life had changed. These days, he worked freelance—his contribution to Leanne's campaign spoke for itself—and he got paid enough not to feel like a total waste of air. Therapy was helping to deal with a lot of issues he'd tried—and failed—to handle alone, mostly out of shame and fear of judgment, especially from his old man.

Living in that house really was killing me.

Apart from his mom sending a few texts early on, his family hadn't contacted him since he moved out, and it had been months at this point. He hadn't bothered telling them that he was married. Maybe it was petty, but it felt good cutting them off. If he'd ever needed confirmation that he was superfluous, a stain they'd rather rinse away, he had it. His therapist's advice on dealing with bad thoughts looped in his head, and he tried to breathe, focusing on work instead. When he got to a stopping point, he texted Dante.

> **Trev:** You busy tonight? Wife's got book club, and I could use some advice.
> **Dante:** I'm there. 7 at Grand?
> **Trev:** Sure. See ya later.

Even this, truth be told, was kind of a big deal. He'd spent so many years feeling like shit that he honestly couldn't imagine anyone sincerely wanting to hang out with him. So he'd never made any effort to become better friends with any of the poker night guys. His family had told him repeatedly that he was a failure and a loser with nothing to offer, and if they felt that way—

Enough of that.

He'd even started riding his bike to run errands, something he didn't expect to enjoy, but those moments felt like freedom, even when it was cold as hell. In the end, he'd bought a low-end electric one, so it still counted as a workout. Sometimes he bundled up and went riding when he needed to clear his head. St. Claire didn't have a bike lane, but most residential streets near the condo were quiet enough that he could race to his heart's content.

"Are you going out tonight?" Leanne asked.

"Getting a drink with Dante. Should I ask to crash at his place tonight? Unless I'm remembering wrong, you're hosting tonight, yeah?"

Leanne waved a hand in lazy acknowledgment. "I am indeed. Thankfully, nobody expects anything from me as a hostess. They'll bring the food, I supply the wine."

"That sounds fun. I should start a book club," he said. "Do you think the guys would be up for it?"

"Maybe."

He crossed to her and kissed her cheek. "So yes or no, do I come back tonight?"

"Hm. I want you here, but we have a lot to talk about, so if Dante is fine with it..."

Trev smiled, trying to seem unfazed. *A lot to talk about? What does that mean, Butterfly?* "Book-wise or gossip-wise?"

"Both," she answered.

"That's cool. I'll ask Dante if he can put me up. If it's inconvenient, Titus will always let me keep his couch warm. Enjoy girls' night, and don't worry about anything."

"Thanks, hon."

After changing his clothes, he decided to eat at Seven Grand as well. He left Leanne fiercely texting with her group chat and muttering over Kalamata olives, whatever that was about. He checked his reflection and headed out, catching a ride to the bar early. Trev ordered a platter of appetizers and a big, juicy burger with a side of sweet potato fries. He'd eaten half his food when Dante showed up.

"Did you starve to death in a past life or something? You couldn't make do with wings until I rolled up?"

"I forgot to eat lunch," he admitted.

"Then carry on, man."

Dante caught up when his steak and fries arrived, and they ate for a bit in companionable silence. "I was glad to get your text, to be honest. Always thought you didn't much like me."

Trev blinked. "Are you kidding?"

"Not even slightly. You barely talk to anyone but Titus, even during a game."

Looking back, Trev realized that was probably right, but it had nothing to do with the other guys. "If I'm being honest, it's because I didn't have much to contribute. So it was better to keep my mouth shut. Besides, I was baked a lot."

"So true. I never knew anyone to like weed more than you. Did Leanne crack down?"

Trev laughed softly. "She did tell me I can't smoke in the condo, but she didn't say anything about edibles."

"I haven't done shit since I became a dad," Dante said. "Trying to set an example, but also, I didn't want to give my ex anything to use against me."

"That's partly why I wanted to meet up."

"To talk about my ex?"

"Not exactly. But you're the best person for me to ask about this since I'm not tight with Miguel at all."

"Are we tight now?" Dante joked.

"Whatever, dude."

"Nah, I'm glad, though. It's hard making friends past a certain age. But this is something you can't talk to Titus or Calvin about?"

"Titus is too deep in the friend circle," he said. "And Calvin is a player."

Dante lifted his beer mug. "Heard that. Man gets more ass than a Greyhound bus."

"Basically, I'm wondering, before your divorce, if you found out your wife had a secret, would you dig into it?"

The other man stared at him, eyes wide. "What kind of a secret? Is she cheating on me? Spending—"

"No, nothing like that. Like, maybe she was in a secret society in college or something."

Or a cult.

"First off, that woman couldn't keep a secret to save her life. But if she was up in Skull and Bones or whatever, I'd likely let it be. There's a reason she didn't tell me."

That made total sense, so Trev raised his beer mug. "Thanks for the advice."

"*Was* that advice? You think Leanne's in something like that?"

Trev shrugged. "You just told me not to worry about it. I know for sure she's in a book club, and that's enough for me. By the way, mind if I come home with you tonight?"

Dante laughed. "Sir, you better pay for this meal first."

CHAPTER 22

LEANNE HARDLY LET THE DOOR close behind her husband before she fired off an emergency alert to the coven group chat.

Since everyone should be on their way over anyway, it ought to expedite the arrivals. Vanessa must've broken land-speed records because she showed up five minutes later, well ahead of the rest of the witches. She surveyed Leanne from head to toe with a puzzled look.

"You seem fine. What's the problem?"

Quickly, she summarized what'd happened after the election and what Gladys suspected that Trev had overheard, though she didn't reveal her nomination to the witch council. Stunned, the other witch dropped heavily onto the sofa, eyes wide. "That is trouble with a capital *T*. You're sure he—"

"No," Leanne cut in.

But she glanced around the apartment with a telling look. If Ethel could spy on others, a good diviner could be listening right now. Grimly determined, Vanessa pulled her supplies out of her bag, and Leanne set up her own, and they joined hands to create a quick but protective shielding spell. That should block unwanted eyes and ears for the time being, but it was a stopgap, not a solution.

She tried to stay calm but bounded to her feet, pacing anxiously. "It's not supposed to be like this. I ought to be gloating right now. Or, at the very least, subtweeting Dan Rutherford."

"There's no point," Vanessa said. "He doesn't manage his own accounts, and even if he did look, he's not sharp enough to realize you're referring to him."

"A valid point."

"Let's get back to your problem. The council might turn your man into a squirrel!"

That was a joke, but not a funny one. "Thanks for the reminder. I wasn't nearly stressed enough." She sighed and sat across from Vanessa. "For now, they have no proof, just a suspicion. I've done everything but tell Trev to deny everything and stay cool, but—"

"That's not a solution. The only reason the council hasn't already stepped in is because technically no rules were broken. Nobody informed him of anything. So they'll probably debate the issue internally before reaching a formal decision."

In such cases, generally the council ruled to protect witches. That was why the council existed, after all, but it occurred to Leanne that using magic against mundanes—even if it was to protect witches—was no different than the hunters severing a witch's connection to magic and making them forget that part of their life entirely. Actually, she thought it could be argued that it was *worse* since mundanes had largely stopped believing in magic altogether.

Witches going underground made sense before, during all the purges. If they hadn't hidden, they would've been annihilated by a fearful, superstitious populace. But it had been hundreds of years, and maybe it was time they rejoined the world officially. From certain comments Ethel had made, Leanne suspected they weren't the only supernatural community currently lurking in the shadows either.

I've been tapped to join the council. I just need to shield Trev until my term starts, then I can change things from within.

Finally, she said, "For now, I need protective charms. Nothing that will hurt another witch but strong enough to keep them away from Trev."

Vanessa raised both her perfectly shaped brows. "You're all in with this one? I thought he was *convenient*." She stretched the word out, smirking like she received dividends for messing with people.

I made her feel like I was leaving her behind. This is the least I deserve.

"I don't know, but what I *am* sure of is that he doesn't deserve to live out the remainder of his days as a chipmunk. He fell into this mess trying to help me, and frankly, he's been a godsend. He keeps Junie in check, handles my socials, plus he cooks and cleans."

"And fucks like a champion?" Vanessa guessed.

Leanne groaned. "I'm pretty sure I never said that."

"You used the words 'surprisingly awesome,' and I speak fluent Leanne."

"Whatever. Do you think the rest of the coven will help me with the protective charms? They'll be stronger if we work together."

"Damn, you're really worried about this little fixer-upper."

"Don't call him that," Leanne snapped.

Vanessa held up a hand, smiling so wide that it showed off her white teeth and her dimples. "You're in so deep that you can't even see the shore. Of course we'll help you. Even if we don't understand your choices, we've got your back."

"Are *you* feeling better?" Leanne asked.

"Much. People act like it doesn't happen, but friends tend to drift when one of them couples up. I don't want that to happen to us."

"It won't," Leanne said fiercely.

I wish I could tell her about being picked as a council member. But if Leanne broke the rules or made waves, saving Trev would become impossible. *I can't help* anyone *if I get turned into a hedgehog.* With a faint sigh, she got the glasses and set out the wine. Just in time, because the rest of the witches turned up soon after—only a minute or two separating their arrivals. It stood to reason since driving from one side of St. Claire to the other took fifteen or twenty minutes, depending on the route chosen and traffic.

Leanne greeted everyone, offering hugs to Priya and Danica. Margie, Ethel, Clem, and Kerry abstained. She could see them assessing her condo, trying to spot any changes due to Trev's influence. But he'd confined his traces to the guest room, which... was a little worrying, now that she considered it, like he didn't think his tastes and preferences belonged front and center in their lives together.

"I gather this isn't the usual meetup," Ethel said briskly. "There are some quality shields already in place. Worried about eavesdroppers, are you?"

Priya came over and took Leanne's hand. "Is it serious?"

Kerry sighed. "I thought we might get some peace after the witch hunter left town, but it seems like we go from one crisis to another these days."

Eyes narrowed, Clem scowled at Kerry. "He has a name, you know."

"Let's not fight," Margie said.

Danica agreed and added, "Why don't we hear what Leanne has to say first? Congratulations again on the city council win, by the way. I'm so excited for you."

That was the kind of thing many people *said*, but Danica was one of the few who actually meant it. Leanne spared a smile for one of the sweetest witches she knew and glanced at Vanessa, who knew her well enough to understand she was asking for a breather. She'd already told the story once, so her bestie took over from there, laying things out more succinctly than Leanne could've managed since her emotions were all over the place. Right now, it took all her composure not to fall on the floor and just start crying.

I can't handle it if anything bad happens to him because of me. I just can't.

"So, basically, you're asking us to side with you when the council might be coming for your mundane husband," Kerry said.

Priya shot her partner a look, but the other witch merely shrugged. The others wore varying expressions. Danica seemed the most sympathetic, likely because Titus and Trev were close, and if things had gone differently, it could be her in this situation instead of Leanne. Clem and Margie both wore neutral looks, while Priya seemed mildly vexed with Kerry.

Ethel broke out into unexpected laughter, aiming at Leanne with dual finger guns. "If you'd asked me to put money on who'd ask me to rebel, I wouldn't have wagered on you. Yet here we are."

"Well?" Leanne prompted. "Who's with me?"

A long silence followed, and she half expected some of the coven to walk out. Only none of them did. One by one, they started unpacking their spell components, setting up the supplies necessary to craft protective charms. Leanne's eyes filled with tears, and she tried to blink them away before they fell.

She failed. "Thank you all so much."

The rest of the witches surrounded her, hugging her from all sides, then Vanessa spoke. "We're with you. Let's save your husband."

Spending the night at Dante's place turned out to be fun as hell.

His friend lived in a two-bedroom apartment on the first floor. That was a good decision so neighbors didn't hear his kid running around. The place was decorated in early bachelor chic with rummage sale finds and strange, amateur watercolors Dante's various aunties had painted. Soon after they got back, Bettina, Dante's ex, dropped his daughter, Evonnie, off for the weekend, and she was a bundle of energy; she had just turned eight. She liked video games as much as Trev. The three of them played *Crash Team Racing* until well past her bedtime, then Trev listened from the front room as Dante read the kid a story.

It was sweet and wholesome, but a pang of sorrow went through him that Dante couldn't work it out with Evonnie's mother and that he seemed to be going nowhere with Margie as well. Sometimes people's scars made it tough for others to get close.

He sent Leanne a message to let her know where he was, not because he had to, but he didn't want her to worry.

At Dante's place tonight. His daughter is here. Cute kid.

He wanted to ask her stance on children but couldn't bring himself to do it since he wasn't even sure if they were in an actual relationship. She'd recruited him more than proposed, laying out the ways in which she'd find him useful. And he'd done his best to meet those terms and conditions, yet he stayed anxious that, at any moment, she'd say, *And scene! That's a wrap, we're good. The husband role is being eliminated, but thanks for playing. You get a hearty handshake and a waffle iron.*

Sitting on the couch at Dante's house, bad thoughts rushed at him like a freight train. He tried to use techniques his therapist had taught him to head off the spiral, but he still couldn't embrace the idea that he was worthwhile, despite months of trying. Too much self-doubt, fed and watered by his family until those seeds grew into a monstrous plant. Like the one in *Little Shop of Horrors*, it would devour him if he let it.

Eventually, Dante joined him in the living room and put a game on the TV. From what he recalled, Dante was into the Chicago Bulls, and sure enough, that was what they ended up watching. Trev paid scant attention to the players as his friend pointed at the TV and got really involved in all the calls and plays.

Titus texted later that night. Bored. Doing anything fun?

Trev: Hanging out with Dante.
Titus: What, seriously? Why didn't you invite me?

Since he'd kind of been avoiding Titus since Sarah's revelation, he had chosen to hang with Dante because their relationship was simple. It wasn't like he had been trying to hurt Titus's feelings, though, just busy processing his own. And it had been so long since he had more than one friend that he'd forgotten there could be complexities to navigate.

Sighing, he waited for a commercial break to say, "So I might have started something without meaning to."

"*Viva la revolución*," Dante said.

"In *our* group."

"Uh-oh. Lay it on me."

"Titus just asked why he wasn't invited to hang out with us tonight. He asked what I'm doing, probably because Danica's with Leanne at book club."

Dante nodded. "You don't have to tell me. Margie's there too. Though I wouldn't be seeing her this weekend anyway. We don't hook up when I have Evonnie."

"How often—never mind. It's not my business." Trev changed his mind about digging into his friend's relationship, if it could be called that.

I can't even sort my own shit out.

"I know what you were about to ask, and...once a month, if that. Usually when Chris has something on and Evonnie is with her mom."

"But Titus?"

"That's *your* problem, dude."

Sighing, Trev decided honesty was the best policy, so he wrote: We had stuff to talk about, and I asked to crash on his couch since Leanne's hosting book club tonight.

Titus: My couch isn't good enough for you anymore?

Trev: Sorry if you thought we were exclusive. I can't be tied down to one couch.

Dante leaned over to read his screen and broke into quiet laughter. "Are you flirting with him or what? But for real, it *is* hard to bind somebody to a couch, unless it's one with removable cushions and wooden armrests."

Trev regarded him with equal measures amusement and trepidation. "Is that personal experience? And...does this look like flirting? We always joke around this way."

"Honestly—and don't take this the wrong way—but I had a bet going with Miguel and Calvin."

Trev tilted his head, wary but curious. "About what?"

"We thought you and Titus would end up together."

Trev laughed. "Were you shipping us?"

"Maybe a little," Dante mumbled.

"Did you lose money?"

"Twenty bucks. Miguel bet you'd both find other people, so that lucky bastard is up forty dollars because of Danica and Leanne."

From all angles, Trev turned the idea over. "I wouldn't have been opposed to it, but I don't think Titus was ever into me that way. We're friends, and for a long while, I suspect he felt sorry for me. I was..." *No need to sugarcoat it.* "I was a mess for years, dude."

"You had some stuff to work out. When relationships end, there's always one person who takes it hard, usually the one getting left."

Trev nodded because there was no arguing any of that. "You're a wise man."

"If only my ex believed that."

"I never asked about the divorce when it went down, but if you want to talk about…" Trev trailed off because maybe that was intrusive.

"There isn't a whole lot to say. Bettina and I had only been dating a few months when we found out about Evonnie. We weren't in love, but I proposed because it was the right thing to do. Bets said yes for the same reason. But…you can't hold a relationship together with that. We're not compatible at *all*. She'd pick at the way I wash the dishes. I couldn't stand her crap all over the bathroom. There was nothing dramatic about the ending. We just realized twenty years of bickering would hurt Evonnie more than an amicable breakup while she was a baby."

"That's a mature way to look at it."

"The hardest part is being divorced already. I feel like people look at me different when I'm dating now. One failed marriage, check. Already got a kid, check. Without knowing me, they make all kinds of judgments about my character. I'm already working against a bias." Dante tried to smile, but it didn't reach his eyes.

"Who knows, you and I could end up in the same boat," Trev said, trying to take a light tone toward it.

Evidently, it didn't work, judging by Dante's expression. "Did something happen between you and Leanne? For you to be talking that way."

"I don't know," Trev said. "Life comes at you fast. I do want to believe things will work out, but I can't fully trust they will."

"Well, whatever happens, man, I'm here for you." Dante patted his shoulder and went back to watching the game.

Trev's phone vibrated again. Stop trying to make me jealous. But seriously, I'm glad you're connecting with Dante. You're awesome, and lots of people care about you.

Trev took comfort in that assertion even as he fought the certainty that the rising wind presaged rough weather, and this was the calm before the storm.

CHAPTER 23

IT WAS 3:00 A.M. WHEN most of the coven departed, finally satisfied with the superior spell work that should protect Trev from all encroachment.

After everyone else left, Leanne said to Vanessa, "Why don't you stay?"

"Sleepover?"

"Sleepover!" she confirmed.

They put on Vanessa's favorite show, but neither of them paid much attention to it as Leanne listened to the family stuff Vanessa had been dealing with on her own. It wasn't like the other witch needed her to solve anything, but before Leanne took a detour, they had been each other's first stop with news and complications. She had no plans for that to change, even though she was married now. *Sort of. Mostly?*

"Thanks for listening," Vanessa said quietly when she finished venting.

"Always. What are you planning to tell your folks?"

Vanessa's father owned a regional restaurant chain, and her parents had been pressing her to move back to Atlanta and take over the company. She was currently working in graphic design while putting together enough sculptures for an exhibition, and she had zero interest in business management. Sighing, she shook her head.

"Hell if I know. Dad doesn't understand why I can't do my 'little art projects' while working for the family business, but it'll eat up all my bandwidth, and I won't have the energy to chase my own dream. I'll be too busy living his."

"I can relate. I still haven't decided if I'm meeting my bio dad yet."

Vanessa shook her head. "You're out of your damn mind. Get in, get out, get paid."

"You really think I should?" Leanne asked.

"I don't understand how this is a question. He was a deadbeat your whole life, now he's scared because his number is up, and even a wicked old witch can't be sure our views on eternal life are correct. He's trying to hedge his bets in case the mundanes are on to something. Man wants to clear his conscience, I say let him. It's practically a charitable act."

"When you put it that way—"

The keypad at the front door beeped. She hadn't realized it had gotten so late, but here it was, well into the morning, and they hadn't slept a wink.

Trev greeted Vanessa warmly, asking, "You look great. How've you been?"

"I'd spend an hour filling you in, but then I'd be too tired to drive home. Somebody told me you're an amazing cook, when am I getting an invite to judge for myself?"

"Anytime you want. If you give me your number, we can set it up."

Leanne smiled as the two most important people in her life swapped contact info. "Sure you don't want to stay for breakfast?" she asked.

Vanessa shook her head. "We snacked all night long. Only thing I want to do now is crash like I'm in college again."

Smiling, she headed out, and Leanne finally felt like things were fully okay between them again. She didn't want to be the one who only showed up when she needed something. Trev came over and hugged her; she snuggled against his chest, realizing belatedly just how much the long night had taken out of her. The last time her eyes felt this grainy, she'd waited all night to be first in the doors at Bloomingdale's in Chicago because some college friends convinced her that would be an awesome way to spend the day after Thanksgiving.

"Did you have fun?" he asked.

Was she imagining it, or was there a certain gravity to the question? *Nah, my imagination is running away with me.*

"We did. Vigorous book discussion, followed by gossip about our partners. I had so many entertaining things to talk about."

Trev smiled like he hoped he was in on the joke, not the butt of it. His family really had a lot to answer for. *I should hex them too.* Leanne wished she could claim she wasn't the type, but in all honesty, she could be petty as hell. Just look at how she'd hexed Mayor Anderson right before his big interview. She smiled at the delightful memory, wishing she could've seen for herself whether he'd developed hives or welts.

Yeah, no two ways about it. If the rest of the coven is nice, I'm extra witchy. No regrets, no apologies.

"Sounds like an awesome time," Trev said.

"It was. Before I forget, I got you a present."

"What?" He froze with a comic expression of disbelief. "But it's not my birthday. Or Christmas. Or—"

"It doesn't have to be a holiday for me to treat you," she cut in.

"Wow. Okay. I'm ready."

She felt a little guilty calling this a present. They'd repurposed a necklace she already owned, one she'd received from Junie as gift but didn't much like because it wasn't her style. She preferred delicate chains and small pendants, while this was a polished stone on a leather strap. It would suit Trev much better, and the tourmaline had been receptive to the layered protective charm. Now this pendant would repel all but the strongest magic, and if the council meddled with Leanne's spell, the breaking of it would signal her that Trev was in trouble.

The leather strap was dark brown; the stone was deep green. When she picked it up, the magic purred against her palm like a kitten. She placed the "gift" in his cupped hands. He regarded the necklace with a silent question in his hazel eyes.

"Do you like it?" she asked.

"It looks like a…healing crystal?"

"Something like that. It's supposed protect you and bring you luck. But mainly, I want you to feel it against your heart and think of me throughout the day."

His wary expression warmed into a smile. "That's so sweet, Butterfly."

Immediately, he dropped it over his head and tucked it underneath his shirt, allowing her to relax a bit. Then she walked over and hugged him.

"So glad you like it. You don't wear a lot of jewelry, so I wasn't sure—"

"I love it. Between this and the ring, I'm all set."

Maybe she shouldn't but... *No, I have to.* "It's important to me that you wear the necklace. Don't take it off, okay?"

A frown creased his brows together, and he eased her back in his arms to study her face. "Not even to shower?"

"The stone is waterproof, and the strap can be replaced."

"Okay. I'll wear the necklace 24/7." He paused, worrying his lower lip with his teeth, then finally asked, "Are you ever planning to explain...anything?"

He definitely knows something is up.

"When I can. When it's safe."

When I've changed things from within.

Even with the shield against divination in place, it wasn't safe to say more. The work that lay ahead was daunting as hell, as she now had *two* systems to transform, but why the hell would she think small? If she succeeded, it would shift the way all witches lived, and it would change what witches were allowed to achieve as well. If Leanne had her way, one day she'd run for mayor as a witch...and win.

But first...

"Okay. I'll accept that. And be patient." But Trev's frown lingered, making it clear he wouldn't be content with her vague assurances forever.

Frankly, in his shoes, she'd probably already be asking dangerous questions. *Hell, in his situation, I'd probably already be a squirrel.*

"Thank you," she said from the bottom of the heart she would've once claimed was untouchable.

"You're my wife. I trust you. And while I'm in that ballpark, I feel like I should tell you before you hear it from someone else. In fact, I should have told you much sooner, but frankly, we had so much going on that I forgot."

Her whole body iced over. "What?"

"When I met Dante a while back, I ran into Sarah, my ex. I wasn't *trying* to see her, it just happened, and we didn't talk long. But—"

"Sweetheart."

"What?"

"I don't care if you ran into your ex." Her whole body practically felt featherlight with relief. This was such a huge, steaming pile of nothing that it didn't even deserve a mention.

"Really?" For some reason, a flicker of disappointment darkened his eyes.

Wait, is he upset I'm not jealous? That's so cute.

"Because I trust you," she explained. "And because I know you want no part of her after how things ended."

"That's so true," he said, brightening visibly.

"Now, if you tell me somebody was trying to get your number, then I might have to investigate and pull some hair," Leanne added, mostly to revel in how he perked up.

"I did get a few looks that night," Trev said. "Not near as many as Dante, to be candid. But once they noticed the ring, they moved on."

Smiling, she traced a fingertip around the simple silver ring he'd chosen in Vegas. "It is clearly part of a wedding set."

"I know. I love that."

"Wearing half of a wedding ring set?"

Smiling slightly, he clarified, "Being married to you."

"It's working out great for me too."

He pulled her with him onto the couch and settled into a snuggle. "This is the life. Let's not move for the rest of the day."

"But—"

"Must you crush my modest dreams?"

"We'll need to eat. And pee. Eventually."

Trev laughed. "There you go again with your relentless logic."

"Are you misquoting *Futurama* in my vicinity?"

"Actually, yes, but I'm surprised that you know that."

"That's from Fry's ex, right?" Leanne asked.

"Got it in one. Let's watch cartoons all day, like real functional adults," he suggested.

She considered the offer then made a strong counter. "Only if I'm allowed to eat ice cream out of the carton."

"You drive a hard bargain. I'll get the spoons."

The sheer easy joy of being with him buoyed her up like she was full of helium. Trev delivered her favorite gourmet ice cream from the freezer and cuddled up to her, feeding her bites as they queued up a cartoon marathon for the afternoon. She'd never been with anyone like him, who didn't ask for anything or make demands, as if just breathing the same air was enough.

And she feared down to her bones that such precious, simple happiness couldn't last.

A ringing phone dragged Trev awake a few days later.

It's mine.

He answered with a groggy, "What?" without looking at the screen.

Junie spoke so fast that it was a little hard to follow. "Sorry to bother you so early, but I thought Leanne should know. Her dad is in the hospital, and it looks like he doesn't have long. If she wants to meet him…"

Suddenly, he was wide awake, gazing at his sleeping wife, wishing he didn't have to dump this on her like a bucket of icy water. But she'd said that if the old man made it until after the election, she'd decide then. It was time. So he whispered, "I'll let her know. Text me the information about where he is."

Almost as soon as they hung up, his cell vibrated with the name and address of the hospital, along with the room number. Bracing himself, he went to wake her, but her eyes opened on their own, and she lay staring up at him, her eyes too bright. She reached up to touch his cheek as if he was the one who needed comforting.

"Looks like I'm destined to do this, huh?"

"Do what?"

"Play out the sad goodbye scene for a father I don't even know."

"That's up to you. If you choose not to go, I get it."

"No, let me shower, and then we'll take off. How far is it?"

Quickly, he checked as she got out of bed. "Looks like a couple of hours, the other side of Chicago in the northern suburbs."

"Okay. Will you drive?"

"Absolutely. I showered last night, so I just need to get dressed."

He did that in a hurry while she went to the bathroom, and then he went to the kitchen to make her an omelet and toast. The coffee was ready by the time she came out, looking preternaturally perfect as always. Though he'd only lived with Sarah for a short time, he knew it wasn't normal how fast Leanne got ready. Her makeup always looked flawless, and it should've taken at least half an hour to do her hair. As ever, he didn't mention it, except to say:

"You look beautiful. Hungry?"

"Maybe I shouldn't be under the circumstances, but I am. Thanks, hon."

Frankly, he envied her a little. If something happened to Wade, he doubted Tanner would even call him. His mom probably wouldn't either. For them, it was so easy to write him off, glad Leanne had shown up to take Trev off their hands. Now they could focus on the good son. He forced himself to let go of that bitterness. Sometimes a tree had to be pruned to live, and that was how he felt about putting his family behind him. Trying to earn their approval might have eventually killed him.

"I'll head down first and start the car, get it warmed up for you," he said since he'd finished eating first.

She stood abruptly and clutched him in a worryingly tight hug. "I don't deserve you."

"What?"

"You're always doing stuff like that without being asked. You're the kindest person I've ever been with, and I…" She drew a breath, swallowing whatever she'd almost said. "Now's not the time, dammit. Not when we're in a rush."

"For what, thank-you sex?" he asked in confusion.

"That would be fun, but no. Are you wearing the necklace?"

"Every day."

Her fixation on that worried him a little, but if it gave her peace of mind, the pendant didn't bother him. In fact, he liked knowing how much it meant to her. It wasn't a ridiculous assumption to imagine that he mattered as well, right? Sometimes it felt like they truly were married, like forever and all, but the fear of being discarded lingered. They'd agreed to keep things flexible, which meant either one of them could call it quits at any time.

That's like trying to build a house on quicksand.

Ten minutes was long enough to warm up the car. He had it toasty when she burst out of the building, practically running, even in heels. Leanne skidded on an icy patch on the pavement, and he half came out of the car, even knowing he was too damn far away to save her. Yet she caught herself, slipped a few steps, and kept coming. That was Leanne, graceful and self-sufficient even in the middle of a stumble.

She said she doesn't deserve me, but it's the other way around.

He reached across to open her door for her, and she slid into the car, breathless, in a burst of nearly winter wind. "Go, go, go, they're after us," she joked.

Sometimes she was like this, charming and silly, and he would've kissed her, except they were on their way for her to meet her dying father for the first—and probably last—time. So it didn't fit the mood. Instead, he touched her cheek with a chilly hand then mapped the route on his phone and put the car in reverse. Leanne buckled in as Trev backed out of the parking spot and passed through the checkpoint at the gate.

"Do you want to talk?" he asked.

"About what?"

"Anything."

"You already know most of it. Junie wasn't great at being a single mom. I pretty much raised myself. I earned my own money from the time I was eleven or so. I took a course at the hospital in CPR and babysat neighborhood kids. Frankly, their parents shouldn't have trusted me. I was a kid myself, but..." She lifted a shoulder.

"You grew up fast."

"I had to," she said bluntly. "Because Junie wouldn't. As for my dad, you know as much as I do."

"Then, if you don't feel like—"

"I didn't say that. Actually, I owe you an explanation about how I ended up with two divorces behind me when I'm not even forty."

"Only if you feel like telling me," Trev said, though he'd frankly love to know.

It was one of the things he'd wondered most about. Who were the husbands who preceded him, and why did they fail? And how could he avoid their mistakes? But he didn't have the courage to ask when he wasn't even sure of his own footing with Leanne.

"Today we have nothing but time while we drive. Up front, it was my fault, both times. Garrett traveled a lot for work, and it never left my head—the fact that he could do whatever he wanted as soon as he left home. I accused him of having one foot out of the door, but it was me who didn't trust him. I asked for a divorce, but I did it..." She sighed. "As a preemptive strike, because I knew...well, I *suspected* he'd get tired of dealing with my shit."

"So you left first." Based on what he knew of her, that made sense.

"Exactly. With Malcolm, it was a lot calmer. Looking back, I don't even know if we loved each other. But he made a compelling case. He said we looked good together, we made *sense*. He painted an enticing picture, and I thought I could manage my end, but then he got a promotion, and they assigned him overseas. There was no doubt in his mind that I should pack my shit and move to Japan. He didn't even ask if I wanted to."

"He left because you wouldn't move?" Trev asked, quietly appalled.

"I mean, Malcolm wanted me on his arm. He had the big-money career, so it made sense, according to him."

"For you to upend your life?"

"I disagreed, and we got divorced. I—"

"You said the divorces were your fault, and maybe I agree with you about the first one, but the second? Don't even think it, Butterfly. Malcolm sounds like a prick."

She shifted in her seat, her eyes sparkling so brightly that he struggled to focus on the road. "You know what? You're right."

CHAPTER 24

AT SOME POINT, LEANNE MUST'VE drifted off.

She woke as Trev pulled into the hospital parking lot a couple hours later. That wasn't like her at all. She generally preferred to be alert and in control, but he made it easy to let her guard down. She lacked the mental energy to focus on figuring out why with the white building looming. He circled past the emergency entrance to the one allotted for visitors before pulling up in front of the automatic doors.

"I'll catch up," he said.

She took a breath, nodded, and slid out of the car. Reflexively, she smoothed her tailored pencil skirt and checked to be sure her blouse was still neatly tucked in. There was no need to check her hair and makeup because even if she was a bit rumpled from the nap, the glamour spell should cover any minor dishevelment. *Unless they already hate me. In which case I'll look even worse than I actually do.* Nothing she could do about that, however.

Leanne paused at the check-in desk to register as a visitor. They took her ID and gave her a lanyard with a number on it before allowing her to pass beyond the lobby. Security was tighter than she remembered, but the precautions made sense. Nerves made her hands tremble as she pressed the call button; she tried to calm down as she got in the elevator, but the closer she got to this meeting, the worse she felt.

I don't even want to do this. Why am I?

Maybe the simplest answer was closure. To put a face to the witch who'd fathered her then thrown Junie away. When Leanne thought about it that way, she wanted to hug her mother. She must've thought she'd found the one, since she'd chosen to get pregnant. Or knowing Junie, maybe she'd imagined a baby would guarantee that her lover stuck around?

If I was a bargaining chip, that tactic failed spectacularly.

The elevator doors opened, revealing a white-and-beige hallway. Every item on the floor was carefully muted, no bright colors, and even the pictures on the walls showed sepia colors behind the glass. The furniture was all metal or vinyl, easily sterilized—impossible to forget this was a hospital where stuff might get spattered with bodily fluids. A nurse in white shoes hurried past Leanne as she stepped into the hallway.

Her father was in room 514, down past the nurses' station. The two at the desk were busy comparing notes and didn't speak as she walked past, her heels clicking on the shiny tiled floor. As hospitals went, this one was nice, likely expensive as well. A man stood in the hallway, shoulders hunched and head bowed. From this distance, she couldn't tell much about him, other than that he was well-dressed, dark hair threaded with silver. Magic trickled from him, likely intensified by the grief of his—their—father's imminent death.

The sweep of it felt...familiar in a way that disturbed her. Before, only Junie felt like this to Leanne, but now she had this stranger echoing her energy signature. He heard the click of her heels and straightened, spinning to face her with his features set. No smile, no scowl. Just a blankness she couldn't interpret.

"You must be Leanne," he said.

"I am. Under the circumstances, I won't say it's nice to meet you."

"I never imagined I had another sister," he said with a visible air of exhaustion. "You probably have no idea who I am. Brian Seaton." He didn't extend a hand for her to shake, and thankfully, he made no attempt to hug her either.

"That makes you my..."

"Oldest brother. I'm fifty-four."

"You're only four years younger than my mother." That...was a regrettable thing to blurt.

He flinched. "Yes, I was seventeen when..."

Your father and my mother had an affair.

"Is everyone else inside?" she asked, rather than prolong the most awkward encounter of her entire life.

"They are. It's just my brother, Paul, and my sister, Ruth. Our partners aren't here at the moment. We thought it best if we didn't overwhelm you with new faces."

"I appreciate that." She stepped forward, moved to pull the door open, but Brian stayed her with a brief touch on her arm.

"Dad doesn't have long. I suspect he's been holding on for you. I don't blame you for not coming sooner—it's so much to take in—but he's suffered a lot the past couple months. I understand if you're not kindly disposed toward him. I doubt I would be either. But it would mean a lot to the rest of the family if you could *say* you forgive him, even if it's lie."

"To let him go peacefully?" she guessed.

Brian. Paul. Ruth. Her siblings had names now. So did her elusive father, Dennis Seaton. She stared at the paper placard outside his door, the man Junie had loved and failed to keep beside her, the one who had chucked them both. She raised her face, wishing she felt nothing—that tears didn't sting the back of her eyes.

Just then Trev strode up and registered the scene. He hugged her immediately. "You got this. I'll be right here if you need me."

Bracing, she separated from him, opened the hospital room door, and went inside. The smell hit her first—sickness overlaid with cleaning products, a faint mustiness that no amount of lemon solvent could scrub away. Paul stood by the window, staring out at the parking lot; he appeared to be the youngest—in his midforties, which still put him seven or eight years older than Leanne. He resembled his brother, Brian, though Paul lacked the same distinguished air. The woman, Ruth, had bright-blond hair that came from a bottle, and she wore plenty of makeup, unsuccessfully trying to conceal dark circles and pallor that came from spending all her time at the hospital.

More magic washed over her, much fainter from Paul and Ruth. Realization hit her like a ton of bricks. *They've been feeding him their energy to keep him going until I got here.* It was no coincidence Dennis Seaton had managed to hold on while waiting for Leanne. His two youngest children had given themselves over to fulfilling that last request, and this display of filial devotion choked her up a bit. While he might've been shitty to Junie and

Leanne, he must have been a much better dad to Ruth and Paul—that they'd go this far. The council disapproved of witches sharing magic in this fashion, as it skirted perilously close to necromancy.

Yikes. I must have that in my lineage as well.

Despite Ruth and Paul's best efforts, Dennis Seaton looked like he had one foot over the threshold already. His skin was waxy and thin, bruises up and down his arms from bloodwork and IV tubes being moved. Witches tended to live a long time, as they were immune to certain human ailments, but other illnesses were unavoidable. She couldn't see much of his face with the oxygen mask covering the bottom part. His eyes were closed, and Leanne had a hard time imagining him healthy and alert. His magic fluttered within him, a dying trickle that filled her with sorrow for never knowing him when he was hale, when he might've taught her about spell work or some important father-daughter truth she'd never learn.

"Dad." Ruth pressed his hand. "She's here. Wake up. You wanted to meet her."

At first, there was no reaction. Leanne wondered if she'd left it too late. Then her father's eyes opened, a weak and watery gray with blue flecks and darker circles around each iris. *I have his eyes.* That absurd thought shook her. An unsteady breath shuddered out of her as he raised a shaky hand, reaching toward her. She didn't want this, didn't want any of it; it was too bittersweet to say farewell at their first meeting.

I never had a dad, and now he's dying.

But she stepped forward anyway, taking his bony fingers in hers. He was so cold that she nearly let go, but he held tight.

"Sorry. Sorry. I..." A coughing fit took him, then he managed to say, "My fault. Sorry."

Granting Brian's request was nothing, she realized. "It's okay," she said. "I have a good life. My husband is outside waiting for me, I have a degree in communications with a minor in political science, and I was just elected to the city council in St. Claire. You can go with my blessing. I don't hold anything against you."

Ruth let out a little sob, and Paul turned from the window with an incredulous look. Brian made some vague gesture preventing the younger brother from articulating his skepticism. Leanne covered the old man's hand with her other one and held on as he gasped for breath. A single tear trickled down his papery cheek, then the machines went wild.

Five minutes later, Leanne lost the father she'd never known.

———

It didn't take long before Leanne staggered out, pale, trembling, and shell-shocked. Trev caught her when she stumbled, and the rest of the family emerged from the hospital room, the woman weeping openly while her brothers tried to comfort her. Hospital staff ran in, but death could only be delayed for so long.

He had no idea what the hell he was supposed to do in these circumstances. They couldn't expect Leanne to help with funeral plans, right? Would they expect her to attend? Quietly, he took his wife's hand and tried to convey support while people whose names he didn't even know cried in front of him. The oldest brother conferred with the hospital staff in a low tone, presumably making arrangements.

Leanne squeezed Trev's hand. When he leaned closer, she whispered, "Should we go? I have no idea what I'm doing here."

Before they could make a break for it, one of her brothers strode over. "I just want to thank you again for making the trip. You did everything—"

"Except show up on time," the other man sneered. "You're not even part of our family! Your mother seduced our dad, and yet *you're* the only one he cared about seeing at the end? Do you have any idea—"

"Paul," the older one cut in sharply.

While Trev wasn't necessarily Junie's biggest fan either, it wasn't fair to blame a twenty-year-old girl for the choices a grown man had made. Plus, he felt the way Leanne recoiled, and hell no, he wasn't having that. "I get that you're upset," he said coldly. "But my wife did your family a favor. If your grief means you can't be civil, then we're done."

He pulled Leanne with him toward the elevators, ignoring the older man's attempts to get him to slow down. Finally, she tugged on Trev's hand. At least she looked amused now rather than shaky. He'd never seen her so uncertain before, and damn, it nearly did him in.

"I didn't know you had that in you," she said.

"Too much?"

"Hell no, it was hot. I thought you might even punch Paul."

"Is that the younger one's name?"

"Yep. Brian is the oldest, Ruth is the middle one, I think, and Paul is the spoiled baby."

"That tracks, according to his behavior. Think he's mad because he's not the youngest anymore?" Trev asked.

Leanne lifted a shoulder in a careless half shrug that spoke volumes about how invested she was in this family drama. "Who knows? I'm out anyway."

"You don't have to be," Brian said.

He'd managed to catch up to them at the elevators. "I apologize for Paul. It's been the hardest for him. He took a leave of absence to stay with Dad, and he's seen the most of..."

His deterioration?

Trev couldn't bring himself to say that aloud, but it probably applied. If Paul had been watching his old man weaken day by day, it explained his hostility at least. Leanne waved a hand, dismissing the explanation.

"I didn't expect any of you would be happy to meet me," she said bluntly.

Unexpectedly, Brian said, "I am, though. You have nieces and nephews if you're interested in meeting them. If you have kids, they'll have cousins. It's up to you, of course. If you'd rather not pursue a relationship with us, I get it."

"Do I have to decide now?" she asked.

Brian shook his head. "Take your time. You're welcome to attend the funeral."

"It seems hypocritical. I didn't know him."

When Leanne glanced at him, Trev said, "It's up to you. I'll go with you if you want to."

"We'll see," she said.

Trev knew her well enough to read her misgivings about this whole situation, so he put himself between her and the brother she didn't know if she wanted. "We'll let you know. Sorry for your loss."

The man took the hint and let Trev guide his wife into the elevator. Before they shifted down even one floor, he tucked her against his side, and she buried her head in his chest. Her whole body shook, so he stroked her back, holding her as they left the hospital. It was cold outside, everything brown and lifeless.

"I don't know how I'm supposed to feel," she finally said. "I keep waiting for it to hit me, but I feel more like I just opened an emergency exit door on a plane. Like, it's always a possibility in the safety talk, but you never expect that you'll actually have to *do* it."

"However you feel, it's okay. There's no manual. It seems like Brian is open to having another sister—"

Leanne broke into frenetic laughter. "He's practically old enough to be my dad, hon. He's fifty-four. Our father was like eighty or something."

Quickly, Trev did the math. *Holy shit.* That meant the dirty fucker had been in his forties while messing around with Junie, a girl less than half his age. It probably wouldn't help to say so, but... *This is so messed up. What am I supposed to say?*

"Junie sure did favor the ashen ferrets," he said.

"What?" His wife stared for a few seconds then started laughing again.

As he walked her back to the car, he explained the silver fox/ ashen ferret thing, and finally, Leanne's smile seemed natural, less tinged by the awfulness of everything. "That's so Junie. I hope you don't mind my copping that."

"Nah, I did the same. It's so quotable."

She narrowed her pretty eyes with their ridiculous lashes, as if visualizing. "I can see the memes already. 'Why silver fox when you can ashen ferret?'"

Relieved she seemed to be feeling better, he opened her car door and put his hand on her head as she got in. "Are you hungry? I suspect you didn't finish your breakfast."

"I could eat."

"Let's stop somewhere on the way home?"

"Sure. Am I awful for not being devastated? For not really wanting to see any of them again? My main impulse is avoidance. I know Brian was trying to make me feel welcome, but I really just feel...pressed. I was minding my business, living my life, and—"

"No. You're not awful." He could only tell the truth. "Meeting you is the best thing that's ever happened to me. And I won five hundred bucks on a scratch-off lotto ticket in college."

She pretended to rock sideways in shock as he started the car. "Five hundred dollars? *I'm* better than winning the lottery? Seriously?"

Yeah, she was joking, but he wasn't. "Seriously. You saved my life. I doubt I would've been able to climb out of the hole I was in if you hadn't reached for my hand first."

Leanne bit her lip and shifted in her seat, glancing away with what Trev thought looked like a guilty expression. "I wasn't trying to do that. I just wanted to bang you."

"That's where it started," he said as he put the car in gear. "But would you agree it's not where we are now?"

He held his breath, waiting for her response. *We're more than roommates who have sex, right? We're building a life together.*

She changed the subject instead of addressing his words. "Don't get serious on me, hon. I've had enough of that today."

The pain startled him, blazing in the center of his chest so fiercely that he rubbed it back and forth, trying to soothe it away. Trev swallowed hard. "Right. Sorry. Find us a restaurant on the way home. Whatever you feel like eating will be fine."

What was I thinking? She's never said she has feelings for me. I'm...convenient. I tick all the boxes, right? I just need to keep quiet and play the part. His wife had all kinds of secrets, and it looked like she had no intention of ever letting him in. After talking to Dante, he'd been trying not to be curious, not to wonder, or cross the line, but he was damn sick and tired of feeling precarious, like one wrong move and she'd be out the door.

Unfortunately, he'd caught feelings, and he ached so bad because he wanted more; he wanted...everything.

CHAPTER 25

FOR THE PAST MONTH, THINGS had been different.

Leanne couldn't put her finger on it, but...something was up with Trev. Sure, he did the same work in terms of household chores, but he was more...remote, responding politely but not warmly. And he didn't come to bed when she did. He spent more time in the guest room gaming if he wasn't working online, then he'd sometimes crash on that bed.

When she'd asked about it, he'd said, "I don't want to bother you."

She'd started to say that him coming to bed could never be a bother, but then it had occurred to her that he might *prefer* that distance. It wasn't like they had a regular marriage, and she couldn't demand cuddles as part of the agreement. So she kept her mouth shut and tried to pretend it didn't upset her. Her relationships always had an expiration date, and this one had lasted longer than most. It wasn't like she'd thought she could keep him around forever.

Maybe it's time to let him go?

By now, he was likely earning enough to get his own place;

he was doing simple websites in addition to his social media stuff, but dear gods, it hurt to think of him packing his stuff. The condo would be so empty without him, and—

I will miss him so much.

Just the mere prospect of him leaving swept her at the knees, and she crawled into the closet to hide because she couldn't stop these tears. The last time she'd wept like this had been at the coven meeting—when she'd been so scared the council might take Trev.

She hadn't reacted this way even after watching her father die. Instead, she'd thrown herself into writing proposals in preparation for assuming her seat on the city council and built up some business for her freelance PR and marketing work. As she sobbed silently into a pile of clean laundry she hadn't gotten around to putting away, she could no longer deny how much she'd invested in this relationship without even realizing it.

She didn't even know if it was *safe* for him to leave. The council had been observing Trev for the past few months, but if he knew anything, he wasn't letting on. It was almost Christmas, and they'd even decorated a tree together, a small one she'd bought on impulse that had to be assembled from the box. It had lights on it, and she'd gone shopping at the holiday bazaar for ornaments, hardly aware that she'd begun to believe they'd need these things for next year and maybe the year after as well.

But...he's already checking out.

Witches didn't share the religious celebration, and they honored another holiday calendar altogether, but Leanne secretly enjoyed the lights and food and decorations for this time of year. So many things could be improved by adding peppermint. She tried to stop the tears by thinking of other things, but they just kept falling, fat and hot and heartbroken.

Finally, the question surfaced, the one she always tried to bury like a body in the back of her mind. *Why am I not enough? Not for Junie. Not for Garrett. Or Malcolm.* Or anyone she'd dated in between. There had never been anyone who lasted, who fought her self-imposed isolation and held on with both hands, who made her believe she was worth keeping.

In time, she cried herself out and silently blessed the glamour spell that would hide these ravages. Leanne put the laundry away, apart from the T-shirt she'd been crying into. And only then did she notice it was the one Trev had worn the night he showed up to her first speech. Shivering, she hugged it to her chest, feeling ridiculous and juvenile. If she was as brave as she pretended she was, she'd just fucking *ask* him what was wrong.

But his answer might scar her for life.

With determination, she tucked the tearstained shirt in the hamper and opened the closet door. Thankfully, Trev wasn't home. He was riding his bike, something he did a lot lately.

When Vanessa texted, she seized on it like a lifeline. Not busy, what's up?

Don't forget the winter solstice festival. Can you get away?

Shit. She had almost forgotten, between her distant husband, the older brother who kept texting her, her political career, coven stuff, and her secret seat on the witch council. Sometimes she felt like pulling her hair out because too many things were happening at once, and she didn't know how to deal with any of it.

I'll be there.

After checking the calendar, she realized it was happening tomorrow night. She hadn't been involved in the planning this year, as Gladys's coven tended to take over big community events. And she wished with all her heart that she could share it with Trev, demonstrate how amazing it was to be a witch, all the little secrets and joys he could never experience.

And then, it was like a switch flipped in her head. Or her heart. Maybe both.

I want that so much. I want it with him.

When she started her term on the witch council in January—ironically the same as the city council—she would lobby relentlessly for witches to come forward. In this day and age, the secrecy was both ridiculous and unnecessary, and it impacted quality of life for those with nonmagical partners. That word was better than "mundane." Not being able to do magic didn't make people lesser, just different. Leanne couldn't speak eight languages even if she could cast a spell, nor could she bake delicious cinnamon rolls.

Closing her eyes, she tried her best to banish her fears. There were so many now, fluttering in her brain like the endearment Trev used for her had multiplied, butterflies everywhere. Terror that he'd leave her before she could sort things out, or worse, be taken by the council, worry that she couldn't achieve the goals that would allow her to live as she wished.

I want him to stay. If Trev's having second thoughts, I'll change his mind.

When he got home an hour later, she had food ready. Nothing fancy, but judging by his surprised smile, he appreciated it. Then she hugged him, the way he used to do to her and buried her face in his shoulder.

"What's wrong, Butterfly?"

Wow. He hasn't called me that in weeks. Didn't realize how much I wanted to hear it.

"Nothing. I just missed you."

"You did?" He pulled back slightly to study her face. "Have you been crying?"

Leanne tried not to display her shock, but she had no idea how successful that was. "How do you know? I put a cold compress on my eyes," she added hastily, because it wasn't like she could admit her face should be layered with the usual protective glamour.

"That's a yes," he said.

Be brave, she told herself.

"It seems like something is bothering you. I miss...us."

"Us?" Trev repeated the word with an expression she couldn't read. "The last time I tried to talk about that, you shut it down. Hard."

"What—*oh*." He must be referring to that day in the car. Leanne winced, realizing how hurt he must be if he'd withdrawn over that. "I didn't mean *ever*, hon. But...my dad had literally just died. Is it so surprising I didn't want to—"

"You could have brought it up," he cut in. "At any point. But it's been *weeks*. How am I supposed to feel about that? Are you sure you're not just trying to patch things up so I won't give the wrong vibe when we start attending public events next year?"

She drew back, stunned. "Do you really think I'd do that?"

He shrugged. "I don't know you that well, do I? You won't *let* me."

———————————

Trev knew he was hurting Leanne, but he couldn't stop talking.

He'd kept a lid on this shit for too long. And all those nights he'd slept in the guest room, when she never came looking for him? Not even once. That hurt so bad, he could barely breathe. It underscored the fact that she didn't really care about him. She needed a warm body, someone capable of wearing the right clothes, and he'd been...available.

Not just available. Desperate, frankly.

Come on, tell me I matter. Apologize. Say you want this to work as much as I do. Please, Butterfly. Don't send me out into the cold.

"I guess we need some time," she said finally. "I'll stay with Vanessa for a while. She has a spare room. I'll tell her..." She paused, apparently unsure what to say.

"This is your place. I'm the one who should leave."

He packed in a hurry, hardly looking at what he was grabbing, then he headed for the door. All the while, he kept hoping like hell that she'd stop him, say the magic words, but only silence followed him out. Trev went in a rush, feeling like the ground was crumbling beneath his feet. All that time, and this was how it ended.

Fuck. I don't even have the right to be mad. She never lied to me. Not once. I just wished...ah, fuck this.

Dante lived the closest, but it would be rude as hell to show up uninvited. He texted first, a succinct—I could use somewhere to stay for a bit.

Dante: I'm home. Evonnie's not here, there's a princess room with your name on it.

Smiling hurt a little, but he rode over with his bag slung over his back like he was Santa instead of a fuckup with nowhere to be for the holidays. Dante didn't even make him knock; the man opened the door and gave him a hug.

"Fighting with Leanne?"

"Yeah," Trev said, because the truth was too much to explain, even to a friend.

"Give her a day or two to cool off, then apologize. If you want the relationship to work, it doesn't matter who's right."

Trev couldn't bring himself to admit he'd stormed out like a drama king because she'd pressed suddenly and unexpectedly on the wound he'd been hiding to the best of his ability. Until he couldn't anymore. And it was frankly kind of cruel of her to ask for things to go back to how they had been before, when she...

When they...

Whatever.

"It's good advice," Trev said, stepping into the warm apartment with a sigh of relief.

"Gonna snow later, you got in just in time. Is Titus gonna be mad?" Dante teased.

Trev had compartmentalized his complicated feelings about Sarah and the fact that Titus had kept that fairly dire secret about her cheating. He tended to avoid issues he'd rather not deal with, and it took him a while to work up the courage to face conflict rather than pretend it didn't faze him. But sometimes, it was necessary.

I'll handle this today.

"I'll message him later," Trev said. "You mind if he comes over for a beer?"

"Not even slightly. These days, I work, play with Evonnie every weekend, and then there's our monthly poker game. My sisters come over to liven up the place when they can, but mostly, I'm on my own."

"Unless you're hooking up with Margie."

"Haven't seen her for a bit," Dante said with a frown.

"You think she's trying to phase it out?" Trev asked.

"I don't want to talk about it."

Since he could relate so hard to that, Trev nodded. "Fair. No relationship talk. Either of us slips, we do a shot."

"Sir, I have work in the morning."

"Then you better not slip."

At Dante's urging, Trev carried his bag to Evonnie's room and set it in the corner. His friend hadn't been joking; the room was decorated with so many ruffles and sequins that Trev might turn into a Brony standing here. It was supercute, and he smiled at the mental image of himself tucked into this pink canopy bed for the night.

No need to unpack. He wouldn't bother Dante for more than a day or two. Hopefully, he could either get his head in order and apologize to Leanne, or failing that, he'd have to follow Junie's path and answer a roommate ad. All those options were better than the basement. His family would probably say "told you so" over his marital failure and commune over how they saw it coming from the start.

God, this sucks.

He messaged Titus and said he was hanging out with Dante tonight then asked if he wanted to join. Within five minutes:

> **Titus:** Danica canceled our date. Apparently the whole book club is heading to Leanne's place. Something you want to tell me?

Fuck. In addition to the Sarah thing, this was another reason why he'd been seeing Titus less. Their partners were completely wrapped up together, and Trev didn't want his best friend feeling like he had to take sides. He sighed, staring at his phone.

We had an argument, he finally sent back.

> **Titus:** YOU? Did she diss the smell of your favorite weed?

Wow. Though he knew Titus was joking, that still stung. Trev took a breath and counted to ten, but he still sent Fuck you a minute later, without remorse.

Trev felt even shittier when he rejoined Dante in the living room. The other man had a game on, but he didn't seem to be paying it much attention since it wasn't the Bulls. Sighing, Trev tilted his head back to study the imperfectly updated ceiling. He could see traces of where the popcorn had been scraped away then painted over, so it had a strange, textured look.

"Is this how you pictured your life as a little kid?" he asked.

"You kidding? Nah. Not even slightly."

"Sometimes life is just..." Trev struggled to find the right words, ones that would express some of how he felt without alarming Dante too much. "So much effort, you know?"

"That's one way to look at it. And you're not wrong."

"How are you viewing it?"

"You never know what's gonna happen if you don't stay in it. Sure, today could be the same as yesterday, but it's not written yet. Tomorrow is..." Dante paused, maybe thinking of how to finish that thought.

"Endless possibility," Trev offered.

"That's exactly it. Bets is dating somebody new, and I think they're serious. It's weird for me because I'm not feeling great about Evonnie living with Tyrone and maybe one day calling him 'Pop.' But I want Bets to be happy. If I'm honest, I want it for me too."

"Does this count as relationship talk?"

"Hell nah. We're talking about Bets, not me."

"I'll let it go this time."

"And besides, life isn't just about that. It's little moments where things worked out better than expected. Like getting the last roast chicken at the deli."

"I never thought about rotisserie chicken as a silver lining," Trev said.

"You should! It's low effort and delicious."

"True enough."

Before long, Titus showed up with snacks and beer. First thing, he said, "I'm sorry. That shit wasn't funny. I was pissy because Danica left me hanging, but I shouldn't have said that."

"I don't even smoke these days," Trev said quietly. "Just

edibles now and then. And people do it for reasons other than fun, you know, to manage pain and stuff."

Frankly, that was part of how he'd used it as well, though his wounds were emotional. He wasn't trying to dig into any of that tonight, however. He stepped back so Titus could greet Dante, and Trev decided he might as well address the elephant in the room.

"Yeah, so you want to explain why you never told me Sarah was cheating on me before we broke up?"

Dante dropped the bag of chips, picked them up, and headed straight back to the kitchen as Titus froze, wearing a distinctly deer-in-headlights look. "How'd you find out?"

"She apologized for it a few months ago."

"When did you see her? What was she even doing in St. Claire?"

Trev gave him a look. Those questions were deflections, and the answers didn't matter, but he gave them anyway. "She was here for her cousin's wedding, and I happened to run into her at Seven Grand. You *still* didn't answer the question."

"And you're just now bringing it up?" Titus asked.

"You're one to talk." Trev hated this stuff, so much that his stomach churned. *Maybe I shouldn't have mentioned it? I'm being sensitive, just like my family says. Wait, no, he needs to explain.* That wasn't how friends should treat each other.

"Hey, *you* let shit fester." Titus wore a defensive expression, but then he sighed. "I didn't want her to hurt you more than necessary! I told her to make a clean break after I saw her—"

"Right, honestly, I don't give a fuck what Sarah was doing." Trev clenched his teeth around the surge of anger he'd been repressing. "You're supposed to be my best friend—*your* words, by the way. And if I'd known back then that she was messing around, I wouldn't have blamed myself so much. If someone else was involved, the failure wasn't all mine. You don't get that I could've—*fuck*. You should have told me," he finished flatly.

"Yeah. You should have," Dante said from the kitchen.

He's not just Titus's friend. Dante's got my back.

Titus clutched the six-pack he'd brought, looking frankly miserable. "I'm sorry. I made the wrong call. Should I...go?"

Since Trev was already raw from how easily Leanne had cut him loose, he shook his head. "It's ancient history. Thanks for the apology. I'll get over it now that I finally said something. Let's just...chill, like we planned."

This was a prime occasion to get baked if ever there had been one, but he wouldn't do that at Dante's place even if he had stuff with him. Which he didn't. And he was trying to lean on that less. It was one thing to do it for pain relief or recreation, another not to have any other means of coping with his problems.

"Sounds good to me." Dante came out of the kitchen, seeming glad the drama was over.

With some faint tension lingering, they all settled in front of the TV with beer and chips. Trev noticed Titus kept stealing glances in his direction, and finally, Trev mumbled, "What?"

"Are we *really* good?" Titus asked.

"Yeah. Well. We will be. I messed up by not telling you about my wedding. You made the wrong call with Sarah. It's—"

"You're both messy," Dante cut in.

Titus laughed first, then Trev joined in. At least it felt okay hanging out with the guys. The game didn't really register; he kept thinking about Leanne's face, wounded and stricken. Would she look like that if she didn't care at all?

Did I make a huge mistake? Well, it's definitely not my first.

CHAPTER 26

LEANNE HAD NEVER FELT LESS like celebrating.

But the other witches had done their usual incredible work with setting up the winter solstice. The field was magical after a fresh snowfall, with fairy lights shining through polished ice. Vanessa stuck close to her side, adorable in a cherry-red puffy coat with a fuzzy white hat and matching gloves. She looped her arm through Leanne's and guided her to the stall where they were selling mulled wine, rich with cinnamon and cloves.

"Gorgeous. This is the best time of year to be a witch," Vanessa said, after a long, luxuriant sip.

"You say that no matter what rite we're celebrating."

"That's true. It's good to be a witch. Period."

Leanne tried to smile, but she couldn't make her face cooperate. Instead, she glanced away, admiring the outdoor skating rink that had appeared by magic and would be no more than a damp patch in the dirt come morning. Witches glided hand in hand, bundled against the cold, and it would have looked like a Norman Rockwell painting, except there were no sparkling illusions in those pictures, with magic cascading in golden sparks.

"Do you ever wish things were different?" Leanne asked.

"I mean, yeah, obviously. Every time I go to the freezer and find I'm out of mint chocolate chip ice cream. But besides that, uh, what things?"

"Do you wish we could join the modern world? Come out, so to speak."

"Wow. I don't know. Sometimes when I'm dating a really fine mundane, I wish I could tell them what's what. But I don't know..."

"How well it would go?"

Vanessa nodded, eyes locked on distant fun. "Being Black and a known witch? I don't know. But enough of that. Let's find the party! And if we can't find it, we'll start it."

Dammit, I actually want to talk about this, it's—

Important.

The lights of comprehension switched on. So this was how Trev felt, back then. No, to be fair, it must've been worse for him because she was his wife. While Vanessa might be Leanne's bestie, she didn't share her life in the same way. But still, it hurt when someone chose not to hear you out. She hadn't meant to hurt Trev, just as Vanessa hadn't meant anything bad either.

More to the point, she couldn't confide in Vanessa or anyone in their coven. There *was* one person at the Yule festival she could talk to, however. Leanne didn't follow Vanessa; instead, she veered toward Gladys, who was peeling chestnuts and laughing at something Ethel said. There was a beautiful fire blazing up toward the ink-black sky—amazing that all this could be concealed by a bevy of skilled illusionists.

"Can we chat for a bit?" Leanne asked, trying to sound casual.

Apparently, subtlety wasn't her strong suit because Ethel shot her a sharp look and rose from the fireside. "I could use a pork pie or some fried honey bread, or...oh hell, why bother making excuses? I'm out."

"Let's walk through the ice palace?" Glady suggested.

The older witch was bundled against the cold, almost as wide as she was tall with all the layers. Leanne followed Gladys into one of her favorite features, the garden of ice sculptures. Deer so vivid, they looked like they could leap into motion at any moment in the localized snowfall cascading over this one spot in the festival.

"This should be far enough," Leanne said.

"What's on your mind?"

"I have a serious question to ask, and the answer matters to me a lot. Depending on what you say, it could change...well, everything."

Gladys smiled faintly, her eyes crinkling beneath a fine dusting of snow. "That's quite a lot to rest on a conversation carried out beside two frolicking penguins."

Just then, the penguins in question began to move, spinning and sliding on the ice. Leanne never stopped feeling delighted by this display, but she had to focus. "Still applicable. So here's the question: How do you feel about me proposing the great reveal when I become a council member?"

"I suppose that depends on what you mean."

"Okay, laying all my cards on the table, I plan to do it anyway, but I want to take your temperature on the idea first. I intend to suggest we change our codicils regarding nonmagical partners and announce ourselves to the world. This is my wheelhouse, so I'll do my best to control the spin."

"And how do you foresee it unfolding?"

Leanne began with confidence, "Two stages. First, we ratify the motion to permit witches to tell their nonmagical partners the truth. I think it's important our loved ones are looped in before we move to the next phase."

"And then?"

"Next, we reveal ourselves to the general public. If we spin it well, so many pathways will open up."

"How do you figure?" Gladys asked.

"Well, for instance, we can monetize our work openly. Look at Danica and Clem. They pretend to fix stuff the slow way. Imagine how cool people would find it if they could actually watch them do their repair work? Ethel could sell her charms openly in her online shop, and witches could stop worrying so much about blending in. We'd be able to just...live. As ourselves. And share our lives with whomever we choose. I was thinking that if we start the process, others might come forward as well. We've lived in the shadows forever, but I want to believe there's a place for us, now. That the world has changed enough."

"You mean other 'special' communities?"

Leanne nodded. "Though we've lost touch, the archives indicate we're not alone among humanity. The point is, this needs to happen, and *I'm* the person to push it through."

"You talk like you're a bulldozer," Gladys said.

"I'm the witch who just won a seat on the city council."

The older witch smiled. "I like your confidence. For the

record, this is exactly why I chose you. You make big moves, and you follow through. You asked what I think? Do exactly as you've said you will. Change the world, Leanne. I believe in you."

Her chest tightened. "Thank you. Your endorsement means a lot to me."

"Then I take it we're done? Because I aim to eat a lot of delicious food tonight."

Leanne shook her head. "Not quite. I'm telling you up front, I made a protective amulet for my husband, just in case. And I plan to tell him everything as soon as I'm allowed. I don't want to fight the council, but if anyone even looks at him sideways, we'll have a problem. You can pass that along to the powers that be, if you're still holding sessions."

At that, Gladys threw back her head and laughed. "Look at you, little fire starter. You're willing to fight the whole council for your man?"

"And then some," Leanne said grimly.

"We're on hiatus anyway, so I can't share your warning, my dear. And then you'll be online in the new year to get started on that sparkling agenda." With a faint smile, the older witch headed back toward the bright lights of the Yule revels.

She needed to keep Trev safe for two more weeks...and how the hell could she do that if he was somewhere else? Once she started on the council, it should be less dangerous, and soon after—if her initiative went well—she could tell him everything and see if he could accept her with no secrets in the way. If he could, if—

Well, best not to count on it. But...she *hoped* with all her heart.

"Come home," Leanne shouted as soon as Dante opened the door.

He laughed. "Leanne! How're you doing? Thanks for asking about *me*, by the way."

Trev could hear their whole conversation from the front room, and he stepped into view just as Leanne flashed a rueful smile. "Sorry. Hey, Dante, how are you?"

"I'm all right. Better when you take his mopey ass back with you."

"May I come in?" she asked.

Trev didn't know how to act as she breezed past Dante and kicked her shoes off in the foyer. He'd never had a wife before, let alone left home after an argument. *Am I supposed to apologize?* At this point, he could admit that maybe he'd overreacted.

"I'm sorry," she said immediately. "On the way home from the hospital, I cut you off. And I was so thick that I didn't even realize I'd done it, let alone that I hurt you."

Wow.

Trev had never been in a relationship where he didn't apologize first, no matter what actually happened. Sarah had a way of turning everything back on him. Like, if he was more successful, she wouldn't have snapped at him. And it got to the point that he'd stopped even wondering if it was his fault because it *always* was in some fashion.

When Leanne hesitantly approached him and reached for his hand, he realized he'd been quiet for too long. "Are you still mad?" she asked softly. "If you are, I can give you more time. But...I do think we should go home and talk—without making Dante witness our convo."

"I'm not. Mad, that is. I'll get my stuff together." As he turned to walk away, she hugged him from behind.

Startled, Trev breathed in the sweetness of her scent—orange blossom and juniper—unable to believe how good her touch felt. Not only did she show up to ask him to come home, but she'd also made amends in front of his friend. No excuses either. Which…he didn't know how to feel about any of it, really. It was a testament to how fucked up his connections had been to this point that he found any of this shocking. His family? They obviously didn't give a damn. And Sarah… They hadn't been a good fit, and their relationship had turned toxic.

"I really am sorry," she whispered. "And you should know I missed you a lot. The condo doesn't feel like home without you."

He turned and wrapped his arms around her, burying his face in her hair. "You're making me feel all sparkly, Butterfly."

"That's the plan."

"All right, I need y'all out of my living room. You're making me feel sorry for myself," Dante announced.

Trev pulled back and pressed a gentle kiss to his wife's forehead. "I'll be right back."

As he headed for the princess room, he heard Leanne say, "I need to get you a present. Thanks for being there for Trev. You're a good friend."

"I sure am, and I enjoy expensive Scotch."

"I'll see that bottle of Scotch and raise you a selection of gourmet smoked meats."

Dante called, "This woman's a keeper, man. She's offering me booze and meat!"

Trev laughed, shoving his clothes back in the bag faster than he'd packed them in the first place. Then he took a cursory look around, making sure everything was in order in Evonnie's room. Since it all looked good, he hurried out, eager to go home.

Leanne reached for him and twined their fingers together. To Dante, she said, "We'll see you later."

He nodded. "Better make sure you invite me to the next party."

"Definitely."

The drive back was silent but not tense. Trev stole looks at Leanne, unable to believe she cared enough to come looking for him. For the past five years, it had been like living as an invisible person. But now...he left footprints when he passed, and—

I shouldn't be this touched.

Junie was waiting for them in the parking lot when they pulled in, her old car idling in a visitor's spot. She bounded out onto the slippery pavement and almost fell, a fairly absurd figure wrapped in clashing colors and a proliferation of scarves. Slip-sliding toward them, she windmilled her arms as she nearly crashed into Leanne.

Trev caught Junie and kept her from knocking his wife down. *Why is my mother-in-law such a kid?* But he smiled at the hopeful light in her eyes, the tremulous smile she kept pinned to her lips even though he could see that she was braced for a brush-off.

"Sorry to just drop in, but I haven't seen or talked to you since..."

"Since the old man died?" Leanne guessed.

Biting her lip, Junie nodded several times. "Are you okay?"

"I'm fine. This is an exception, mind you, because I really do prefer making plans beforehand, but...do you want to have dinner with us?"

Junie's eyes widened. "Really?"

"Sure, come on." Leanne beckoned, holding on to Trev's arm as they moved toward the condo building.

"Have you done any grocery shopping?" he asked quietly.

His wife angled an amused look at him. "Of course. I know better than to let the fridge get empty. To say nothing of the cabinets."

"Then I'll make something delicious and quick."

As they got in the elevator, Junie asked, "Have you heard anything from the attorney?"

Every muscle in Leanne's body tensed, and Trev set a hand on her shoulder, silently telling her to chill. She breathed in and out a few times then said, "Actually, I received a letter via certified mail on official letterhead."

"What did it say?" Trev asked, mostly because he knew Junie would if he didn't, and it would irritate Leanne if her mom pushed on this topic.

"I'm not sure. I haven't even looked at it."

The conversation hit a lull as they left the elevator and went into the condo. As the door closed behind them, Junie said, "The reason I was asking was because I got one too."

That surprised Leanne enough that she dropped her purse. "You did?"

"I guess he felt bad and changed his will. When the will leaves probate, I'll have enough to buy my own place, not that I plan to. I like Blair, and I don't want to live alone anyway."

Trev stifled a wave of amazement that Junie knew the word "probate," but he kept quiet. If Leanne was willing to extend an olive branch, he wouldn't get in the way. But he would keep an eye on the woman to make sure she didn't cause Leanne any more problems.

"Do you think they'll contest?" Leanne asked, likely referring to Dennis Seaton's *other* family members.

Junie blinked, pausing in the process of unwrapping herself from all those scarves. "Why would they? It's what he wanted."

"People get weird about money," Trev said. "Now, let me see what I'm working with."

He left the two women talking in the living room as he headed to the kitchen to check the ingredients. Nothing had been resolved, exactly; they still needed to talk. But he didn't feel unappreciated or impotently furious anymore.

She wants me here at least. Maybe that's enough.

CHAPTER 27

"OPEN THE LETTER," JUNIE URGED.

Leanne didn't argue with her mother; she merely sliced the envelope with a letter opener and pulled out the document. The whole division of property was provided, and since she was named, she apparently got to see all of it. But when she got to the section pertaining to her bequest, she dropped the will in shock. *I guess the old bastard really was sorry.* He had been generous with Junie, a few friends had done well also, and the rest of his estate was split four ways between Leanne, Brian, Ruth, and Paul.

"Holy shit," she breathed.

In fact, the numbers were dizzying because there were multiple properties to be liquidated, cash assets, stocks, and...*wow.* If her siblings didn't fight the updated will, running for mayor wouldn't be as much of an obstacle as she'd feared. *And all I did was show up.* But judging by the date of this amendment, Dennis Seaton made this change when he first got diagnosed. *He never planned to make the inheritance contingent on my response.*

"That's incredible," Junie said, after scanning the pages herself.

"Well done, your life is complete. You pulled off the longest con."

Her mother stared at her, open-mouthed in shock, and then Junie dissolved in nervous laughter. "I can't believe you said that."

"I have no idea how I'm supposed to react. I can't cry for someone I didn't know, so if not gallows humor, there's nothing."

Junie sighed. "Sometimes I wonder how it would have gone if I hadn't disappeared and cut all contact with Dennis."

"Why did you do that?"

"I was afraid…" Junie broke up abruptly, her expression suddenly stricken.

"Let me guess, you were afraid he'd make you get rid of me."

"I wasn't supposed to tell you that."

That had to be Trev's handiwork, trying to protect her feelings. But Dennis Seaton had clearly been a selfish prick in his heyday, so it didn't come as any surprise. Some part of her realized she should be shocked and/or hurt by all of this, but it felt like these revelations were about someone else. She'd never had any illusions about her father, even when she'd believed he was a shiftless mundane. The biggest surprise was that the man was willing to pony up assets to try and make amends at the end.

"How do sloppy joes sound?" Trev called.

"Delicious!" Junie shouted back.

In half an hour, he had dinner done: sloppy joes and salad. The man was a wonder, and Leanne took a moment to admire him in the silly apron before she sat at the kitchen island. There were three stools at the counter, so they ate there instead of setting the table properly. Junie cleaned her plate with relish, rambling on about how much she liked her roommate.

After the meal, Leanne said, "Okay, so if you're planning to stay in St. Claire, we need ground rules. I *will* return your calls and texts, but you don't get to decide how fast I do it. No more showing up unannounced. We'll make plans in advance, and you *will* honor my schedule. I refuse to be the bad person if I have other stuff to do. I understand you want to work on our relationship, but I need time…and space. Does that sound fair?"

"Extremely fair," Junie said. "I need to stop and think before I act on impulse."

"You should get that tattooed on your arm," Trev suggested.

Based on Junie's expression, she was considering it. "Maybe in cursive, in a pretty font?"

He nodded. "Exactly."

"Is there a good tattoo place in St. Claire?" Junie asked.

Trev glanced at Leanne as if gauging her reaction to this conversation. "There are a couple of options. I'll check with Calvin and find out where he gets his done."

Soon after, Junie left. Apparently, she'd mainly been curious if Leanne had gotten a letter from the law firm handling the Seaton estate. Once she was gone, Leanne showed the paperwork to Trev, who stared like he couldn't believe his eyes.

"Is this for real?"

"I guess so. It hasn't really sunk in yet."

"If only you'd known," he joked. "You didn't even have me sign a prenup."

She stood and kissed his nose. "The solution is simple."

"Oh yeah?"

"I'm never letting you divorce me. But I hope Garrett and Malcolm don't find out about this. They might sue me for alimony."

Trev paused in stacking their dinner plates in the dishwasher. "Are you serious?"

"Sort of. Malcolm was definitely that kind of guy. Maybe not Garrett. He was pretty hurt that I couldn't trust him while he was on the road."

"Why couldn't you?" he asked.

"Do you really want to talk about my ex?"

He made a face. "Not per se, but I *am* curious about your relationship. I'm looking to avoid their mistakes."

She thought about it briefly. "Well, for one thing, Garrett was ridiculously good-looking. Like, even when I was *with* him, people would hit on him and try to give him their numbers. So, if they were doing that in front of me..." Sighing, she shook her head. "Basically, the more I fretted about what he was doing while he traveled, the more we fought when he came home. Eventually, the fighting got overwhelming, and I left. But it doesn't help to re-tread that ground."

"Yeah, well, I guess I'm not so hot that I make you nervous," Trev said.

"You're understated hot. Because your personality is low-key, you roll under the radar, unless someone has a discerning eye."

He folded his arms. "Am I supposed to take that as a compliment?"

"I came straight for you, didn't I?"

"Still don't understand that."

"You don't need to." She took a breath, bracing herself for this. "We need to talk."

Trev snapped to attention, his shoulders tensing. "Fun beginning, very ominous. Living room after I finish in here?"

"Whenever you're ready."

Five minutes later, she'd practiced what she meant to say in her head ten times when he showed up, perching beside her on the sofa. "Is this about the argument?"

"Sort of. I apologized and I meant it. We're overdue for a relationship talk, but here's the thing, I can't be candid with you right now. I'm not permitted to be. And I know that's annoying and frustrating and mysterious, so here's what I'm asking. Give me three weeks. If everything goes well, I'll be able to level with you then."

"Wow, this is the weirdest 'it's not you, it's me' speech I've ever heard," Trev said.

Leanne poked him. "That's not what I'm doing. Can you give me some time?"

"It's not a hard ask, Butterfly. I'm confused, but I'll try to be patient. Let's just enjoy the holidays and feast on delicious food."

"Speaking of which, am I correct in supposing that you aren't visiting your family?"

Trev flinched ever so slightly, and she leaned over to hug him. He rested his head on her shoulder for a long moment before responding, "I haven't heard from any of them in months," he admitted. "So that's a safe bet."

"I'm sorry, sweetheart. Do you want to—"

"No. I really don't," he cut in.

Leanne was the last person to lecture someone else about forgiving family members no matter what. If Trev chose to cut them off, she supported his decision.

"I'm in favor of whatever makes you happy," she said softly.

That's you.

But Trev didn't say that because of her weird request for a three-week relationship extension. Just when he thought he had this woman figured out, she threw him a curveball. And he'd had her pegged as fastballs all the way. Next thing he knew, she'd be lobbing sliders.

"Should we invite Junie over? I can cook on Christmas."

She contemplated briefly then nodded. "If you want. I wonder if Blair has plans."

"You want to invite her roommate?"

Leanne shrugged. "I'm curious about the person who gets along with Junie so well."

"Fair enough. Should I text your mom about it, or will you?"

"I'm on it," Leanne said. She tapped out the message then glanced at him, seeming strangely tentative. "Now I know why you were avoiding me and sleeping in the guest room half the time. Will you come to bed like before?"

His heart got all soft and melty, full-on cardiac fondue. "Definitely will. Sorry I didn't just tell you that I was upset. But…I wasn't sure I had any right to be. Despite our Vegas wedding, things are still kind of…undefined. Between us."

"They won't always be," she promised. "I just need time."

"I can wait. Just don't make me do it forever."

"Three weeks."

"What exactly is happening…?" He trailed off because she was already shaking her head. "Right, you can't tell me. As in, you're not allowed by the secret society."

Her head snapped up, and her eyes went wide. Quickly, she pressed a hand to his mouth, and with her free hand, she delved beneath his shirt. Trev tried to speak through her fingers, but she seemed genuinely frightened until she found the necklace she'd given him. Then she slumped forward suddenly enough that he wrapped an arm around her in support.

"I suspect that was a joke, but you're closer than you realize to the truth. Have you mentioned this to anyone else?"

"I might have asked Dante what he'd do if his wife had a secret," he admitted, feeling strangely guilty.

That feeling intensified when he felt the shudder that went through her. Her breath came in unsteady gulps, and she sat back, twisting her hands together, but even that wasn't enough. Leanne jumped up to pace, seeming not even to see him.

"This is fine. It's… Everything will be fine. Gladys said…" Then she quickly snapped her lips together, more agitated than Trev could ever recall.

"Just so you know, I'm trying not to freak," Trev said. "But it's not easy."

"I'm sorry. This must be so confusing."

"You could say that. But I promised to give you three weeks. I hope everything makes sense when you're allowed to loop me in."

Leanne's smile seemed to contain more than a little tension. "I hope so too."

"Does this have to do with—"

"No further questions," she interrupted.

Trev laughed because she sounded so pro, every inch the city councilwoman. It sucked, but pushing wouldn't get him anywhere.

Thankfully, his personality permitted him to back off and just... avoid thinking about the issue. In fact, that was his preferred coping mechanism. He used to ward off bad thoughts with weed and video games. Now he rode his bike when the noise in his head got too loud. There were a few edibles in the house, but he didn't lean on them as much as he had, mostly because he was afraid of causing problems for Leanne.

"Fine, let's watch some TV."

She picked the program, and they cuddled for a few hours. He went to bed when she did because he wanted to make up for the past few weeks. In the morning, Leanne said, "I heard from Junie. She'll be over around two on Christmas."

"With her roomie?"

"Looks like it. She asked if she can bring a friend named Noodles along with Blair. Apparently, the three of them were planning to eat canned soup and watch the Hallmark Channel all day. Hopefully our place will be a step up."

"The food will be. There's a spiral ham in the freezer, and I've got a recipe for mashed potatoes to try out."

"You need a recipe for those?" Leanne teased.

"There are different schools of thought. I'm trying these without dairy."

"Almond milk?" she guessed.

"You'll have to wait and see. Since you're messing with me, maybe I won't ever tell you, even if you beg."

Trev remembered that he'd said he would ask Calvin about a tattoo recommendation, so he shot off a text. It took an hour or so, and Leanne left in the meantime. She had stuff to do, relative to taking over from Dan Rutherford on the city council. His term ended in December, so she'd be officially in the role starting in the new year.

Is that what she can't tell me? Something to do with politics? Wow, maybe it really is the Skull and Bones thing Dante mentioned. He knew many politicians got involved in stuff like that, networking and secret handshakes, but Leanne didn't seem like the type. Because from what he knew of such organizations, they were all about maintaining the status quo.

She's not like that. Is she?

Fuck. He hated doubting his own wife and worrying secretly about what terrible situation she'd gotten herself into. But it wasn't like he could extricate her without knowing exactly who she was connected to and what was at stake. She'd seemed genuinely frightened about him even speculating aloud. Did she fear the condo was bugged?

No, you've played too much Ghost Recon.

Later that day, Calvin finally messaged back. Thinking about getting some ink?

Trevor: It's for my mother-in-law.

Calvin: Unexpected. I usually get mine done at Buffalo Brothers Ink.

Trevor: Thanks, I'll let her know.

They texted a little more, as Trev figured it'd be rude to get the info and go silent. He found out about Calvin's holiday plans—lucky dude was leaving for Costa Rica tomorrow—and shared his own. Just like Dante, it seemed that Calvin liked him fine. Trev had been getting in his own way when it came to making friends. If he messaged Miguel, the guy would help him out, and he'd probably be game to get a beer if he didn't have family plans already.

Trev had a session with his therapist, then he got to work on the socials, creating content and scheduling posts. Next, he designed a home page for Hazel Jeffords's cat Goliath, who'd gotten a bit popular after Trev's "fat cats" political post went viral. Most days, he couldn't believe he was getting paid to do this. Leanne even said he wasn't charging enough for his time, but he felt weird about that when he was still taking classes online. He would have a certificate when he finished, but for someone who didn't even complete his degree...well, it was hard for him to imagine the word "expert" applied to him.

As he wrapped up with work, there was a knock at the door. He wasn't expecting any visitors, and they usually had to be buzzed in, so maybe it was a neighbor? Trev opened the door to find a man and woman, both wearing black suits.

"Trevor Montgomery?"

"Vanderpol-Montgomery," he corrected, mostly because he had done the paperwork. These two gave him such a bad feeling with their blank expressions. Trev added, "Who's asking?"

"No questions. You need to come with us."

Raising a brow, he folded his arms. "Nah, I don't think I will."

CHAPTER 28

LEANNE WAS DRIVING WHEN TREV'S protective charm activated.

She was on her way home already, thinking of stopping at the supermarket to pick up a few last-minute items for the holiday feast since they were hosting Junie, Noodles, and Blair, but then the backlash of energy swept toward her, and she stepped on the gas. It wouldn't do her any good if she got into a police chase, but she didn't give a damn. This was a speed first, ask questions later situation.

From the way her spell had snapped, her husband might freaking disappear if she didn't arrive in time. As it was, she nearly chewed her lower lip off as she waited for the gate arm to raise and allow her access to the parking lot. She left her car half sideways in the parking spot.

Leanne pulled off her heels and raced upstairs, unable to wait for the elevator. *But shit, what if I miss them? What if they're dragging him into the—no, I've got this.*

Her hands shook as she keyed the pin. When she dashed into the condo, she stopped short, silently stunned and desperately circling for a reasonable explanation—only there was *nothing* she could say that would negate what she—and Trev—were seeing. A bright protective shield shimmered around him, activated the moment council enforcers tried to take him against his will. Steely-eyed agents in black suits conferred nearby, probably discussing Trev's fate.

Fuck. FUCK. Looks like this is happening now.

She shut the door behind her and called Gladys. "We need an emergency council meeting. The agenda has just been moved up."

"What's wrong?" the older witch asked immediately.

"I have two heavies in my apartment, and I'm not losing this fight. But it needs to go through official channels. Right now, I haven't violated any of the tenets. Technically, *they* did by pushing the matter, and my magic reacted. If they'd left well enough alone, the breach wouldn't have occurred, but the time for this bullshit has passed. You want me on the new council? Get them all online. Now."

"I'll send word," Gladys said. "You should have a link in your inbox within ten minutes. Can you keep things calm for that long?"

"I have to, don't I?" After hanging up, she took a deep breath, squared her shoulders, and faced the intruders. "Did you hear that?" she added.

"What the hell is going on?" Trev asked.

Frankly, he sounded calmer than she probably would be under these circumstances. "I'll tell you everything soon," she promised. "I'm sure you can put some of it together, but if you can't, it will be resolved today."

"Leanne Vanderpol-Montgomery, you have violated—"

"I have *not*. In fact, you precipitated this whole situation with your incautious behavior. But since you started this, *I'll* finish it. I just spoke to a current council member, who's convening an emergency meeting. Now sit the fuck down and wait."

To her astonishment, both enforcers took seats at the dining room table, keeping a wary eye on the room. Leanne crossed to Trev, and as expected, the shield allowed her to phase through it. *Such a relief.* She hugged him because she could, feeling the warm pulse of protective energy around them.

"I'm super confused right now," Trev said. "But first, I want to say that was absurdly hot. Next, I have some theories, but most of them are, like, pretty out there."

"How far?" Leanne asked.

"Like, Salem the talking cat?"

"Huh. You're in the ballpark. That's all I can say now, though. Otherwise, I'll be guilty of what they're currently trying to pin on me. And that's not happening."

He actually broke into soft laughter and nuzzled his face into her hair as magic shimmered all around them. "My life has gotten *so* damn interesting since I met you."

How can anyone be this precious?

"I hope that's a good thing," she whispered.

"So far it is. Provided I don't get turned into a cat for knowing too much or something."

"Is that really the only comparison you have?" she asked.

"I'm stressed! And I play video games more than I watch paranormal TV."

"Fair enough." Leanne moved away from him, keeping an eye on the enforcers as she grabbed her laptop and opened her email.

As Gladys had said, there was a link waiting for her, and she beckoned to the enforcers. "Let's do this in the other room."

"I'll just...chill here, then," Trev said.

Before she clicked the link, she quickly cast the illusionary spell as instructed. All council members were supposed to use this to keep their identities secret. How that was supposed to work with two enforcers watching her do it, she had no idea, but that wasn't her biggest problem. Probably, they'd get their memories adjusted after she sorted out this mess, presuming she got enough votes in her favor. It was hard telling how this would go or who would show up for this meeting. Might even be a blending of the incoming members and those who were ending their terms of service.

Soon, she was online in a video conference with so many people that their shifting facials were only tiny thumbnails on her laptop screen. *Yeah, it must be the old council* and *the new.* Too soon to judge whether that was good or bad for her cause. At this point, she could only move forward.

"I've been accused of allowing my nonmagical husband to discover I'm a witch," she said. "But I told him *nothing* directly. That said, I assert this council stricture is both outdated and unnecessary. Witches shouldn't have to hide from those they love. I move that we strike this codicil from the covenant and allow us to disclose freely. If this motion is carried, I also suggest we wait a reasonable time for those conversations to happen privately, and then...on a preapproved date, we come out to the world."

Immediate outcry followed, so much shocked shouting that Leanne tuned it out. If they called on her to defend the proposition, she would, but for now, it seemed like there was support and opposition already in play. She listened to the arguments for half an hour, until they gradually slowed and came to a lull.

Into that silence, someone said, "This has been proposed before. We always decide it's too risky."

Fuck. If this failed, there would be consequences. For her. For Trev. For the enforcers. *Time to earn my keep.*

"Think about the advantages." Leanne made her case, just as she had with Gladys. "How amazing would it be if we could earn a living through spell work? Instead of hiding our gifts and struggling with a day job that brings no joy. Some witches are lucky enough to find regular work they enjoy, but many are not. And others live in poverty because they're forced to hide who they are.

"It would enrich our lives on so many levels. No more barriers between us and our nonmagical loved ones. We could stop wasting so much time and energy hiding our seasonal rites. In fact, I suspect they would become tourist attractions. People would drive *hundreds* of miles to experience the marvels we take for granted. And witches have been featured in so many modern media adaptations that I imagine we'd receive a lot of support from fans delighted to learn we exist. Old superstitions have largely died out. Folks don't blame witches for random problems anymore. Science has explained so much, there's no need to live like this. Make the right decision. Vote with me. Vote for freedom and disclosure."

"It's time," another council member said.

"Wait, are we voting for both measures together? For the two-step process—speaking to our partners and families, and then later, the world?"

"Correct," Leanne said, before anyone else could complicate the matter.

"It makes sense," another council member said.

A confident voice added, "I'm sending a link to a poll. Your vote is yes or no. Your identity will not be revealed, so none can hold your stance against you. Ready to proceed?"

Leanne voted yes immediately, hoping hard for the correct result.

Trev noticed the glimmering energy ball dissipated as soon as the creepy MIB-looking pair followed Leanne into the bedroom.

But he couldn't deny what he'd seen. That was...magic.

He paced the living room floor, fighting the urge to bail. Because this was beyond anything he could've expected. For real, he'd occasionally thought she got ready too fast or she was too gorgeous to be real, and he'd been baffled by the convo he'd overheard between her and Gladys, but had he ever *really* thought she was a wizard? Or a sorceress? He wasn't even up to date on the correct verbiage. In video games, she'd likely be a magic user. Of course, she'd also be wearing a sexy dress that showed her thighs and be able to cast fireballs and summon lightning too, enchant magical weapons...what else? Oh, in one game, magic users could turn into spiders or bears.

Can Leanne turn into a bear? Fuck. I'm so freaking out right now.

With shaking hands, he went to the liquor cabinet and poured himself a shot. He didn't even look at the bottle and drank it straight, whatever it was. *Ugh. Gin.* To his palate, it tasted like pine cleaner smelled. Trev gulped some water to get the traces out of his mouth.

It seemed like forever before Leanne came out, flanked by the two assholes who'd showed up to try and...arrest him? He was guessing about that, frankly, but based on his wife's reaction, whatever they had planned wouldn't be healthy for anyone involved.

At first, he couldn't read her expression, but she turned to the two and said, "Get out. As of now, your job descriptions will likely change."

"Understood," said the male agent.

They left as swiftly as they had arrived, with absolutely no explanation. Leanne closed the door behind them and slowly turned to face him. Trev thought she was nervous, judging by the way she fluttered her hands as she moved toward him.

"I wanted it to happen," she said slowly. "But...I wasn't sure it would. In a way, it's probably good that it came on like a tsunami. We had to go on gut reactions rather than letting everyone mull it over and maybe second-guess. As it was, it was close. Two votes, our favor. I'm a persuasive speaker."

"You realize I have *no* idea what you're talking about."

"You will soon. I'm sure you've already worked out that those clowns set off a protective spell."

Spell. There it is.

He tried not to let on how unsettled he was by *all* of this because it would probably upset her, but damn. This was a lot. "I did figure out that much, yeah."

"Let's start there. Witches are real. I am one. For hundreds of years, we weren't allowed to disclose that to anyone outside our community."

"By that, you mean...?"

"Other witches," she confirmed.

"Gotcha. But that's changed now?"

She beamed at him with such incandescent joy that he smiled back despite all the uncertainty and doubt roiling inside him. "It did, just now. I pushed hard for that resolution and barely accomplished it. That's what I was waiting for, by the way, why I couldn't have a proper relationship talk with you until I had permission to let you in all the way. I don't want to hide anything from you. I want you to know everything before you decide..."

"Decide what?"

"Whether you can live with a witch."

"I have so many questions that I don't even know where to start," Trev admitted.

"Just ask what comes to mind."

The first thing that popped into his head was, "Is Junie a witch?"

Leanne nodded. "She's a vivimancer. That's not as weird as it sounds, by the way. All witches are born with a strong attunement, and they can usually work within their minor attunement as well."

Trev listened with dawning amazement and wonder. *My wife is a witch. I'm not hallucinating.* "I feel like I just found out that Magic the Gathering is real, but the rules in the manual are wrong."

Laughing softly, she said, "Do you want me to go on?"

"Please."

"The next thing you should know, the book club is my coven. Talking about novels has been our cover for years, but that's where we confer, support each other, and assist with com-plicated spells. Your charm is so potent because I put everyone to work on it."

Silently amazed, Trevor touched the necklace he had on. "You made this because you were worried about what I overheard the night you won the election."

It wasn't a question.

"Exactly. Anyway, back to attunements. There are six types—technomancy, vivimancy, divining, necromancy, enchantments, and neuromancy."

"I never thought video games would help me this much, but I think I can figure out some of those. Can I offer my guesses?"

"Go ahead."

"Technomancers deal with technology, impact or control it. Diviners can probably get information. Necromancy likely relates to death. Enchanters, I think they create magical items. Not posi-tive about vivimancers or neuromancers. The root of those words are 'life' and 'brain,' but..." He shook his head. "I'm not sure, beyond that. How did I do?"

Leanne took his hand, watching his face as if she expected him to recoil. *Does she really think this would change anything?* It's like finding out he'd won the lottery when he'd forgotten he even bought a ticket. For someone like him, this was a bonus prize, not a horrible secret.

"You're pretty close on most of those. Neuromancy does impact the mind, and it extends to illusions and glamours as well. Vivimancers can change living things with magic. That includes healing and creating new plants and animals. It's powerful, but it can also be…dangerous. Necromancy is a rare affinity, and good witches don't meddle with it. I'm unusual in that I don't have a major attunement, but I can dabble in everything. To get powerful results, I need help from the coven."

"What are you strongest in?" Trev asked.

"Neuromancy. I do my best work in glamours. Next, it's probably divination, but I'm weak at it compared to Ethel, so I usually leave it to her."

"Right, your coven…mates?" Trev didn't know if he was using the right word for them, but since Leanne didn't correct him, he ran with that choice. "What are their specialties? If you're allowed to tell me."

"I *am*. That is what's so magical about passing this proposal with the council."

"Guessing you don't mean the city council."

"There is some internal witch stuff I'm not supposed to talk about, so suffice to say, yes, I can tell you what everyone specializes in. Vanessa is enchantments and vivimancy, and her sculptures are literally magical. Both Danica and Clem are technomancers, as you could guess from their business name. They're so strong that I don't even know what their minor attunement is. Kerry and Priya, likewise, only they're vivimancers. Ethel is a diviner with minor attunement for enchantments. Margie is a neuromancer, though not a superstrong one."

"Wow." This was so much information that his head was spinning.

Not necessarily in a bad way, but like, it hadn't quite sunk in that this was all real. He kept waiting for her to crack up laughing and admit this was all an elaborate prank, but so far, her beautiful face remained utterly earnest. He took a steadying breath.

"What?" she asked.

"This might come across wrong, I don't know, but...could I see the *real* you? Without the glamour in place."

CHAPTER 29

MAYBE IT SHOULDN'T, BUT THAT felt like a knife twisting in Leanne's heart.

"Are you worried about what you've married?" she asked.

"No, but I think it's a fair request, all things considered."

She couldn't even argue, so she concentrated on stripping away an illusion she had been crafting for years. In all honesty, she couldn't even recall the last time she'd dispelled it, so she might not recognize her own features without it. Bracing herself, she turned to face him, waiting for him to shout in shock and flee the condo.

"When are you planning to do it?" he asked.

Puzzled, she got up and hurried to the bathroom. To her own eyes, she looked visibly older. Tired, as well. With a few lines around her eyes, and her mouth paler than she'd usually allowed it to be. She came back to face him.

"The glamour *is* gone," she said.

He started to smile then. "But you look the same. You're beautiful, Butterfly."

"What? I do *not*."

Ignoring her words, Trev shrugged. "To me, you look the same."

Just then, her phone beeped with an advisory, alerting all witches to the change in the covenant. That meant Danica could tell Titus the truth whenever she wanted. All over the world, witches could be having this same talk with their partners.

But she couldn't stop here. It was time to step up. To be brave, braver than she ever had been before. No longer would she live like she didn't deserve to be loved, like the person she cared for above all others might still choose to abandon her. She'd done that in the name of self-protection, but really, it was just another word for cowardice—leaving someone before they could decide to do it to her.

"I'm glad you're not put off by any of this," she said then.

"My head is a mess, but...no, it doesn't change anything. I don't care what—or who—you are. You're still the person who crossed a room to pick me out of the crowd. You're still the person who makes me feel like I matter more than anyone else."

"You matter. So very much. And that's the next stage. When we got together, we had so many sensible reasons. Logical motivations. But for me, it's not about that, and frankly, it never was. I was just too scared to admit the truth."

"Which is?" Trev asked.

"I want to be your wife, always. I don't want a temporary arrangement. I don't want to worry you'll get tired of me and take off. I want you to come to bed even when we fight." She paused, knotting her fingers together because the next one was huge. And she'd never said it to *anyone* before, which explained why none of her relationships lasted. "I want you to love me, as much as I love you."

He let out a slow breath, his eyes bright as golden coins. "That's so easy, Butterfly. I've been yours almost since the beginning. But I was so afraid that I didn't have anything to offer. Let's face it, I wasn't a catch when we met, and by most standards, I'm still not. I don't earn—"

"Bullshit," she cut in. "I was making enough money already when we got married, and though I've shifted gears, we're still doing fine freelancing. When you add in the inheritance, money isn't a factor. One day soon, I'll be allowed to freelance as a witch as well. Imagine the money I could earn doing beauty glamours for special occasions. People with skin conditions who can't wear cosmetics at all could benefit."

Trev blinked. "Wow. I didn't even think of that."

"I don't need someone to buy me shiny things. I can do that for myself. What I need is someone who always shows up, who always has my back. And you've been that person for me, even when I failed to offer you the same. If you think you can stand living with a witch, I'm yours for better or worse, just like we promised in Vegas. I didn't realize it at the time, but I meant those vows. I truly did."

"I love you," Trev whispered. "So damn much. Nobody else made me feel like I could ever put myself back together."

"But I didn't *do* anything," she protested.

"See, that's the thing. You didn't have to. I needed to make those changes, and you were so steadfast in believing that I could. And you gave me somewhere to go when I needed it most."

When he reached out, Leanne leaned into him, settling against his side with rising sweetness. *He loves me back. He doesn't want this to end either*. Not content with only his arm around her, she also laced their fingers together.

"You were always amazing. It's rare to find someone who is genuinely gentle and kind. And trust me, I'm aware you have a habit of swallowing your hurt, letting things go because you don't want to upset people. Please don't do that with me, sweetheart. We'll argue sometimes, but coming to a compromise that suits us both will make us stronger in the long run. From now on, don't keep the pain inside. Let me share it."

Sighing softly, he rubbed his cheek against her hair. "I'm not opposed. It's just that there hasn't been anyone for so long that I kinda forgot how it's meant to be."

"We'll figure it out."

Just then, Leanne's phone rang—a call from Danica. She answered and said, "You're on speaker. What's up?"

"Oh my God, did you already tell Trevor?" Danica sounded breathless, changes already echoing through her life.

This was the right move.

Leanne laughed. "I sure did. Why?"

Her friend's voice came across equal measures amused and irate. "Because Titus claims he already knew! I'm adding him to the call, just a sec."

Soon, Titus said "Hello?" like he wasn't sure who all was involved in this chat.

Leanne said hey, as did Trev, then Danica moved forward. "Seriously, I call bullshit. You didn't know anything! I was *so* careful."

Titus startled Leanne by chuckling uncontrollably. Finally, he settled enough to respond. "Honey, your shop is the cleanest in the world. There's never any oil or dust or *any* sign that mechanical objects have been taken apart. Your hands are pristine. Hell, half the time, you even have a manicure, and you didn't even bring a toolbox the day you repaired my oven. How does that make sense for someone who supposedly fixes machines?"

"He has a point," Trev said.

Though the other two couldn't see her, Leanne nodded. "So does it change anything?" she asked, hoping she wasn't about to witness Danica's relationship falling apart.

"Not for me," Titus said swiftly. "I'll keep my mouth shut until the official stance changes. I guess it's nice that she can stop hiding her...witchy stuff when I come over, though."

"I did wonder why Leanne has a locked drawer in the bedroom," Trev admitted.

She shot him an apologetic look. "You can look at it now. It's just spell components. If you're interested, I'll show you how I do the glamour later."

"Tonight, I'd rather do something else," he whispered.

Not quiet enough, though.

"Okay, hanging up now," Danica said hastily.

"Good talk," Titus called. "And welcome to the modern world."

Once they hung up, Leanne kissed Trev delicately on the chin, nuzzling her face against his with all the adoration she'd been hiding. "Thank you."

"For what?"

"For loving me."

He tasted her lips like there was no sweeter flavor. "That's not something I could stop even if I wanted to, Butterfly. So I'll just thank you in turn."

"For what?" It was her turn to ask the question.

"Not breaking my heart."

Even now, Trev could hardly wrap his head around everything he'd heard today.

I'm married to a witch. And I almost got hauled off to…wherever they keep mortals who know too much. That was probably the wrong word, but he wasn't worried about vocabulary. Not with all this information to digest. Titus had said he kind of knew already or at least suspected. When Trev considered, it made sense. He'd only been in Fix-It Witches once, but the place gleamed with cleanliness, unlike any other repair shop he'd ever been in.

Leanne shifted and wrapped her arms around him fully, tucking her face between his neck and shoulder. "I thought you'd leave once you found out."

"Are you serious? Why?" A sudden and shocking thought occurred to him. "Wait, are you immortal or something? How old are you, really?"

She laughed. "Definitely not. I'm thirty-seven. You saw my ID when we got our marriage license in Vegas."

"That's exactly what an immortal witch would say. Those documents could've been fake." He grinned to show he was teasing.

"Is this what I have to look forward to?" she asked with a gentle sigh.

"Nah, this is just me…processing."

"Witches aren't a different species," Leanne said. "We're just...like augmented humans, I guess. You know, some people are supersmart. Others are incredible artists. Some folks can speak multiple languages. It's like that, only our ability is magic. We do have stories handed down about how we came to possess these powers, but nothing that can be proven."

Her explanation made it easier to grasp their situation. "So no differences otherwise?"

"Oh. We're immune to some diseases, and actually, there is *one* other thing..."

"Lay it on me."

"Witches don't get pregnant accidentally. It's a conscious choice, and the act of procreation requires a little magic. When we're partnered with humans, however, our kids aren't always magic endowed."

"That's actually kind of a relief," he confessed, aware she might misunderstand. He hastened to clarify, "That way, when we have kids, it'll be a mutual decision, not a sudden shock. Regarding the magic use, I mean...I won't be any help if our tiny tot suddenly starts levitating all the toys in the nursery."

"I'm glad you feel that way."

"This is incredible. Anything else I should know?"

Leanne appeared to consider the question carefully. "You can talk about this to Titus, obviously, since he's been looped in... and Dante, if Margie tells him. I don't how serious they are. But otherwise, no external commentary until we figure out how best to reveal ourselves to the world. If I know the council, it'll take a while yet."

He nodded, thoughtful. "It sounds like you know a lot about the council."

"I can neither confirm nor deny that statement." But her eyes said he was on the right track; she just wasn't allowed to discuss it.

"This has been a hell of a day," Trev said.

"I'm sorry if you were scared."

"I'll be honest, when they tried to grab me and I suddenly lit up with an energy shield shaped like a hamster ball, that was pretty freaking wild. It's probably a good thing I wasn't...chemically enhanced, or who knows what would've happened?"

Leanne whispered, "When I got the alert that the spell had triggered, I panicked. I was so afraid they'd disappear you before I could get here. But the coven nailed that protective amulet." She pretended to buff her nails on her shirt.

"I was wondering..." Trev hesitated.

"About more witch stuff?"

"Tangentially speaking, I guess."

"Ask whatever you want to know."

He tried to conceal the devilish impulse driving him to press kisses along the side of her throat. "You said witches can't get knocked up by accident. Do you even want kids, though?"

"Actually, yes. I didn't think I would ever find the right person, and I was determined not to raise one alone, like Junie. So, if you'd asked before, I'd have said 'Yes, but it likely won't happen.' Now..."

"Now?" he prompted.

"It's a yes. Eventually."

He kissed the tender spot behind her ear. "Should we practice?"

"You're just trying to get laid."

"Guilty. I have some adrenaline to work off."

"Then let me assist you." She offered him a slow, sultry smile.

Leanne stood, and Trev stared up at her, unable to believe his luck. The whole witch thing still seemed kind of surreal, but he probably would still be here even if he'd learned she was a succubus draining his life force. He took her hand and followed her to the bedroom, admiring the slow sway of her hips.

She pulled the blinds since it was daytime, leaving the lights off. The room was all shadows, sweetly seductive. Then she said, "Illusions aren't my strong point, I'm better at glamours, but I feel like showing off a little. Watch this..."

Trev stood rapt, feeling like Odysseus must've felt on the shores of that rocky Grecian isle, watching Circe turn sailors into swine—awed and captivated and unable to look away. Leanne pulled a few stones and herbs from the locked drawer in her bedside table and manipulated them in what seemed to be a ritual style, then she whispered unintelligible words, and the air above the bed came to life with swirling lights, like ones cast by a spinning, patterned lamp, only without any source. It was achingly beautiful, and he longed to see those colors glimmering across her bare skin.

"Wow," he breathed.

"Get naked."

"You don't need to ask me twice."

He pulled off his clothes in a hurry, only to find his wife already in bed, beautifully bare and reaching for him with gentle arms. She was softness and radiance, all dewy determination, and when they kissed, it felt like the first time. Because it was, in a sense. Before, it had been practical, and while he'd known how he felt, he hadn't been sure of her emotions.

Now he was certain. She loved him.

And he tasted that devotion in each press of her mouth, each sweep of her tongue. She was minty fresh, nibbling at him until he panted her name, overcome with the sheer joy. The lights cascaded over them, seeming to catch the urgency he felt so that the strobes increased along with his excitement. Her skin gleamed blue, then green, then silver, glazing her face with ethereal enchantment.

"You're so beautiful," he whispered.

"How do you want me?"

"Forever," he said promptly.

"It makes me so happy to hear that. Not what I meant, though."

"I want what you want, anything at all."

In the end, it didn't matter the position. They came together in a desperate tangle of arms and legs, kissing and rolling across the bed until he pushed inside her and she wrapped herself around him as the lights flashed faster and brighter, adding to the liquid pleasure sparkling through him. He'd never felt so close to anyone in his life. Trev thrust hard and fast, and then she pushed him back, riding in delicious bounces, her hands holding his.

She came first, gasping and moaning until it drove him over as well. "I love you."

Trev said it back as he came down, cuddling her to him. Leanne stroked him until the shivers stopped. *So good, fucking good.* With her, it always was, even when they were strangers.

For the first time, maybe in his whole life, he felt perfectly certain that everything would work out precisely as it should.

CHAPTER 30

15 MONTHS LATER

"I CAN'T BELIEVE I EVER thought this was a good idea," Leanne said, walking the floor with their daughter.

Not only was this the longest relationship she'd ever been in, but she'd given birth three months prior. They'd talked about it for a couple of months before deciding to give parenthood a try. She hadn't expected to get pregnant the first time she opened herself to the possibility, but it happened so fast that it seemed ordained by fate.

If she believed in that.

And honestly, she didn't. Everything she had was because of her own choices. She'd managed to balance pregnancy with her seat on the city council while debating how to manage the world-wide reveal with the witch's council. Trevor's business had taken off in a big fashion, going a long way toward mending his shattered self-esteem. Therapy sessions helped as well.

Now that he'd established his own company, after marrying a rising political mover and shaker—she would be running for mayor in the next election—who'd inherited some money, his family was trying to patch things up. Trev wasn't too interested, and she couldn't blame him. Leanne didn't subscribe to the tenet that families should always be forgiven no matter what they did or how they made you feel. Sometimes the best solution was a clean cut, but only Trev could decide that. As always, she'd support his choice.

Melanie let out an impatient cry. The baby was tired, but she wouldn't go to sleep, no matter how long Leanne paced and bounced her. *This child is more exhausting than all my other commitments combined.* Thankfully, Trev came in and reached for their squirming, red-faced bundle of joy.

"What's wrong? Mom doesn't know how to hold you?"

Most annoying, the baby settled right down on his shoulder. "I have no idea how you do that. It's like magic."

He flashed her a grin. "Maybe it is."

"You're just in time. I have a conference call. I'll be in the bedroom."

With the guest room converted to a nursery, they'd compromised by sticking a desk in the bedroom. Space was a bit tight now, and they were currently looking for a bigger place. Since Leanne's inheritance—after taxes and lawyer fees—had been sitting in the bank collecting interest for over a year, they could buy any property they wanted. But they both wanted to make sure the place was perfect, their true forever home, because moving was a pain in the ass.

Quickly, she cast the appearance-altering spell, marveling over the fact that she could do so without worrying about being caught. Living as her true self was far more liberating than she'd imagined, and she'd thought it would be great. Likewise, Danica was over the moon, being able to live freely with Titus. Word on the coven grapevine was the CinnaMan planned to propose soon. Clem had gotten her happy ending as well when the former witch hunter returned to town and pleaded for a second chance. Gavin formally applied to join their coven and received enough votes, so he was a familiar face these days.

Her laptop screen flickered to life as she tapped it and joined the witch council meeting. Most of the others were already online. Today was a special day, the agreed-upon date for Leanne to post the press release they had argued over for more than a year. Privately, she thought this was wasted effort, but since she'd gotten her way when proposing her first motion—a rarity, she later learned—she'd figured discretion was the better part of valor. Better not to agitate her peers and let them tinker with the content of the announcement to their hearts' content.

She'd just never imagined it would take *this* long to come to consensus. But witch politics had filibuster in common with nonmagical committees, and now she had far too much personal experience with the excruciatingly slow progress of both. The debate went on for nearly an hour, until she finally lost what remained of her patience.

"If I agree to all the amendments, can we finally post this? I've shared the short list of media sites that I'll be—"

"Yes, yes. All in favor?"

Oh sure, interrupt me.

With effort born of long practice, she held her temper. The poll went up, and at last, they reached a majority in favor. *It's really happening. Today's the day.*

Leanne clicked out of the conference chat before the fickle

council could change their minds. *No take backs. I'm finally doing this.*

Her fingers shook a little as she copied the press release, double-checked the content, then hit send. She didn't bother asking Clem for the viral spell, figuring it would gain traction on its own. After closing her laptop, she rushed out to the living room, where Trev was settling Melanie in her swing. That was the one baby accessory she wouldn't trade for ten million bucks, as it soothed this difficult child like nothing else. Already, she was blinking big hazel eyes, so like her dad's, nodding off as the seat gently swayed back and forth. A few minutes later, Trev pulled Melanie out and settled their daughter in her crib for a nap, then returned to hear Leanne's news. He'd learned to read her well.

"I did it," she said.

"Did what?"

"Told the world about us!"

He moved to her side and wrapped her in a warm, wonderful hug. She'd never get tired of this. "Congrats, Butterfly. You've been trying to come out for over a year."

"They didn't make it easy," she muttered.

To her vast annoyance, the announcement failed to make a dent in the internet whatsoever. *Nobody* freakin' cared. Her meticulously written press release ended up with clickbait article titles like "Good News, Magic Is Real," and everyone in the freaking world ignored the existence of witches in favor of continents on fire, towns being wiped out by freak tornadoes, and diseases running rampant while the economy ate up the rest of humanity's focus.

"Huh," she said a week later after scanning the web for reactions.

Trev bit his lip, obviously trying not to laugh. "You lost to climate change."

"Shut up, it's not funny."

He made eye contact. "It's a *little* funny. Y'all lived with such care and secrecy and—"

"Fine, fine. I should have seen this coming."

But there was comfort in that indifference as well. After the anticlimactic online announcement, Hazel Jeffords joined the coven as its first nonmagical member. She *loved* watching their spell work and always brought her famous baked goods to each meeting to energize the rest of the group. Leanne nearly hurt herself laughing when she saw the bumper sticker on Hazel's car— HONORARY WITCH. Goliath got a new tag on his collar with his name engraved on the front as, *Goliath, Honorary Familiar.* And on the back, *if found, return to Hazel Jeffords, honorary witch*, along with her contact info. She didn't just attend meetings at Danica and Clem's place these days—no, she visited everybody else's houses too.

On the way to the coven meeting, her phone rang. "This is Leanne."

"Ms. Vanderpol-Montgomery?"

Shit, is that—

"This is Dan Rutherford. The mayor's not taking my calls, and—"

Without an instant of hesitation, she cut the call at once and kept driving. These days, Rutherford was screaming "foul" to anyone who would listen, and he was trying to demand a recount on grounds of "witchcraft." Little wonder the mayor was disavowing him, as Rutherford had turned into a vocal, screeching conspiracy theorist. To make the situation even funnier, when Leanne got to Margie's house, she had a text from Mayor Anderson, asking her to play golf.

Leanne laughed as she deleted the message. *Nice try, but you can't make nice now. I'm still coming for you.* Whistling cheerfully, she hopped out of the car and let herself in unnoticed. Like the rest of her coven sisters, Margie's adorable two-bedroom house felt like home.

"Are you *sure* I can't learn to do magic?" Hazel was asking Vanessa as Leanne wandered into the coven meeting, ten minutes late now. Tonight she didn't have wine, and she had a little baby spit-up on her blazer.

"Sorry," Margie said gently. "That's not possible."

Vanessa used that distraction to make a break for it, and she beelined for Leanne, hugging her tight. "You did it, babes."

"*We* did," she corrected.

"I have the best news. A gallery in Chicago contacted me about an exhibition, and I can even sell my pieces with accurate descriptions." Since Vanessa enchanted her pieces as part of the artistic process, this was freaking huge.

Leanne screamed and hauled her bestie into a tight hug. "I am so happy for you! Just tell me when and where. I wouldn't miss it for the world."

"So glad I didn't give up on my dream. Who runs the world?"

Vanessa did a happy little wiggle, proving how glad she was that they'd paved the way.

———

"This is not a playdate," Trev said.

"It counts," Dante argued.

Trev glanced at the girl lounging on his sofa, tall for her age and elegant in box braids. "Your kid could change my kid's diapers."

Evonnie glanced up from her phone. "I'm not doing that."

He laughed. "It was an example. My point is, you can't tell Bets that this counts as any kind of social interaction for Evonnie."

"Leave me out of it," the girl said, returning to the mobile game she was playing.

Dante sighed. "Fine. But if she asks, we were doing educational activities."

"You're not competing with Tyrone. No matter how well he treats Evonnie, he's not you, okay? Take a breath."

His friend seemed to appreciate the support, relaxing on the sofa next to his daughter. "What time is Miguel coming over? I can't believe he's bringing *all* his kids."

Trev laughed. "Yeah, you can call it a playdate when they get here. I think the older two are around Evonnie's age."

The girl perked up. "Are they cool? Why haven't I met them before now?"

Dante blinked. "I...don't know. They stay pretty busy. Miguel's wife keeps the kids in lessons. Dance, swimming, karate. When they're not in school, they're learning something else."

"I'm not doing that to Melanie. I mean, if she says she's

interested, I'll support her, but I won't drag her around otherwise. I want her to play with toys and—"

"We get it, Father of the Year."

Trev quieted, feeling a warm flush on his cheeks. "Was I soapboxing?"

"Little bit. And you've only been in the fatherhood game for a few months."

"It doesn't count when they're oven buns?" he asked.

Dante shook his head. "It does not."

"Bummer."

"Quick question," Dante said.

"What is it?"

"I happened to read this article…"

Trev thought he knew where this was going. "You're wondering if Margie's a witch?"

It made him sad that Margie hadn't confided in Dante on her own. His friend liked her, but she was so closed off and skittish that it seemed improbable she'd ever let anyone in again all the way. *What the hell did her ex do to her anyway?*

"I mean, yeah." Dante punctuated his words with a sheepish look.

"She is. The way I understand it, *everyone* in book club is. Except for Hazel Jeffords. She's just lonely."

"Holy shit," his friend whispered.

Welcome to my world.

Trev got up to check the snacks and set them on the kitchen counter for easy access. There was a selection of fruit, nuts, cheese, and chips—all easily snatched up by grabby hands. Soon, there was a knock at the door, revealing Miguel and his four kids, ranging in age from twelve to four. He and his wife, Juanita, were prolific.

After seeing Leanne scream her head off once, Trev had no idea if he could face her doing that again. He adored Melanie, and he was delighted they had her, but watching his wife suffer hurt his heart, especially when there was nothing he could do. Belatedly, he greeted Miguel with a casual hug and listened carefully as his friend introduced the kids.

"Marco is twelve. Teresa is ten. Manuel is seven. Tatiana is four. Are you sure there's space for everyone here?"

"The younger kids can play in the nursery. I hooked up a console in the living room for the older ones, and I have multiple games that allow up to four players."

Miguel grinned. "I can see you've thought this out. I stand corrected."

"It's only for a few hours anyway to give your wife—and you—a break."

"I really appreciate it, man. She's waiting in the car, so I'm taking off. We'll be back after the movie."

"Not a problem."

Miguel headed out, leaving Trev and Dante to entertain a bunch of children. About an hour in, things settled into a reasonable groove, with Evonnie schooling Marco and Manuel in a racing game. Tatiana wandered into the nursery to check out the toys, and Teresa preferred reading quietly, keeping to herself.

Dante drew Trev aside to whisper, "If my sisters find out I'm babysitting for Miguel, I'll never hear the end of it. They'll *keep* their kids at my house."

Trev laughed quietly. "I won't tell, but Evonnie might."

Without looking up, the girl said, "Oh, I'm *totally* telling my aunties on you."

"Damn it," said Dante.

A few hours later, everyone finally exited, leaving the apartment a mess. Trev was tidying up when Leanne finally got home, and he dropped the dish towel to head straight for her. He'd never get tired of this, never get tired of seeing her smile brightly, never weary of holding her in his arms and breathing her in.

My butterfly. My love. My life. My wife.

"Looks like you had a productive evening," she observed.

"So. Many. Children."

In fits and starts, he filled her in on how the night had gone, and she told him about Hazel Jeffords. This...he freaking *loved* this—the debrief at end of day. No matter how busy they got in life, he adored taking these moments to share everything with each other. When she got to the part about Hazel's new bumper sticker, he cracked up laughing.

"She is too much. To think she got on your nerves in the beginning."

"Right? Now I can't imagine our meetings without her. Is Melanie okay?"

"She's sleeping for now. I just fed and changed her like half an hour ago."

"So...we have a few moments of privacy?" Leanne raised her brows in suggestion, and Trev leaned in for a kiss.

On cue, Melanie let out a horrendous wail. Babies were truly the best at keeping their parents from touching each other. With a rueful smile, he hurried into the nursery and found her yelling. Since she'd eaten—yeah. Judging by the smell, she needed yet another change. He handled it deftly, as he was frankly better with child-rearing chores than Leanne. To him, it seemed fair that he should do the heavy lifting now, as she'd done it for the ten months prior—swollen ankles, stretch marks, nausea, weird cravings, constantly needing to pee, birthing pain. His beautiful witchy wife had run the gauntlet making this precious—

Lights. Just like the ones Leanne had conjured for him the night he'd learned she was a witch. And they danced around the nursery, now that Melanie was clean, dry, and content. If he hadn't already known there was a good chance his daughter would be a witch also, he might be freaking the fuck out. As it was, he stared in wonder for a few seconds.

Then he called, "You might want to check this out, Butterfly."

She came to the doorway, puzzlement melting into a pure, incandescent joy. Sparkles and shimmers cascaded over them as Melanie kicked her chubby legs on the changing table. Trev snapped her onesie back in place and picked her up. The baby waved her fists, trying to catch the fairy lights she'd brought into being, just by existing.

"In the old days," Leanne whispered, "before we could live freely, I'd have sewn charms into all her baby clothes. To prevent a mishap like this."

"It's not a mishap," he said instantly.

"I know. It's such a gorgeous, unforgettable moment. I'm so glad we don't have to hide this anymore." Eyes soft and tender, she leaned over to kiss their daughter on her soft cheek.

"Welcome to the world, little witch. It's different than the one I grew up in."

This moment, this one—he could ask for nothing more. Once, he didn't even have the energy to hope, let alone dream, and then this incredible woman changed his life. Forever.

EPILOGUE

SIX MONTHS AFTER WITCHES STEPPED into the light with astonishingly little fanfare, lost amid other headlines, other paranormal communities came forward as well—shifters, psychics, descendants of the fae, and some said vampires as well, though they remained well hidden and yet distrustful of outsiders. Human governments scrambled to legislate and figure out how to capitalize on these hidden resources, while life appeared to go on as usual.

But it was difficult to predict how life would change, how these new additions to the modern world would cope with this open existence. One thing was certain, however, and it was that there would always be new ground to break, new worlds to conquer for the rising paranormal profile. In time, St. Claire would experience many changes, but one truth remained constant: there would always be new and intriguing stories to be told...

Read on for a peek at
Clementine Waterhouse's story in

BOSS Witch

Available now from Sourcebooks Casablanca

CLEMENTINE WATERHOUSE HAD BEEN FIXING problems for as long as she could remember.

As a kid, when she heard her mother, Allegra, sobbing, she'd be the one to magic up a cup of tea after the latest knock-down-and-drag-out fight that ended with furniture broken and her bio dad, Barnabas Balfour, abandoning them. *Again.* Somehow, that pattern continued with her cousin. Clem was the one who ended up sweeping up the wreckage and trying to piece together whatever was broken.

For the past month, she'd had an ominous feeling about Danica's growing attachment to Titus Winnaker, the mundane baker who was stirring up family drama during a time already way too fraught with it.

A quiet throb started in her right temple as Clem waited for Danica to come home and carpool to their coven meeting. Her cousin dashed in, out of breath, radiating anxiety. Clem didn't push for details, knowing that whatever was wrong, her cousin would explain at the meeting. So Clem headed to the car and drove over to

Kerry and Priya's place, two coven sisters who were among Clem's closest friends. They were also a committed couple who'd just moved in together. Kerry Quarles was an angular woman with blond hair and sharp features while Priya Banik was softly rounded, her bronze skin a glowing complement to her river of silken black hair.

Clem and Danica greeted their hosts with hugs and a bag of yogurt-covered pretzels. Then Danica beelined into the house. With growing concern, Clem watched her cousin pace the cozy living room, chewing her thumbnail as she went. It had been a while since she'd seen Danica this agitated, and Clem swapped a look with Priya while Kerry set out drinks and snacks. In silent reply, Priya lifted a shoulder.

Looks like she doesn't know what's up either.

Kerry and Priya lived in a two-bedroom town house with a good-sized living room decorated in a pale palette with splashes of color and set adjacent to an open kitchen. The furniture was comfortable, and Clem took a seat to wait for the rest of the coven. Margie Bower tended to arrive first. She was a quiet woman in her forties with brown hair and circles under her eyes. Vanessa Jackson got there next; she wore her hair in beautiful braids, and today, she was glowing in a yellow sundress that was the perfect foil for her dark skin. Since they lived on the same street, Ethel Murray came in with her, a plump woman in her sixties with silver hair cut in a pixie style. Leanne Vanderpol rolled in last, a redhead in her late thirties with warm olive skin who favored pencil skirts to show off her curves and who always had on a pair of heels.

Ethel took one look at Danica and grinned. "You got laid. And it was *powerful*."

At the old witch's words, Leanne took a closer look. "Damn. So she did."

"It's been ages for me," Margie said with a sigh. "I demand vicarious satisfaction."

For fuck's sake, she was navigating family interference like it was an active land mine, while her cousin was off boning. Clem's eye twitched as Danica made a shooing motion.

Then Danica said, "I'll take questions about my sex life later. Something big might be looming. Titus told me a big, scary guy barged into the bakery and started yelling about witches. He made threats and flipped the cash register and spiked his coffee on the floor when they asked him to leave."

Fear swirled inside Clem, exacerbating her headache. Though witch hunters weren't usually so overt in their actions, she couldn't assume it was a mundane with mental issues. The safety of their coven depended on staying hidden.

Kerry cursed quietly, addressing Danica. "You've made two service calls there recently. If this guy's a hunter, he could have followed your energy trail."

Danica let out an unsteady breath. "Exactly what I'm thinking. I haven't bothered using a dispersal ritual in ages. I got comfortable. And careless."

Of course she did. She's obsessed with the baker and his buns.

"The hunter hasn't got us yet," Ethel said with a pragmatic air. "My mother told me about one who came sniffing around in the thirties. They didn't find us then either. Try to calm down."

Breathe, Clem told herself. *Stuff like this happens. It'll be okay. I'll find a way to keep them safe.*

Seeing how upset her cousin was, Clem moved to comfort Danica, but Priya got there first. She rubbed Danica's shoulder. "It's not your fault. I suspect that none of us have been as careful with our magic as we could've been."

Vanessa nodded. "It could have been any one of us that pinged on his radar."

With a sigh, Danica shook her head. "But I'm the one who's spiking like crazy. My output is off the charts lately."

"At least you admit there's a problem." Clem tried to sound neutral, but she was angry and scared in equal measure.

How the hell do I put this cat back in the bag?

If anything happened to her coven sisters, she wouldn't be able to live. Clem loved all of them so much, even if she wasn't the most demonstrative, and the idea of anyone hurting them exacerbated her headache. Visceral fright lodged in her brain like a rusty railroad spike. To make matters worse, her cousin didn't even acknowledge her words.

Danica turned to Ethel. "You said there was a hunter here in the thirties. Did your mother tell you how they got rid of him?"

"First, we protect this place so he can't sense our workings," the old woman said. "And then we do a joint casting to confirm if he's the real deal."

"Divination is your forte," Vanessa said.

Ethel nodded. "That's why I'll be taking the lead. Priya, can you lock the apartment? You've lived here for years, and your imprint is stronger than Kerry's."

"Understood. I'm on it." Priya bolstered her wards in each

room, creating a secure site that shouldn't leak any sign of their workings.

Leanne confirmed the seal was solid, then Kerry and Priya procured the implements Ethel requested, white candles and purified water in a copper bowl, along with various ceremonial herbs. The old witch took the lead, intoning softly as she scattered the carnation and mugwort, finishing with sea salt for purity. Without prompting, they joined hands around the table, allowing Ethel to pull from their energies as she peered into the glimmering water.

At first, it was cloudy as she whispered, "Tell us, spirits, true or false, false or true. Him we seek and him we find. Let none hinder this quest of mind. Hunter, the water reveals the truth of you."

The liquid roiled inside the bowl, gentle bubbles that slowly clarified into the image of a large man reclining in a vinyl chair. A leather jacket was slung over the back, and he was drinking a beer in a cheap motel room. He was big, but more, he radiated intensity and determination. At his feet lay a battered leather satchel. He wore battered boots and torn jeans. From head to toe, he promised danger, and if that wasn't enough, he was ruggedly appealing too. Strong jaw, dusted with dark stubble, a shock of hair so black, it gleamed, and his eyes were an eerie silver gray. And though it was impossible, he *stirred* as they gazed on him, glancing around as if he felt the invisible weight of their attention.

Gazing at him, Clem felt…something straightaway. Not fear. Not exactly. It made no sense, but it resembled…inevitability. *Clearly, I need to sleep more. I'm hallucinating.*

Carefully, Ethel drew back, and Danica rubbed her hands together nervously. "Well?"

The old witch stared into the now-quiescent tureen. "We're in it now, my darlings. He's the real deal."

Her coven sisters sat quiet for a bit, each likely wrestling with their own fears. Diverting him might require something of Clem she didn't want to give, but so be it. *I have no plan, but I'm the fixer, right? I'll figure something out.*

Clem squared her shoulders. "No worries. I'll handle him."

Acknowledgments

First, I'll thank Lucienne Diver for being wonderful in all ways. I love how supportive she is and how she's always excited by my weird ideas.

Next, I'm sending all the hearts to Christa Désir. She's the absolute best, and I love working with her. My heartfelt appreciation goes to the whole Sourcebooks team as well. It's so fantastic working with such skilled and passionate booklovers.

Thanks to the friends who support me and inspire me along the way. Thanks to the readers who have been with me for years and still believe in my ability to transport them.

As ever, thanks to my family. They know why. And finally, thanks to my pets, who try to keep me from getting any work done, ever.

About the Author

New York Times and *USA Today* bestselling author Ann Aguirre has been a clown, a clerk, a savior of stray kittens, and a voice actress, not necessarily in that order. She grew up in a yellow house across from a cornfield, but now she lives in Mexico with her family. She writes all kinds of genre fiction, but she has an eternal soft spot for a happily ever after.